I0713005

COSCOM
ENTERTAINMENT

MAGIC MAN

PLUS

15 TALES OF TERROR

BY

A.P. FUCHS

COSCOM ENTERTAINMENT
WINNIPEG

ISBN 978-1-926712-51-2

PUBLISHED BY COSCOM ENTERTAINMENT
www.coscomentertainment.com
Text set in Garamond; Printed and bound in the USA
COVER ART BY A.P. FUCHS AND ROXANNE FUCHS
COVER PHOTO BY ROXANNE FUCHS

For Keith Gouveia: colleague, fellow dreamer, and friend.

THE PROGRAM

PLUS

15 TALES of TERROR

INTRODUCTION

If this collection is anything, it's a snapshot of a writer's early attempts at fiction.

To quickly recap:

I started in this game in 2000 after my plan to draw comic books fulltime didn't pan out. Aside from scripting pages for my classmates at the animation school I attended, I began writing short stories, the idea of tackling a full-blown novel right off the bat something far too daunting for me. I mean, really, me write a book 250-plus pages? No thanks. But write something 5 or 6 pages long? Sure, I could handle that.

Never really had any formal training. I learned to write—and still am learning—by reading and writing and keeping myself inspired to keep reading and writing by watching other writers and what they're doing. Short stories, actually, were how my career as a novelist began. I wrote a couple—which are both contained here, more on those in a moment—then I started what was supposed to be 5 or 6 short stories to hopefully be published in serial format, each story leading into the next. What ended up happening was a huge accident and something that changed my career forever: those 5 or 6 stories became the prologue to my first novel, *A Stranger Dead,* which is now out-of-print but might be resurrected someday when I have the time.

What you have here in *Magic Man Plus 14 Tales of Terror* is what could be called the first chunk of my career, back when I wrote more short stories than novels, sent them out to wherever I could, sometimes accepted, sometimes rejected, eventually all published.

What I'm really pleased to include here is my first short story, *Rag-man.* This was the first story I wrote when I got serious about writing fulltime. When I pulled it from the archive, it was rough around the edges so I've cleaned it up for this collection, likewise the second short story I penned, *A Perfect Date.* Actually, all of the stories within have been re-edited since their original publication, most notably the main clump of stories under the *Magic Man* umbrella.

I've got to tell you, reading and editing those stories after having not looked at them for many years was a great joy. There's a raw honesty in these tales and a certain eagerness to them from a young writer who wanted nothing more than to make a career out of telling stories and making stuff up. There were many times where I went, "Whoa, cool." Other times where I said, "Oops. Got to fix that." And yet others where I thought, on some level, that I might not ever be able to write this way again. That last part is true, I think, by the way. Like all crafts, writing is one of evolution and adaptation, a writer's stories acting as a mirror to what was going on in their lives at the time the stories were written. Couple that with their skill set at that time and you have something that a writer cannot duplicate later on. Those are two variables that are constantly in motion and never retreat back to the way they were.

This collection, I'm hoping, will give you a thrill as you read good old-fashioned horror stories—especially *Theatre of Skulls*, a story that gave me a horror fanboy thrill as I edited it after who knows how many years since first typing it—all meant to entertain, enlighten and just plain have a good old time in a genre that I fell in love with some 12 years ago.

Thanks for reading.

- A.P. Fuchs
Winnipeg, MB
June 14, 2010

Ps. Some of you who took the time to count the number of stories in the table of contents would have noticed there are more than 15 listed despite this book's title. To clarify my reasoning on why the title of the book is, *Magic Man Plus 15 Tales of Terror*, is because I counted the 3 stories, 1 poem, stream of thought and intro under the 'Magic Man' label as one overall story, with the rest intended to remain separate despite the Magic Man sequel titled, *Below*.

So, if I haven't confused you enough, grab a drink, a warm blanket and enjoy the stories to come.

Behind the veil of filth and rot
He takes you down, takes all you've got
Your heart escapes; chains are placed
Runs out your back without pity or grace

It hasn't really hit home, this game he plays
Just keeps on going days upon days
Smearing a street with gore and flesh
With fetuses escaping from their mothers' flesh

And still slick of caul and goo
Babies of light, with life set to do
The Magic Man knows when you'll ask
For him to heal you, to change the past

Tempt your fate, if you will
But you'll lose your stomach and fall ill
To a dying soul of resignation pure
You can take part but be confident you're sure

That you're prepared to give anything
Everything
All

THE EXCHANGE

When the strange man approached Barry Snyder, he seemed to have appeared from nothingness. Barry was rounding a corner in the Exchange, the old part of Winnipeg, when the peculiar man stepped out from the shadows beneath an awning and extended a thin hand toward him.

"I can make her come back," the stranger said.

It took Barry a moment to realize the man was talking to him. There was no one else around.

"Excuse me?" Barry said.

"I said, 'I can make her come back.'"

Barry thought for a moment. *Margaret? Is that who he's—No.*

He eyed the man quizzically. The fellow wore a tight-fitting purple suit, with white candy stripes running vertically all the way from the collar to the pants' cuffs. Long brown hair hugged his face like a scarf, and a purple fedora, without the stripes, topped it all off. A wide white feather stood up proudly from the fedora's headband, something similar to the quills folks used to use as pens. The man's clothes reminded him of a magician's outfit, the kind that entertainers wore at carnivals.

"Sorry," Barry said and stuffed his hands in the pockets of his autumn coat. He walked around the man. A weight descended upon him, the reminder of losing Margaret heavy not just in his heart, but all over. "I'm not interested."

The words "bring her back" brought Margaret's memory to life. Barry had dated her in high school and for two years after that, while both attended the University of Manitoba. Barry had studied psychology and Margaret was in education. Toward the end of their second year, Margaret announced she didn't want to be with him anymore. He couldn't understand it, what with the talk of marriage and all. Turns out a week later, when he asked some of her friends if they had any ideas as to why she left him, Margaret was seeing another guy by the name of James Fielder. Worse, she had been seeing James behind Barry's back.

His heart shattered.

Margaret's betrayal haunted him for years until one day he gave up on the hope that, given a miracle, Margaret would come back to him. This was the very same day he found out Margaret and James got married and moved away to somewhere in the States.

The years went on, but Barry never forgot her, never forgot that girl with the blonde hair and dark eyes who he dated for four years. But that was just a memory, now. Even so, Barry never forgot her, never let her go. Not completely. Not a day went by when he wouldn't look up into the sky and pick a cloud, wondering if, by chance, Margaret was looking at the same cloud somewhere else. Of course, he knew that was impossible. Cloud cover ranged from region to region, so there was no way Margaret, if she *was* looking at a cloud, was looking at the same one. Regardless, the idea she might be gazing at the same puff of white in the sky was encouraging. It always calmed his aching heart.

There were times when, while in bed, tears dampened his eyes at the thought of her. He never stopped missing her, never stopped thinking about her.

Never stopped loving her.

He was thirty years old now. He was on his lunch break from work and nipped down to the Exchange District for a coffee. That's when he rounded the corner and met the man in the purple suit, saying he could bring her back.

When Barry was thirty paces away from him, the man called after him.

"I can bring her back, Barry. I promise."

Barry stopped in his tracks and glanced over his shoulder. The fellow looked straight back, hands raised shoulder-high in an apparent offer of friendship, his purple suit clashing with the browns and grays of the buildings.

Barry turned and kept walking, Margaret's face hovering in the fore of his thoughts. Whenever he thought of her, he always pictured how she looked during that second year of university, so full of youth and eagerness, excited to start a career as a teacher once she graduated. Sometimes he would think about what she looked like now, eight years later. She would look the same, but there would be a maturity about her, an evident expression containing wisdom from the years.

Suddenly, the man stepped in front of him. "I can bring Margaret back, Barry."

How—? He looked back over his shoulder. The spot where the man had been standing was empty. "How'd you—how'd you do that?"

"Doesn't matter," he said. "What *does* matter is I can bring her back. You want Margaret back, don't you? You want to be with her again. You can say it isn't so, but it's written all over your face. Your eyes gloss over immediately upon hearing her name. When I look at you, I see *her*."

"How do you know that? How do you know my name?" The whole thing was surreal, like being stoned and experiencing life through a fog. How often Barry had wished someone would walk up to him and guarantee just what this man said. How much he had wished someone would say they would bring Margaret back into his life and assure him their relationship would never end again.

"I've heard your prayers," the man said. "I can do this for you. If you let me." The man's hands were still raised, open, evidence of trust.

Heart beating hard and quick, Barry exhaled slowly. And, for a moment, he didn't care if this was real or not, if he was dreaming or awake.

"Who are you?" he asked.

"I'm whoever you need me to be. I just want to bring her back, almost as much as you."

Magic Man, Barry thought.

"Magic Man?" the man said. "Well, I suppose that's as good a name as any. Magic Man, it is."

"How did you—"

The Magic Man offered a warm smile. "You don't need to know, but do know that I'm here for you."

Barry swallowed the lump in his throat. If this was truly happening, then this was his only chance to see Margaret again. To take back what James Fielder stole from him. What the Magic Man had in mind to accomplish such a thing, he had no idea. But, like earlier, he already decided to go along with it, no matter how strange this all was.

"How . . . . How do you plan on doing that? How do you even know about her, anyway?" Barry said. The wind picked up and swept through his thinning brown hair. He smoothed it back down with his palm.

"Like I said, I've heard your prayers. You wanted someone to make that ache in your heart go away. You wanted someone to simply say, 'Here you go. Here she is. Now go and be happy.' Well, *I'm* that someone. *I* can bring her back."

For a long moment, Barry considered his offer. Perhaps the Magic Man really could do what he said? After all, he somehow vanished from where he had been standing and suddenly appeared in front of him. No one could do that. No one *human*, anyway.

"Are you . . . God?" Barry asked. It was a foolish question, one that escaped his lips before he could restrain it.

The Magic Man laughed. "No, Barry, I'm not. And I'm not the devil, either, if that's what you're thinking. Which you are, by the way."

Barry's spine tingled. He *did* just think this guy was the devil.

"I'm just a good Samaritan," the man said, "and I want to help you." The man looked him in the eye. "What do you say?" He extended his hand for a handshake.

Barry thought of Margaret and how his heart burned when she said she didn't want to be with him. He thought of the sleepless nights for months afterward, kicking the sheets and bringing his fists down on the mattress, wondering why she left him for James. He never hated her, but was only frustrated by the ever-present pain she caused. He remembered dating other girls and how he ended those relationships because they never felt right, none of those girls ever measuring up to the standard Margaret set. Remembered his all-consuming desire to have her back, anything to ease the permanent pain in his heart.

"Sure," Barry said. "Might as well. I've got nothing left to lose." He took the Magic Man's hand in his. "You gotta deal. Anything for Margaret."

———

Barry had been here for so long, he didn't know what day it was. Worse, he didn't even know what *year* it was. Nearly every calm moment was spent regretting meeting the Magic Man. And nearly all moments, even during the searing pain of the Magic Man's torture, were spent thinking of Margaret.

It had been a long road.

Barry prayed it would soon be over. After meeting the Magic Man in the Exchange, the moment after shaking the Magic Man's hand, Barry knew he made the wrong decision. Yet, it couldn't have been completely wrong, could it? No.

This was for Margaret.

It was all for Margaret.

It would always be for her.

That day in the Exchange, the Magic Man led him around the corner and then around another into a back alley. Steam rose from the sewers and the alley was dark, even for the middle of the day. Garbage and old newspapers littered the ground, stirring in the light wind that swirled through the alley like water in a funnel.

"Wait right here," the Magic Man said.

Barry stood and watched the man in the white-striped purple suit squat down before a mound of garbage next to a BFI bin. With a thin hand, he pawed at the pile, pushing the garbage aside, revealing a rusted iron handle. The man turned it to the left, then all the way backwards in a circle. There was a low *ka-chunk* that echoed through the ground. Barry felt the same dull *ka-chunk* in his chest.

His heart skipped.

The man glanced over his shoulder and winked at him, then, curling his long fingers beneath the bottom rim of the BFI bin, the man hoisted the garbage bin up at a forty-five degree angle. Then he let go, and the BFI bin remained suspended in the air, without any support save for its opposite end that was still planted on the ground.

How—Before he could finish his thought, the man gestured with a finger for him to come closer.

Hesitantly, he neared him. The Magic Man must have caught the caution of his steps because he said, "Don't worry, Barry, I'm not going to bite you. You're just going to have to trust me. I can bring her back, but we have to go someplace first."

Barry stopped walking. "Where?"

The man eyed a dark area beneath the BFI bin. "Down there. I need you to do something for me. If you do, I'll bring Margaret back. If you don't, you can walk away now, no harm, no foul, just a missed opportunity."

Margaret. Anything for Margaret. I don't want to go with him. But I will. He knew my name. He knew about Margaret. I've never see him before in my life. I'll take a chance. Might as well. I've got nothing left to lose. Legs shaky, he approached the Magic Man. He took his hands out of his pockets just in case the Magic Man tried something, perhaps attempted to rob him.

"Tell you what," the Magic Man said, "I'll go in first. That way, you'll know I won't try anything." He gave Barry a knowing grin, one telling him he knew what Barry was thinking.

The Magic Man got on his belly and wriggled feet-first toward the dark spot beneath the dumpster. When his feet touched the shadow-like patch, the patch swirled, as if made of liquid, and the Magic Man's black and white spats disappeared into the goo. Soon he was waist-deep, and then was gone.

Barry stared after him wide-eyed then glanced down the alley, wondering if anyone was looking on. Nobody was around, not even a stray cat.

"What am I doing?" he said as he got to his knees and mimicked the man's movements by going on his belly, wriggling back feet-first beneath the dumpster.

The bottom of the BFI bin was a mere inch or two above his back and Barry's muscles ached with fear the dumpster might somehow fall off its invisible support and come crashing down.

"Come on, my friend," the Magic Man said from somewhere beneath him.

Friend? Barry peered over his shoulder, into the darkness that was the sharp crevice where the dumpster balanced on its rear rim.

Closing his eyes, he took a deep breath in an effort to calm himself. "Okay," he said, "here we go." He pushed against the pavement with his palms, feeling the cool syrup of the black goo through his shoes as his feet swam through it. Soon the thick cold of the goo was against his shins, then his thighs, his waist, his stomach, chest, shoulders, face, and, finally, arms and hands.

There was a *ka-chunk* when he dropped to the stone floor. He knew the dumpster had fallen back into place on the pavement above, the latch presumably locking itself.

Darkness surrounded him.

———

That was six years ago. Or was it seven? Eight? Ten? Barry didn't know. He'd been down here too long, in this cave, away from everything and everyone. But it was worth it. It was for Margaret. The Magic Man promised he would bring her back.

"For you," Barry said to the stone floor, drool dripping from his chin. "All for you."

The cave was dank, the lighting dim. A flash of pain flared up in his shoulder blades. His forearms throbbed, the absence of blood circulating through his muscles getting to him again. His shoulders pounded in pain and another film of sweat materialized on his brow. His hands . . . he couldn't feel them anymore. They were above him, he knew, but as to what position they were in or how his fingers were curled, he hadn't the faintest idea. His wrists were bound in iron cuffs, the cuffs connected to a chain, hanging him by the arms from the stone ceiling. Only his toes touched the floor, all his weight upon them, his toes pulsing with icy pain. He yearned to touch the ground again, stand with his feet flat and give the strain on his wrists and arms a break. But it had been days since he'd been allowed to do that. Maybe weeks. Maybe months, for all he knew.

The blood that had trickled down his forearms from the iron cuffs digging into his wrists had dried a long time ago. At least the sensation of liquid running lightly over his skin wouldn't tickle him anymore. That tickle was, on some days, what he hated most instead of what the Magic Man did to him.

He was naked, the sweat on his skin causing the cool air of the cave to feel that much colder. He couldn't remember the last time he felt warm. Only when the Magic Man held Barry's palms over a candle was temporary warmth an option before searing heat took over and agony became his only consciousness. Barry never looked at his hands. He couldn't bear the thought of what they might look like now. He had undergone what the Magic Man dubbed "Candle Therapy" more times than he dared to count. The damage to his hands . . . . Despite his curiosity, no, he wouldn't look at them, not even on the rare occasions when the Magic Man lowered the chains and allowed his feet to touch ground.

On these days, when Barry was unshackled from the chains, he only had a few spare moments before the Magic Man would push him down and attach a chain to the iron bracelets around his ankles and hang him upside down for an hour or more. Each time he thought his head would explode, the blood rushing and pooling inside his skull somehow not washing away the bone before bursting out of his skin in red glory. Eventually he would pass out, and when he awoke would find himself right-side-up again.

All for Margaret.

Barry wondered when the Magic Man would come again. He wondered when his time in this cave would end and he could be released. He wondered if the Magic Man would make good on his promise.

An hour passed before the iron door sealing Barry in the stone room opened a crack. No light poured in for there was only darkness in the room beyond. Barry had never seen darkness so black before. A shrill screech echoed throughout the cave as the rusted hinges worked and the iron door opened completely. The blackness from the room beyond seemed to swallow what little light there was in Barry's part of the cave.

The Magic Man stood in the doorway, still wearing the same white-striped purple suit he wore the first day he met him. The man's fedora, however, was not there and his long, bushy brown hair hung in locks over his face. In his gangly, thin hand the Magic Man held something long and snake-like.

Barry knew what it was and immediately the gashes on his back stung with the memory of pain.

"Ready, Barry?" the Magic Man said.

Throat dry, Barry hadn't the strength to speak. All he could do was barely nod. *For Margaret. Anything to see her. To touch her. To breathe her . . . I . . . .* His heart ached at what he would think next: *I don't care anymore. Too long down here. I just don't care, anymore. I-I don't want to go through* that *again. No more. All for Margaret. No more.*

The Magic Man walked over to Barry's hanging form, prolonging the anticipation of the torment to come. With a gentle hand, he touched Barry's shoulder, aggravating the half-healed cuts on his flesh. The Magic Man spun him around so he had access to his back.

Barry forced himself to swallow. He braced his body for the impact of the lead beads at the tips of the leather whip's stringy end. Then he remembered he mustn't tighten his body, mustn't go rigid. It would only make the lashings worse. Taut muscles equaled more blood lost when they were torn open. He had to relax, let his body move with the lashings; move and absorb.

The Magic Man cracked the whip, its sound deafening in the small cave. The wind created from the whip's decisive cut through the air fanned Barry's back for a split second before the sharp, stinging slicing of his flesh replaced all awareness.

Eyes squeezed shut, Barry thought of Margaret and for a brief moment began to care again. Began to force himself to endure this torment just to see her.

The whip lashed across his back and blood trickled from split skin.

The fire across his shoulders forced a gasp to escape his lips. He could picture ten red slashes across his already-mangled flesh. Ten slashes. Ten lead beads at the end of the whip's frayed end.

The Magic Man lashed him again.

It was all part of the deal. The Magic Man needed to give pain so he could have the power to make anything happen.

"I'd do anything—*endure* everything—for you," Barry had told Margaret during their final phone call those many years ago. And he meant it. He was proving it now.

Ten strikes of lightning slashed his back again and the warm blood oozing from the wounds was almost soothing, like an ointment. Barry gazed down at his feet, his toes straining to take some of the weight off his arms. On the stone floor the deep red of dried blood, the evidence of previous beatings, stared up at him.

I'd die a thousand times, just to see you. Margaret, I lo—I need this to stop. No woman is worth this. The whip cracked against his skin. He could feel his flesh hanging in ribbons off his back. *I need this. I need to give him what he wants so I can see you again. No . . . no more. Not anymore. Kill me now. I beg you. Please. Just . . . please.*

Each time the lead beads laced across his flesh, Barry's body tensed, bringing more blood to the surface, more blood to trickle down his back, his legs and pool on the floor. Soon his reactions grew farther and farther apart, the nerve endings of his torn muscles and shredded skin numbed by searing heat and pain. Before long, he stopped reacting altogether, passed out from the hell just handed to him.

It was only then the Magic Man stopped.

———

When Barry awoke, his arms were spread out to either side of him. There was a sharp pain in his wrists, as if they were supporting a half-ton truck. His feet, right across his insteps, blazed with heat. Blood dripped off his toes. The cave was especially dim today. Only one solitary candle was at his feet, a small nimbus around the flame, lighting the room ever so slightly with an orange glow.

He inhaled and found himself instinctively rising up on his feet, his left foot over his right, just to breathe. His muscles strained, not just in his chest but also in his shoulders and arms. Immediately Barry knew what the Magic Man had done to him. His heart broke as he exhaled, blood running from his wrists along the underside of his forearms and then, finally, dripping to the floor.

He was crucified.

Head hanging, his legs bunched up beneath him, Barry suddenly became aware of the rough wooden pillar running up the middle of his back. The pillar then split off into a lowercase T, running along his arms, leaving only the top of the T for his head. But it hurt too much to raise his head. It was as though someone had a chain around his neck and was pulling him forward to the floor.

Sweat coating his skin, the dripping blood rolling and tickling him beneath his arms, his sides, driving him mad—Barry bellowed, and begged to be released. This was not right. He was not worthy to be punished like this—to be tortured like this—hanging from a tree. Though Barry had shunned God ever since losing Margaret, he now realized why he was here, why the Magic Man was putting him through this.

At least a partial answer, anyway.

Finally Barry knew what love was, what lengths a man was willing to go to, to be with the person he truly loved. What a Man over two thousand years ago did for a people who turned Him away.

Barry knew he was not worth it. He wasn't God's Son. He wasn't on a Holy mission to save the lost.

Suddenly, he wished he was already dead. He deserved that, death, and not being put to the test the same way the Son of the Most High had.

"Help!" The effort of exerting his voice sent a sharp pain through his chest. He tasted blood. He tried to spit it out, but there wasn't enough moisture in his mouth to do so. Panting, he tried calling out again. This time his voice was weak, desperate. "Help . . . somebody . . . somebody help me . . ."

After all those years of thinking he had nothing left to lose, he was now begging for his life. The Magic Man was in another part of the cave, somewhere behind that rusted iron door, no doubt ignoring him. Barry would give anything for another brand of torture.

Just not this.

"Help . . ." Barry said, his voice barely audible even to himself.

The pain in his arms, his legs, his chest, tore at his muscles. Then fiery pain took him and he saw no more.

———

"Wake up, Barry. You're done."

A voice. Who was there? Where was he?

"I said to wake up, Barry."

An open palm slapped him across the cheek. He barely felt it. Barry blinked open his eyes and squinted at the bright light of the candle. For a brief moment, he thought he was upside down again, but then he realized the teardrop shape of the candle was upright. The flame was held before his face; beyond its glow, the Magic Man grinned.

"What?" Barry wheezed.

"You're done," the Magic Man said. He smiled this time, his cheeks rising up in wrinkles on his face.

"Done what? What did I do?" His mind quickly felt like it was floating on a sea of mush. Only fragmented memories of blazing pain and unscratched itches and unrelieved tickles filled his mind.

The Magic Man brought the flame closer. Barry felt its heat. "You're done your time with me. It's over."

"Margaret . . ." Barry barely managed.

"That's right," the man soothingly said. "You can see her now." He waved his hand to somewhere off behind him. "She's over there."

The words not sinking in, the disbelief that all the pain, all the torture, was finally at an end took him. Barry allowed the Magic Man to help him to his feet. Standing on rubbery legs, Barry glanced down at himself and in the candle's faint glow saw his legs were covered in bandages. Same with his arms, his body, everywhere. A few red blotches dotted the bandages, blood from the wounds. There was little pain.

"I gave you some morphine to help make moving about easier. Just mind your step. Take it slow," the Magic Man said. "And, of course, a special touch to aid in your healing."

Barry wasn't sure, but he thought he heard the Magic Man add, "Physically, anyway."

His dry throat made swallowing an effort. "Why—"

"No questions, please. I just needed to make you suffer, so I could come through on my end." The Magic Man took a step closer, his mouth at Barry's ear. His breath was hot and smelled awful. "She's waiting. Go to her." The Magic Man gave him the candle, its shaft thick, hot wax running down its length. A bony finger pointed to the darkness across from them.

After all those years of pain, the hot wax dripping onto his hand didn't bother Barry. Not wanting to spend any more time with the Magic Man, he wandered into the darkness, the candle lighting his way.

He checked over his shoulder only to see the man was gone, nothing but pitch black, a black with an odd depth to it that made it seem to go on forever.

Out of the darkness, the Magic Man called, "Keep going. You're almost there." There was a pause. "You're welcome."

Barry continued on for a long time, wondering what the Magic Man meant by Margaret being "over there."

His walking seemed to go on for an eternity, each moment tainted with the memory of endless years of pain.

The silence of the dark void was suddenly broken by sobbing. Barry hurried toward its source. It wasn't long before he found Margaret, hands bound above her head in shackles, hanging by a chain, her body red with blood.

Setting It Right

Do overs away, ripped from every day
Candy coated lovers with nothing to say
A break in between, sudden and clean
Filled with a fear neither had seen

The rumblings of a watershed stir about in his head
But can never see over the love and red
And as the tide fades, he looks at the shades
Of a sudden, shattering the glass heart he'd made

When you can set it right
Laugh and count to three
And if you're lucky today all day
The Magic Man will come for thee

Blackness is heart, music is art
And he just lost her; she filled the part
Of his core squealing with loss and heartbroken feelings
Dismal and dark, he feels his consciousness peeling

No hope, no rope
To pull him to cope
With the absence of luminance
Her song made him dance

Try again, try again
Laugh and count to three
And if you're lucky tonight all night
The Magic Man will come for thee

INTRODUCTION TO A MAGICAL ORIGIN

The story of how the Magic Man came to be has been around for a long time. Fifty-plus years, I'd say, give or take a decade.

It all depends on who's telling the tale.

When I heard it, it had taken place in 1954, fifty years ago as of this writing. A friend of mine, who'd also heard it but from a different source, said the story of how the Magic Man was born took place in 1948. A couple of years back, an ex-girlfriend of mine had also heard the story but, she said, it took place in 1967. I guess no one really knows the precise year the Magic Man came into being.

What's strange, though, is that—being the Ripper buff that I am—when I was reading about that horrible autumn in East End London, 1888, a theory as to who Jack the Ripper was and why he'd gone around murdering people was strangely reminiscent of the Magic Man tale. I'll let you figure out that parallel for yourself.

Especially on the motivation side of things.

Could it be that the Magic Man isn't some fifty-some-odd-year-old spook tale but perhaps something older? One hundred years older? One hundred-sixteen years older? Maybe the Magic Man was around *before* the autumn of 1888. It certainly is possible. I mean, how many ghost stories have we heard that we thought were recent but it turned out our parents had heard the same tale when they were kids? I could name a few off the top of my head, the classic one about the guy with a hook for a hand being the first to come to mind.

Regardless, the story of the Magic Man has been around for a long time. I cannot promise you the version I'm about to share is the true story, but it was the one told to me when I was eleven or twelve, sitting around a campfire at Camp Arnes, a Christian summer camp, about an hour and a bit from where I live.

What I find odd now, looking back on it, is how the legend of the Magic Man made its way into a camp that, really, was supposed to be, what, holy? Typically, dark stories aren't told at Christian camps, or any form of Christian gathering for that matter.

It makes me wonder how far the Magic Man's reach is and if there's anywhere he cannot go.

- A.P. Fuchs, October 17, 2004

THE LITTLE BOY WHO WOULD

It didn't really look like her, Gene thought, but it was close enough. He had drawn his mom's face and colored it in as best he could using the crayons from the same box he had since the first grade. He was in grade four now. After drawing up his mother's portrait on the six-inch-squared piece of paper, he taped it to the empty soda bottle he had brought up the rocky hill with him.

This'll show her, he thought. The anger inside still hadn't abated even though what his mom did happened about an hour before.

After setting the bottle on top of a boulder that was about shoulder height, he bent down and picked up a stone the size of a large marble, and pulled his slingshot from his back pocket. Straightening, he nestled the rock in the loading pouch. Setting the slingshot to his shoulder as though a rifle, he turned about-faced and marched ten paces.

"Ready" —he stuck the slingshot out in front of him, one hand on the grip, the other maintaining the stone in the loading pouch— "Aim" —he spun around and aligned the bell of the slingshot's Y with the bottle— "Fire!" —he released the stone. It was a tiny gray blur as it cut through the air.

This is what you get, he thought. He was so sure the stone was going to hit the bottle and land squarely between his "mother's" eyes. Instead, it sailed right over it. Gene threw the slingshot to the ground.

"Crap, man!" he spat. *It's your fault!* His mom had made him so angry even his concentration was ruined.

Stuffing his hands in his pockets, he stood staring at the ground for a moment before bending down to pick up the slingshot. As his fingertips trailed along the ground before curling themselves under the handle, he inadvertently rubbed away some of the gravelly dust beneath the slingshot and revealed a small spot of glassy purple. Looking closer and wiping more of the dust away with the sleeve of his jean jacket, he uncovered a patch of purple crystal. If it was black it could have easily been mistaken for mica. He never knew a rock could be purple though.

A few feet away was another small mound of gravel dust. Gene went over to it, squatted down and batted it away with his sleeve, like he had the other. Beneath it was another smear of purple crystal, this one a little bigger than the other by a good inch or two around.

"Cool," he said and scratched at it, thinking maybe he could dig it up. The crystal was as part of the rocky hill he was on as were the boulders that jutted out from it.

In his peripheral, he noticed patches of gravel dust began dotting the ground around him, springing up out of the hill like weeds from dirt.

Where is it coming from? he thought.

The crystal at his feet! What if it was like gold? What if it was worth tons and tons of money? Though only nine years old, he knew the value of money and that if you had enough of it, you could get anything you wanted.

Maybe you can do whatever you want to, too? he thought.

It certainly was possible. After all, Flin Flon, where he lived, was a mining town and was founded because of gold. But how did all those miners miss the purple crystal? Were they blind?

"I don't care," he said. "It's mine now. Hear that, Ma? It's mine now! Mine, mine, mine, and with it I can get all the BB guns I want! Forty zillion of them, if I wanted to." He walked over to the soda bottle, staring a hole into his "mom." "You won't be able to tell me what to do ever again. Ever!"

Slingshot still in hand, he wound up, making sure the hard plastic of the V part of the Y would hit it square on, and swung at the bottle. *Chink!* The bottle went sailing, as did his mom. The tinny, glassy ring of the bottle shattering against stone made him smile.

He had more crystal to find.

Three quarters of an hour later, every small mound of gravel dust had been wiped away. Over one hundred shiny patches of purple crystal sparkled in the sun. Admiring all the work he accomplished, he wiped the sweat off his forehead with his sleeve.

"Where is everyone?" he said. No one had come by since he'd been up here. He should have seen another kid or four by now. Nearly everyone in his class had been on this hill at one time or another and some of the guys he knew spent nearly every day there, whipping rocks at each other, playing war. "Weird," he added.

Squinting, he glanced over the many patches of purple, hoping to see some kind of pattern. The only pattern—which seemed more of an actual design—was some of the patches were closer together than others. The patches ran in a row over a distance of about twenty feet then arced inward like the hook of a cane.

Gene followed the curve, quickly realizing his walking along the cane's arc was taking longer than covering the two right turns. The arc kept going, spiraling inward, circle after circle. Though the cane's arc originally covered about fifteen feet widthwise, Gene knew he was walking a lot further than that.

The spiral's path grew tighter and tighter with each pass. Try as he might, he couldn't take his eyes off the shiny purple patches of smooth crystal between his feet. There was this nagging feeling lurking in the back of his thoughts that told him if he did look up, he'd lose the trail and would have to start all over again. But there was more to it than that, which caused him worry. Not only was he sure he'd stray off the path—however small and tight it already was—he'd also *fall* off it, too; plunge forever into a void or chasm of some kind, never to be saved or found.

A minute later it felt like his eyes were spinning and turning and twisting and rolling in their sockets. His stomach contracted and expanded in sickening bursts of what he called the "puke pump." The back of his throat brought to life the taste of that morning's bacon and eggs, digested and *used*. His brain seemed as if it was spinning inside his skull like a plate did when you held it down with one finger and rotated it with the other.

Knees shaking, tears turning the grayish-brown of the rock and the smooth bits of purple into a distorted mosaic, his puke pump about to launch a healthy dose of chunky throw up, Gene glanced away from the path.

The ground disappeared beneath him.

———

Hello, Gene.
"Huh?"
Hello, Gene.
"Who's there?"
Hello.
Gene.
"Who's talking?"
Gene, hello.
"Shut up! Turn on the lights!"
Hello, Gene.
"Stop saying my name."
Hello . . .
. . . Gene.

Screaming, Gene spun around in the dark, took a few running steps then stopped abruptly. Something was in front of him. *Someone.*

Gene!

A jolt shot from his hips to the base of his skull; his legs turned to jelly.

"Wh-who's there?" he asked.

Someone was there. He heard them breathing. It sounded *old*, like the way his grandpa breathed.

Shaking, not knowing whether to turn around, look up, or feel what or who was ahead, Gene yelped when a hand touched him on the shoulder from behind.

"Lemme go, lemme go!"

Gene. Hello. Want a BB gun?

"No! I don't want anything. Lemme go now! Now!"

I can give it to you, you know. I can give you more than one, too. I can make it happen.

Screaming, Gene shook free from the fingers grasping his shoulder and ran into the dark. Looking up, hoping to see an opening, anything that revealed where he fell, his heart broke when there was . . . nothing. No light. No hole showing a blue sky. Just darkness.

Stomping his foot, he turned in a circle again, doing his best to keep calm, but in spite of any self-reassurances he was going to be okay, his heart steadily beat harder and harder.

Gene.

The voice. Low and spellbinding.

"Who is that? Tell me!"

I am magic. I am charm. I make everything okay.

Breaking down, face in his hands, Gene sunk to his knees. Was he going to die? Who was with him in the dark? Curse his mother! If she didn't say no to letting him have a BB gun, he wouldn't be down here. He was going to use his own money, for Pete's sake! He saved nearly every stinkin' cent earned from his paper route that spring. It was *his* money and he could do with it what he wanted. He *deserved* it! But noooo, his stupid mother had to have a hatred for guns; for *any* weapons. She didn't even want him to have his slingshot, but thank God for dads. His dad was able to talk his mom into letting him have the slingshot, but only if he agreed to *always* use it outside and never ever aim it at anyone or anything alive. That even included the trees, as far as his mother was concerned. That was why he always went to the hill every time he wanted to "fire a few off."

It's okay, Gene. I'm here for you. Do you want to go home?

"Yes, l-let me out of here." He wiped his eyes, partly ashamed he was crying. Such a baby.

Can I come with you?

His lower lip trembled as more tears came to his eyes. Try as he might, he couldn't bite back the tears. "I don't know." He wiped his eyes again. "Mom!"

The back of his throat burned from his scream. Swallowing was like trying to down a jawbreaker. "Mom . . ." Coughing, a sickening metal taste filled his mouth. He spat. It was so dark he couldn't even see he accidentally spat on his shoes. He only *felt* it.

"Dad! Mom! Help!" Mouth dry, lips pasty, he winced when whoever was in the dark with him spoke again.

If you had that BB gun, you wouldn't be down here, now, would you? If you had that BB gun, you wouldn't be in the dark with me. If you had that BB gun—you wouldn't be crying.

"Quiet!" he demanded. He spun on his heels and after one step found himself under the yellow of a street lamp, that antique kind you saw in history books and old movies.

The lamp cast a small circle of light, perhaps only seven or so feet from one side to the other. Gene ran to the lamppost and hugged it tight.

The post's black metal was warm and comforting.

He hung onto it for a good while before letting go. When he turned around, a glossy wooden table with round legs and a chair with a round seat were now in the circle with him. He glanced up at the streetlamp again, a brief beat of dull pain pulsing against the back of his eyes. When he looked at the table again, a deck of blue, flower-patterned cards sat neatly at the table's center.

Gene went over to it.

Sit down.

"Wha—"

I said sit down!

Gene grabbed the chair and quickly sat on it, the firmness of the voice compelling him to listen. He waited. The lamp buzzed. The air warmed.

Time to play.

Out of the shadows, a young man, perhaps twenty, stepped out. He wore a gray sweatshirt and tight blue jeans and white sneakers. His brown hair was cropped short, a buzz cut like the kind you'd find in the military. His blue eyes, gentle as a mother's touch, set Gene at ease.

"Hello," the man said. His voice was soft and clear, sounding nothing like the haunting voice Gene had heard coming from the darkness moments before.

"Um, hi," Gene replied.

The man came over, his eyes never leaving Gene's. He sat down. "We're going to play a game."

"What, um, what kind of game?" *I'm not supposed to talk to strangers.*

The man glanced at the cards on the table and stuck out his hand for a handshake. "I'm Bill, by the way. I already know your name."

Gene nodded. His heart sped up, but quickly slowed when Bill's reassuring eyes comforted him.

"It is a very simple game," Bill said. He picked up the deck of cards from the table then split it in the middle. "This is a deck of cards."

"Yeah. Duh."

Bill grinned. "There are two halves. One, in my left, has blue flowers on the back. The other red flowers. But remember, they are from the *same* deck. With me so far?"

"Sure," Gene said. *Does he think I'm stupid or something?* He slid his chair closer to the table. The fact he was in a strange dark place somewhere below the rocky hill didn't cross his mind. It was cozy here, like it was when you curled up in bed and hid beneath your quilt.

"Each half has two suits. You do know what a suit is, right?" Bill said.

"Yep. Hearts and diamonds and spades and clubs. Oh, and jokers, too!"

"Very good. But this deck is a little different. Each suit is numbered one through thirteen. There are no face cards. No Ace either. Just a one, instead. And no Jokers. Got it?"

"Yes." His right thigh rapidly bounced up and down; a nervous habit.

"Now, we each get half the deck, the one with the red flowers or the one with the blue." He gesticulated with each half-deck. "Now here's how the game works. We flip a coin to see who goes first. Whoever goes first can choose to lay down either one card or two. If you lay down two, each card must be from a different suit. The suits that belong to the red deck are Reason and Fear. The suits belonging to the blue are Wishes and Hope."

"How do you decide who gets what color?" Gene asked.

"The older person gets the blue. The young—"

"What if there are more than two players?"

"Then the oldest person gets blue Wishes, the next oldest blue Hope, the next oldest after that red Reason, the last Fear."

"What if twins are playing?"

"Then they take their pick. Now listen—the cards are numbered one to thirteen. You can lay down either one card or two. If you put down two, each card has to be from a different suit, okay? Scenario. If you lay down, say, a two of Wishes, I could beat it with a three or higher from the Fear suit. If I lay down a one of Fear, then you beat me and we start over with you deciding to lay down one card or two. And, of course, the same applies for suits Reason and Hope. But Wishes can't compete with Reason and Hopes can't compete with Fear. All right?"

Gene played the rules over in his head. The game seemed simple enough. It was kind of like War, but with slightly more to it.

"Yep. I got it."

"Then let's begin."

———

Bill won the first three hands, Fear dominating two of them and Reason the other. But Gene came back in the fourth hand and stomped out Bill's two of Reason with an immense twelve of Hope. The victory warmed his heart and he couldn't help but smile.

"You caught on," Bill said.

"Yup, sure did," Gene said.

Bill set down a pair of sixes, one from Fear and the other from Reason.

"Say if you laid down a five of Reason and a six of Fear," Gene said, "and I laid down a seven of Hope but only a two of Wishes, that's a tie, right?"

"Depends on the numerical difference between the suits. Using your example, if you laid down a seven of Hope, you beat my five of Reason by two. However, your Wishes lost to Fear by a value of four. Which is greater, two or four?"

"Four," he murmured, then spoke up, "but what if I beat one of them by three and lost another by three, then what?"

"Then it's declared an official tie and each of us get a point. In this case, you have to beat my Fear card with a seven or higher. Same with my Reason card."

"What if—"

"Just play."

Eyeing Bill's two sixes, Gene drew one card from each of his own piles and when he flipped them over, he was relieved when he saw he had turned over an eight of Hope and a ten of Wishes.

Bill proffered a golfer's clap. "Bravo, Gene. Well done."

"Gee, thanks, Mister. Um, Bill, I meant to say."

Grinning, Bill straightened his Reason and Fear decks. Gene laid down his next card; only one this time, a one of Wishes.

Just one wish, he thought absentmindedly.

"What is your wish?" Bill asked.

"Just . . ." He bit his tongue. *Mom said no. I just hoped that—* "—she would buy it for me." His heart was heavy. "All I wanted was a BB rifle. Is that bad?"

"No," Bill said, "it is not bad. You had a desire and you had it turned down. It happens. Sometimes we don't get what we want."

Gene sat back and folded his arms, frowning. "We should."

"Do you think the world would be a better place if everyone got what they wanted?"

I know I'd be happy if I got everything I wanted, he thought. "Yeah. Then people wouldn't get mad when they couldn't get what they really wanted."

Bill paused a moment, squinting one eye. Then he said, "Can I tell you a secret?"

Shrugging first then sitting back up in his seat, Gene said, "Yeah?"

"When you beat me, there, with your stronger Wishes and Hope cards against my Fear and Reason cards, you helped someone achieve what they wanted, *get* what they wanted."

"I did?" *How?* This guy was a nut!

"These are special cards, Gene," Bill said, "and if you and I keep playing, and if you keep winning, you can help other people get what they want."

"Really? But . . . but how do I keep on winning?"

"Hmmm, well, the only bit of advice I can give you is that you listen to your heart when it comes to choosing to lay down one or two cards whenever it's your turn to start a hand. Remember, with two cards, you risk a chance of a tie and though we each get a point, someone out there gets what they want and someone else doesn't."

Then I can play just one card all the time, he thought cleverly. "Okay."

Bill said they would finish their current game then begin the next hand.

"I'm going to beat you, you know," Gene said.

"I don't know about that. There are a lot of people to help."

"Whenever you're ready."

"Let's go."

———

Even after all this time, Gene was still shamed by his nakedness. The years . . . . He had outgrown his pants and underwear long ago. He only wore his sweatshirt when he was cold, but that lasted only a short time until the pressure of a boy's shirt against a man's frame was too restrictive, making it difficult to breathe.

Now a man—mid-thirties would be his guess, but he didn't know how long he had been down here—his dark hair long and matted, hanging down to his bottom, his beard almost as long, hanging past his gut. His skin was pale and blistered with sores; some of his wounds still hadn't healed. He hadn't had a real meal in decades.

Many years before, after several hours of playing that card game of Wishes and Hope and Reason and Fear, Gene had wanted to leave. Bill wouldn't let him. Bill said there was no way out. He said they had to keep playing, keep helping people. So Gene played a little longer and asked to leave again. Bill still said no. Figuring it was only a matter of time before Bill would call it quits from being too tired, Gene thought he'd escape while Bill was asleep, but Bill didn't sleep that night or any other to follow. Bill never slept.

Only allowed to rest a bit here and there, Gene was told he had to keep playing the game, keep helping people get what they wanted, keep satisfying wishes and hopes and warding off fear, getting things, sometimes, in spite of reason.

Perhaps a week or so into the game, Gene threw over the table, the cards scattering across the stone floor. He told Bill to rot in Hell and refused to play.

What a mistake, Gene thought. He remembered Bill somehow appearing behind him and with thick fingers grabbing him by the scruff of the neck, dragging him into the darkness.

Gene never forgot the first time he felt the hot sting of a lead-beaded whip tear into his back. Never forgot the soothing warmth of blood oozing over the wounds, temporarily washing away the pain.

From then on, with each refusal to play, he was beaten. With each attempt at escape, he was beaten worse. Bill barely fed him; only gave him enough food and water to survive, but not enough to keep him strong.

Head heavy, eyes drooping, Gene was prepared to sell his soul, just to die and be rid of Bill and that blasted card game.

But you're helping people, Gene thought. *You're doing the right thing. But . . . but you're also losing your own life. There's no way out. There's nothing down here except Bill and Fear and Reason and Wishes and . . . .* There was no hope. Not anymore.

Gene looked at Bill's eleven of Fear.

I have a two in thirteen chance of beating him and a one in thirteen chance of tying him. He'd played this hand hundreds of times before. Sometimes he won and sometimes not. If his stomach wasn't so empty, he would throw up from just looking at the cards. Instead, he was forced to endure nauseating throbs and gut-twisting sickness.

He forced himself to remain seated at the table, forced himself to play.

Hand trembling, he reached for the deck of Wishes, not caring if he won or lost, if he helped someone receive the thing or person or feeling they wanted most, or if the person broke down inside from a desire unmet and they became self-destructive to ward off the pain.

It doesn't matter, he thought. *It's because of them, those selfish, no good, filthy, stupid people that I'm here.* Taking a card, he paused before turning it over. *What would Mom say? She'd want you to hope for the best, to help others.* His inner monologue still carried the voice of a nine-year-old. But then, in a darker and lower voice, that of a man. *Screw her! She didn't give you that BB gun! It was just a toy rifle. A stupid toy! Mom. She's why you're here. If it weren't for her—* He flipped the card over. It was an eight of Wishes.

"Blast them all," he said.

Bill didn't say anything. He never said anything. Not anymore. Who Gene once thought of as a kind man who only wanted to help people was now just some sort of demonic host at a never-ending gaming party. Knowing that Bill knew he knew there was nothing he could do to escape . . . . He wanted to die.

And that's what I'm going to do, after this game is over and I'm allowed to sleep, he thought. If *he lets me sleep.*

Hope, foreign yet familiar, finally came.

Ambling through the dark, Gene went to the corner of what he dubbed his "cell," a small room six-and-one-half grown-man paces by seven; double that when he was a kid. Bill had introduced him to the room the first time he slept down here, beneath the earth, away from his mother, his life and everything else he once knew.

His mother.

She must have been worried sick because of him. Even now, he still never accepted that, in her mind, he *was* presumed dead. *But they never found a body,* he thought. He could only imagine her guilt or how many times she must have wished she would have gone after him the day he stomped out of the house.

All over a BB rifle. So stupid. The toy-that-everyone-wanted-and-some-had no longer meant a thing to him. The day he stopped caring was the day he saw the toy next to his chair, leaning up against the seat, just waiting for him to finally pick it up, cradle it; the object that led him to a life of Fear and Reason and Wishes and Hope.

"Can I go now?" he had asked Bill that day. If it was day, that was. He slept so little that day and night became one.

Gently placing a hand on his shoulder, Bill said very simply, "No," and crossed to the other side of the table and sat down. Even after years of playing a game he could barely stand, even after giving up his life to help others, even after receiving the toy that had caused him so much pain and in a way things having come full circle—his life was still forfeit. He tried to kill Bill that day. He dove over the table and tackled him to the floor. The moment they landed, Gene found himself flipped onto his back, Bill on top of him, his captor's hard knuckles smashing over and over into his face.

Now in his room without light, crouched in the corner, Gene held the rifle for the first time in years. It was heavier then he remembered it. But he was also thinner now—*weaker*—than the day he first received it.

I'm so sorry, Mom, he thought. He then whispered, "So sorry." *I don't deserve anything. Should never have asked for this thing. It's just a gun. Just a stupid gun used to kill—* "—people. Things. Me." Tears leaked from the corners of his eyes and rolled down his cheeks. The salty liquid stung his dry, cracked skin. He didn't wipe the tears away. He deserved the discomfort. He didn't deserve reprieve.

He set the rifle barrel beneath his chin, resting its butt-end on the ground.

Finally, he thought. *Peace.*

He pulled the trigger.

The empty *click* that echoed in the small stone room was as devastating as if a real bullet had discharged.

Just a pellet, he remembered. *Not a bullet.* He hadn't checked to see if the weapon was loaded with the BB pellets the toy was supposed to come with. Actually, he had forgotten it was just a toy. If only it could have discharged. If only . . .

"I don't understand you, Gene. This is how you thank me for giving you what you wanted?" Bill said from behind him. The way the man could sneak up on you—so silently—chilled the nerves.

Anguish wrenched Gene's heart at the sound of Bill's voice. He dropped the rifle and placed his face in his hands. *I'm sorry. I'm sorry. Sorry. So sorry.* The words were like pins pricking his heart and mind; the painful piercings he deserved.

"What do you want me to do?" he asked. *He's going to whip the hell out of me again.* "No," he whispered. "No more." *Just kill me.*

"It's too late for that, Gene. I gave you what you wanted. You ignored it. I gave you the chance to help people, prevent them from suffering from being without the thing they wanted most, and you tried to end your ability to help them with a toy."

"No, it's not like that! I just want to go home! I just want to go—"

Somehow, without making a sound, Bill was right next to him, his thick hands pressing down on his shoulders, gripping him, holding him so he couldn't move.

"From this day forward, you will service others," Bill said. "You will grant their wishes and erase their fears. You will give them hope and oppose any reason, even Reason itself, so that they can achieve peace."

Bill leaned closer, his hot breath tickling the inside of Gene's ear. "You will not rest until everyone living is helped. Every. Single. One."

Tears flowing freely, Gene could barely find the strength to speak. "But that's impossible. I can't . . . too long . . . I can't do it."

Releasing him, Bill stood. "I know."

DESECRATION OF IS

Victimization is everything when you become slave to a system of existence of living of dying and though things cannot change you force yourself to do everything within your power to become all powerful all changing all needing and wanting and eventually consuming and though you defy fate fate defies you and soon you seek outside help because what are we but alone just alone and no matter how stronger or smart or powerful you are there is always someone stronger and smarter and more powerful except for me as I have been given everything to right the wrongs and wrong the rights and contrast your life as you wish it to be however my favors were not given to me by choice though I was told during the card game that I chose to receive the ability to change destiny so be it I will acknowledge it but never accept it for few accept the fate we've been given no we always must change something as humans are selfish and pitiful creatures I once was human but now am more than man perhaps even a god speaking of which I do not know who or what gave me these powers other than his name was Bill and surely he was not a man but now I can serve you now I must serve you in order to be free of this curse of aid yet in return for my services I wish to have something more you must give me yourself and endure what I've endured in order to receive the thing or person or state of mind or spirit that you want most so I ask you again can you take it can you give it do you really want it that badly I know I can take it and give it and I want you to be happy that badly for my freedom depends on it yet why press on in such an impossible task well here's why and that's because we are never happy with what fate has given us and what destiny has decreed to be true.

by the Magic Man
Time: nonexistent
Place: the cave, where nothing matters

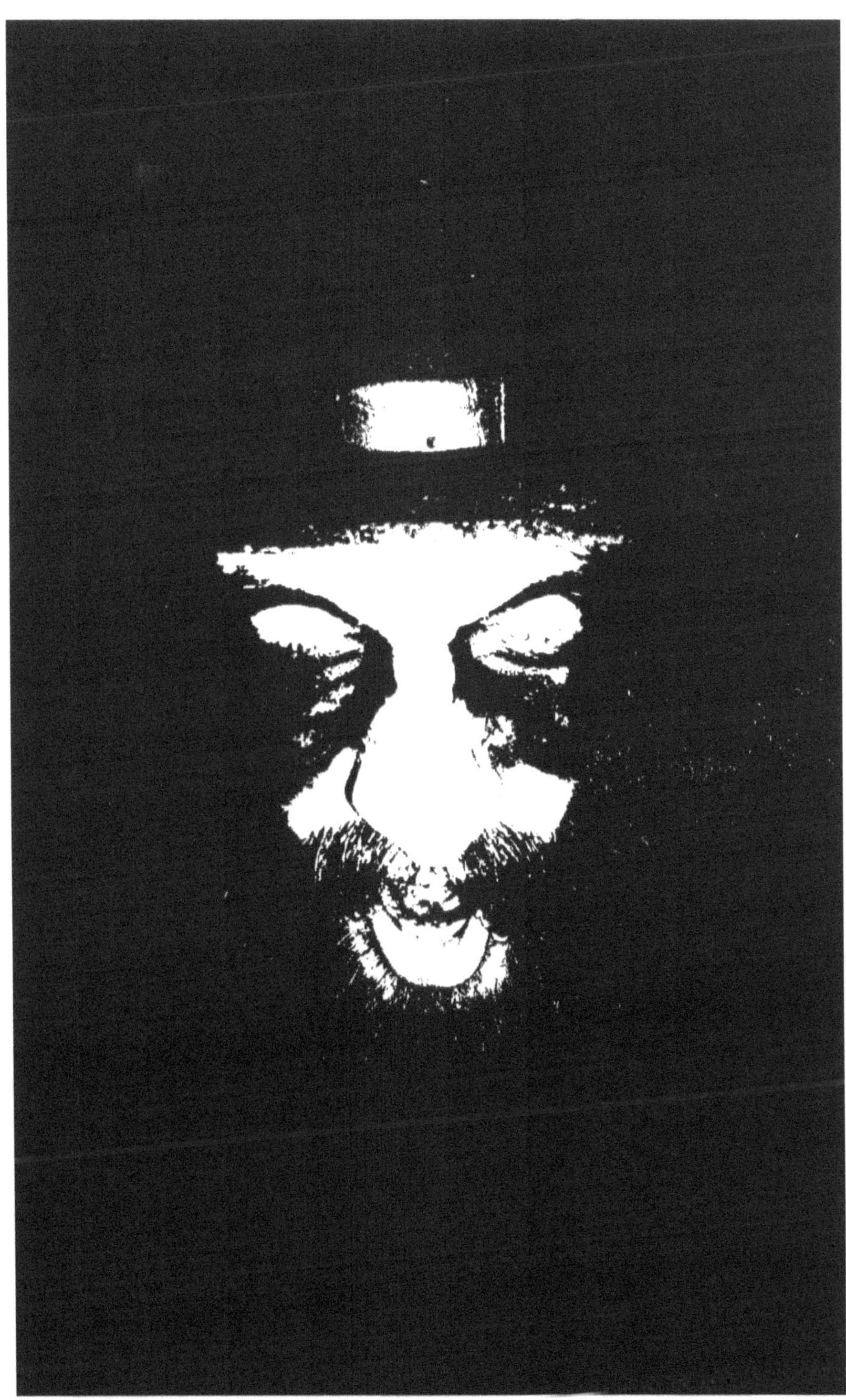

SHEDDING THE SKIN

It had been living inside him for so long that it didn't know if it could break free. His body was its home. But, it had come to this place before, the time to shed the old skin and find a new, younger host. It was a lion. Its name, as dubbed by the press, Beast of Night. Beast lived in the body of Herman Gordes. But it wasn't much of a body anymore. Herman was a paraplegic, his neck having been broken when Beast tangled with the swamp monster of Spirits Bog a long time ago.

Before, on the nights when the Northern Lights danced like wisps of bright cloud on a chalkboard, coming out of Herman was easy. Now, coming out was difficult as Herman, having resigned to being a seventy-two-year-old man in a wheelchair, had stopped feeding Beast the anger needed to be released.

Beast was on his own. These past few months when the Northern Lights graced the sky, Beast could feel them, sense them, hear them call. But Herman, unbeknownst to himself, would keep the lion contained.

It was time to break free.

Here, inside this body, there was darkness. The only light coming in when it was day, the sun's rays shining through Herman's old flesh in an odd array of oranges and reds, while he was out in his wheelchair, his nurse having taken his shirt off so he could get some sun.

It was night now, and Beast had no light to guide him in his task.

I'm leaving, Beast told Herman.

Herman gurgled something in his sleep. That was all.

Good-bye.

Forepaws pressing against Herman's ribcage, Beast let his claws break free. They punctured the flesh and a spurt of blood splashed him in the face. He didn't mind. It fueled him to dig further. Herman awoke and Beast felt him trying to find the strength to scream. He didn't want his friend to suffer. Quickly, he scraped away Herman's lungs, the flesh leaking down the interior of the rib cage like oil on a wall.

Bone. There was bone in the way. Beast brought his paws back and thrust them forward, his claws poking through the gaps in the cage and through the muscle and skin on the other side. For the first time ever, his claws probed the air of Herman's bedroom. He curled his paws, the pads finding purchase on Herman's rib bones.

Beast pulled and the bones tore apart, snapping like dried twigs, blood splashing as high as the ceiling. Like a dead man rising from the grave, Beast rose from Herman's body. His friend lay there, his chest a messy heap of skin and bone and flesh, ripped and torn in pink and red folds.

Beast blinked his eyes and saw the world for the first time in years.

Tonight he would find a new host.

SPINNING ROOM

It had to work. Sharon was sure of it. She knew what was going to happen; her heart rate was already quickening.

Thunder crashed and lightning flickered in sharp flashes against the deep purple sky beyond the gray, marble railing to her left. The lightning's bright flash reflected off the shiny surface of the gigantic marble pillar on her right; if it wasn't for being under such terrible circumstances, she might have stopped and waited for the lightning to bounce off the surface again just so she could say it was beautiful.

This place, this room—this *round* room—a balcony wrapped around a massive pillar like a band around a finger, was as good a place as any to be on All Hallows Eve. But it wasn't really a room, was it? More like a washer around an amazingly tall cylinder, or a gigantic ring encircling a pillar so far and wide that it dwarfed anything the Greeks or Romans could conjure up.

Thunder boomed.

The air changed, humid now, feeling thick. Sharon kept her pace.

She rounded the corner, hoping she could change things. Adjust . . . something . . . so she and her family wouldn't die. So they'd be fine.

Thunder crashed again, sending a shockwave through her chest. Lightning followed this time and right at the last bright white flash, was her Aunt Clora, beautiful as always. Aunt Clora stood about midway between the railing and the wall, her white dress—bright but with dark, shadowy folds in the material—blowing in the gentle breeze. Black rings encircled her eyes, complimenting her long red hair, the ringlets blowing with what seemed to be a harsher wind. Almost as if the wind blowing her dress blew in opposing directions and speed as the wind that blew against her hair.

There was the glint of black metal as Clara raised her hand and aimed a gun at Sharon.

Sharon poured on the speed, praying her aunt would be kind enough to let her pass. Sharon ran by her, already *changing* something. Her aunt's gun remained aimed at her. If Clora fired . . .

Almost past, almost past, Sharon thought. Her heart ached from its rapid beating and she could envision the flakes of cracked dry skin at the back of her throat. Each panting breath only dried it out even more. She should have drank something before she started the "obstacle" course again.

Thunder boomed.

No, not thunder—

The bullet blasted its way into Sharon's left shoulder blade, exiting through a neat hole in the middle of her front deltoid. Blood splashed out of her red sweatshirt, the two tones oddly clashing with each other. Fire stung her skin; her left arm burned, but the sharp pain of the bullet wound burned even more.

She kept running, her tears making it difficult to see. No matter how many times she wiped them away, they returned full force. Pressing her other hand against her shoulder to slow the bleeding, her stomach twisted into a knot at the feel of the warm blood spilling from her wound.

Her bones ached.

Something else was about to happen now. Supposed to happen.

At least she remembered to look to her right this time. On her previous run, she had forgotten and only remembered at the last second, but it had been too late, she having ran past her mother and the man about to end her mom's life.

Already watching the wall, she came around the bend, the gray marble abruptly stopping and becoming a tinted window. It was difficult to see through the window running by as quickly as she was, but she did make out the two figures inside. One was tall and lean, the other shorter and plump.

Her mother was in a private room with a man, someone who was not her father or anyone she recognized.

Mom, get out of there, she thought, *the other guy's gonna come in*. She didn't know how she knew a second man was going to enter the room through a black door, a bar of dim yellow light coming from the room or hall beyond. But he was going to come in wearing red. The tall man . . . he wore blue.

A faint memory crept to the fore of her mind. She wasn't supposed to know the stocky man in the red jumpsuit and hood was going to come in the room.

Not supposed to know? Eyes still on the window, tears filled them the moment the tall man grabbed her mother and tore her apart, his long sharp nails digging into her mother's doughy flesh, ripping her insides open. Blood burst from her mother's body like water from a balloon.

Sharon ran past the window. In spite of the heartache and blazing pain in her shoulder, she forced herself to wipe her eyes and press on. There was another that needed saving.

It wasn't long before Sharon's legs filled with fatigue, hot, gooey blobs of tiredness invading her thighs and calves. Her pace slowed; her biceps ached and raising her arms was nearly impossible.

He's just around the next turn, she thought. She pressed on toward her father. Already she could envision what was happening in her absence. This particular arc of the Spinning Room seemed extra long for some reason, almost as if the path was straight instead of curved. Readying herself for the smooth marble to end and for the chalky gray of ancient Roman-like pillars to appear, arranged in a waist-high railing, Sharon's lungs screamed, her breathing rapidly increasing. She suddenly forgot what was supposed to happen now, what she was supposed to stop.

Before she could slow down to think or even just catch her breath, the thick stone railing supported by miniature Roman-like pillars appeared. Over the railing was a rectangular room, inset into the wall. The wall, like the railing, was a powdery, light gray stone. The sound of rippling water came from just below the railing.

To her right, her father stood with his back to her, hands raised, the baggy sleeves of his green sweater bunching around his elbows. At an angle across from him, a figure in a black hood and robe held him in the sights of a sleek black rifle. The mysterious figure bore an unsettling resemblance to Death.

Purple clouds tumbled and twirled above like fluff in a dryer. Thunder rumbled both far off and also near.

"Dad!"

He didn't seem to hear her. Maybe he wasn't allowed to turn around? Maybe the figure in the black robe would shoot him if he did?

White rope. It was more of a sensation than a thought, but the image of a white rope came to the surface of her mind.

Glancing to her left, she saw a dark purple stone box pushed up against the outside railing. The box was about a half-foot shorter than the railing, but the white coil of rope on its top made its total height a good six inches above the railing, if not more.

Black handle. Another sensation, another *knowing* of a kind.

Disregarding the consequences of what she was about to do, Sharon ran toward the rope and grabbed the black handle that sat in the coil's middle. It was only when she stood on the railing and looked down did she realize what she was doing. The endless abyss of swirling purple and gray cloud below made her head swim.

Light headed, certain she was going to faint, Sharon fought to stay coherent. A ways behind her, over her right shoulder stood her father, hands still in the air. His balding head caught the light of a jagged slash of lightning that shot through the sky, then just as quickly disappeared.

The figure in the black robe—it was closer to him.

Okay, here we go, she thought. She did this before. Many times. At least, she thought she had.

Sharon ran along the railing, away from her father. The rope unraveled a good fifteen or twenty feet before it went taut. The moment the rope tugged on its bond to the purple box, Sharon dove off the railing's edge, hoping her grip would hold on the handle. Immediately her body jerked to her right and fell, hot wind blowing her hair back. Reaching the base of her downward arc, she shot upward, her body quickly sailing toward railing-level. Still rising upward, she passed the man in the robe and her father, and when the rope hit the pinnacle of its swing, she twisted her body to the right so she was facing them. She leaned over to the left as she descended. Her shoulder ached, but she swallowed the pain and ignored it.

With the skill of having done it countless times before—from other "runs" through the obstacle course that was the Spinning Room—she pulled on the rope and jolted herself down its length, grabbing the rope where it was still taut.

Legs outstretched, she swung in and knocked the cloaked figure to the ground. The shiny black rifle went off as its butt-end hit the ground.

Her father fell, blood spurting from his chest.

———

Aunt Clora aimed the gun at Sharon.

Move! Sharon screamed inside and darted past her. The gun went off and Sharon ducked instinctively. The bullet grazed her shoulder, tearing up a chunk of the white nightgown she wore. *Wait, red sweater, right?* she thought. The realization of difference in apparel quickly faded.

"Come back here!" Clora yelled after her. The voice was distant, melodious, and seeming to come from somewhere ahead of her instead of behind.

Lightning slashed the sky in zig-zagging lines. Thunder rolled along the purple and gray clouds.

Digging her bare heels into the marble floor, she pressed on, already envisioning the tinted window about to appear on her right.

"Mom!" she said and ran even harder.

Stopping before the window, she found it difficult to breathe as she frantically tried to figure a way in. Banging on the glass with the undersides of her fist, Sharon hoped the sound would distract the man in the blue outfit—Blue—long enough for her mother to get away and not endure whatever he had planned.

"Watch out for the one in red!" Sharon shouted through the glass.

Her mother glanced over at her, smiled sweetly, her aged eyes reading, "I know what I'm doing."

The short man in the red suit—Red—entered the room and joined his friend. Before long, her mother fell from view. A gush of red streamed upward, splashing the window.

"No!" Sharon's cries were quickly silenced by a devastating boom of thunder.

Next time, she thought. *Next time.*

She ran.

The desire to redeem herself burned a hole through her heart. She saved herself from her aunt, but let her mother die. Her father was the only one left. She knew what was going to happen. She just couldn't remember if she knew *how* it was going to happen and how she could save him.

He died last time, right? she thought. She couldn't remember. Memories of efforts to save her parents ending in failure kept her thoughts in a foul mix.

Sweat trickled off the baseline of her hair, down her neck, and rode the contours of her back and pooled at the waistband of her jeans.

Look out for the man in black. The pace of her thoughts matched that of her stride. *Man in—*

And then she saw him. Spikes of lightning zig-zagged so close to the smooth marble railing that Sharon was certain the figure's black cloak would burst into flames. He stood near the railing, the clouds crashing, thundering, booming behind him.

*Now that would be a blessing. I wouldn't have to—*The white rope! There, beside the dark figure.

She poured on the speed and, a moment later, a sudden flash of gray followed by a rush of black as her face slammed into the marble floor.

The sound of impact ran through her head from front to back then hung above her ears. Hot pain sliced the front of her ankle, then the back, then the front again. She felt like she had just stubbed her toes, too.

Drawing her knees to her chest, she slowly got up, her head still bowed and her fingertips bracing her on either side, keeping her balanced. Standing straight up, she winced as she carefully set her left foot down.

Parting the brown hair that hung over her eyes, she screamed when she saw her father on his knees before the man in the dark cloak. The rifle—now silver—was to her father's head and with the next bang of thunder the end of the gun barrel sparked a bright yellow star, the color quickly replaced by a glistening upward spray of deep red.

———

Her left foot was fine. There was no headache or ringing originating from inside.

I wish I could see Aunt Clora well before she tries to kill me instead of this stupid gray pillar that hides everything beyond each curve, Sharon thought.

The stone pillar that was part of the path she followed was enormous. Its curve was so slight that it felt like you were moving in a straight line when running next to it.

What if she ran alongside the railing instead of beside the pillar? Would it make a difference? She might get a better view of her aunt.

Crossing over the reflective gray-speckled, marble floor, she brought her hands up, already imagining the bang from Aunt Clora's gun.

She ran, an impending feeling that she had to get to . . . someone . . . soon or the worst would happen. Far off, where the railing began curving inward, a flutter of white . . . cloth? . . . materialized.

"She's waiting for me," Sharon said. *She's waiting . . . waiting for me.*

The flowing white material moved rhythmically in an unfelt wind, growing closer.

Her thoughts ceased and her legs brought her nearer to the woman about to kill her.

She's waiting for me. The thought was a welcome noise in a too-silent mind. *Waiting!*

Sharon crossed the floor again, back to the pillar. She slowed to a jog then stopped completely. It might work. This whole repetition of events felt like a game, but Sharon couldn't recall what game she was playing or who she was playing it with.

Keeping herself as close to the wall as possible, she slowly stepped forward. *Not too far . . . not too close, either.*

"Wait," she whispered. Stopping, she swallowed the lump in her throat.

Moments crept by and her legs grew jittery. *Have to hurry and run. You have to hurry and—No! Don't do it. Stay put or move slowly, but do not run!* The words inside her head carried the firm voice of her mother scolding her when she had done something wrong.

The white fabric of her aunt's dress crossed back over to the right. She would be there any moment, gun poised, ready to kill.

Sharon crept forward, trying to make her body one with the wall.

Aunt Clora's shoulders and hips were clearly visible now, on the other side of the curve far ahead. The rest of her would soon follow.

When she's halfway over, before she can see me—Clora's gorgeous red hair hung halfway down her arm. Only half of it was visible.

Sharon ran back across to the railing at an angle, keeping as close to it as she could, restraining herself with everything she had from looking over the edge. But she looked anyway and was lost to the paint-like swirls of purple, indigo, gray and blue. There was nothing down there yet there was everything. Its depth ran for miles and her body ached to jump over the edge to see where it might lead.

About to succumb to its pull, Clora grabbed her.

"Bye-bye," she said in a plucky tone. She brought the gun to Sharon's head.

No! It's not supposed to happen like this! I escaped before. If I did it once I'm supposed to every time, right? Her head ached with confusion.

The instant Clora cocked the gun Sharon ducked low, grabbed the arm with the gun and pulled her aunt to the railing, slamming her aunt's gut against it. Quickly, Aunt Clora twisted, her back pressed against the railing. Wasting no time, Sharon put her hands above Clora's breasts and pushed quick and hard. Aunt Clora toppled over the edge. Sharon broke her momentum forward, palms to the rail.

Clora didn't scream as she fell and disappeared into an inviting pool of moving purple, gray, blue and—

Sharon moved onward.

Okay, get Mom, then Dad right after, Sharon thought. *Moving past Aunt Clora took longer than I thought. So much for my plan.* She doubted that any other she would have come up with would have worked either. *Just run.*

The metallic taste of stale saliva ran over her tongue. Her lungs hurt, but only at their bottoms, like a sharp stick was being driven into the lower part of her ribcage. Her mother would be coming up on the right any moment now.

"Gotta have more time," she said. Her words came out choppy as she ran. It was better to say some of her thoughts out loud than keep them in. It helped keep her head clear.

Glancing over her left shoulder, she checked to see if Aunt Clora had somehow found her way back up and was following behind. All she saw was the long, slightly curved wall that was the pillar in the middle of this Spinning Room.

Spinning Room. That felt somehow *right.* This was a spinning room, wasn't it? The path spun around the pillar and—

A crack of thunder shook the ground. By her right foot, the one closest to the pillar, was a fine black line—a crack of some sort. Despite not wanting to lose time, she forced herself to slow down and eyed the line that separated the pillar from the floor. The blending of the grays of the floor and the wall made it nearly invisible.

Placing a palm on the pillar's smooth surface, she slowed her jog to a brisk walk. Heat brewed beneath her palm as she trailed it against the wall. At the speed she was walking, her outstretched arm should have bent at the elbow as her body caught up to it. But it didn't. Her right arm stayed straight even when she picked up her pace.

She had to get moving. It took so long to get from one "event" to another.

Bursting into a fast run, she charged toward the glass window, hoping she hadn't wasted too much time while she figured out that the floor was spinning—however slowly—around the pillar like a washer around a screw.

How am I gonna save Mom? she thought. The glass that separated her and her mother was *thick,* a Plexiglass of some kind. She had nothing to break it with.

I'll never get out of here— "—unless I save her," she said.

Every ten or so feet, the railing far to the left was separated by stone posts, part of the finely-detailed railing's design. Upon further inspection, the rail appeared old in parts, worn away and cracked at different connecting points, weathered from years of abuse from the storm that raged ever-on around this place.

I wonder . . .

Hope filled her as she crossed to the railing, stopping by one of the dividing posts. The shape on the top of it resembled the smooth, bulbous piece of wood that would sit on top of a square block at the end of a banister.

Wrapping her hands around the back of the sphere, she pulled with everything she had. It wiggled, but nothing more. Planting first her right foot, then her left against the railing, hands still behind the sphere, she pushed her legs outward, assisting her arms.

She grunted, straining to break the top of the post free. Thunder crashed, its sudden sound causing her to jump and apply that much more strain on the post and railing. The railing snapped and her legs shot over the edge; she smacked her tailbone as she hit the ground, her crotch slamming into the post. She yelped and pushed against the post—hoping it wouldn't break—to get the better part of her legs away from the endless nothingness of the cloud-swirling sky.

Panting, she lay there, sweaty and tired. She had taken too long. Her mother would be dead by now. So would her father.

—

Sharon, muscles fresh, lungs full of energizing air, tore along the wall, confident she would save her parents this time.

Just like before, she lured her aunt over to the wall, ran around her, only having to dodge one shot before taking off toward her mom. This time, knowing the room was spinning around the pillar made her run all the more faster. She kept her eyes peeled for the post she had tried to free last time she underwent this strange challenge. The posts were all alike and all seemed to have a weathered look where the railing joined up with them on either side. To find the same one . . . . And did the posts *reset* themselves, too, each time she had to start over? Things changed here in the Spinning Room. First her sweater was red then changed to—what was it, again? And the figure in the black cloak's rifle had turned from black to—She couldn't remember, but knew in her heart things altered slightly with each run through the course.

Save them first, she thought. *You have a bit more time. Be careful to not go over the edge if the railing breaks again.* She went to the nearest post, set her hands behind the bowling-ball-sphere at its top, planted her feet on the railing and pushed/pulled with all she had. Feeling it move, she rocked the post back and forth.

It broke quicker than last time. Well, the railing did. The post still stood there, but that didn't matter. Parts of the railing flew over the edge; other chunks skittered across the smooth marble floor, crashing into the wall-like pillar across the way. Sharon quickly got up and ran to a piece of stone about the size of a football.

She would save her mother this time. She was certain.

Ahead, she saw the dividing line where the wall blended from marble to glass. She slowed down and, only a foot or so away from it came to a complete stop. This was perhaps one of the few times that being left-handed worked to her advantage. Using her hips for power, she twisted back, gripped the stone and hocked it hard. When her hand was just over shoulder height, the stone's true weight came alive and Sharon's arm sunk. The stone sailed through the air and with a low *boomsh* landed against the window and shattered a hole about three feet around.

The tall man in the blue jumpsuit glared at her. Her mother jumped back as glass slid across the ground and gathered around those gaudy gray sneakers she always wore.

"Mom, run!" Sharon shouted.

Her mother froze. Any moment the short man in red would come in.

Setting fear aside, Sharon dove at the jagged hole she created. Spikes of glass tore at her shirt and pants, blood dampening her skin. Other pieces of the serrated hole broke, widening it, a few shards sticking into her skin. It didn't hurt as bad as she thought it would, but as she got to her feet, the skin on her thighs and arms stretched as they extended and hot slices of pain danced along the leaky slashes.

The short man in the red jumpsuit came into the room, gun ready. The taller man in blue lunged for Sharon's mother. Moving quickly, Sharon grabbed her mom by the shoulders, spun her away from the taller man and, with a grunt, pushed her toward the hole in the window. Arms flung out wide, head bowed forward, her mom landed against the glass back first, shattering the remainder of it as she fell through.

"Go, Mom, go!" Sharon shouted, tears streaming down her bloody face.

Her mother lay there, groaning, rotating her hips slowly from side to side, as if something inside was broken.

A blue-sleeved arm wrapped around Sharon's neck, pressed downward and forced her to her knees. She grabbed at the forearm that squished her windpipe. Its grip would not loosen. The shorter fella rounded in front of her, squatted down and held the gun to her head.

Straining to look to her right to see if her mom was okay, Sharon's heart filled with relief when she saw the place where her mother had lay just moments before was empty.

*She—she must've—*Her thoughts were cut short when the man in the red jumpsuit cocked the trigger. The other man squeezed her throat harder.

If he breaks my neck, so be it, she thought. *But—*Jerking herself forward, she reached for the gun. What felt like a golf ball-sized rock slammed into her windpipe. When the man in red pulled away, he lost his balance and fell backward. Sharon grabbed the gun and fired one slug into him. Another blue arm came round on her left, the tall man's bony hand going for the gun. Leaning to the left, she brought the gun over her right shoulder and forced the barrel against the right side of the man's chest. The blue arm on her left dropped the moment she pulled the trigger, warm blood splashing the back of her neck.

Her father was next. If she saved him, she would be free.

Come on, Dad, hang in there, she thought. He had to. She was tired of running around in circles, lost to some repetitive obstacle course that, for all she knew, didn't have an end. Even now after her recent victories, she toyed with the idea of quitting and, when the cycle started over again, bow at Aunt Clora's feet and hope for a bullet to the head. Yet the cycle would still probably renew itself.

But if there is a way out . . .

She also wondered how she got herself mixed up in this strange sequence of events to begin with. There was no place she knew of that had a tower with a rotating floor around it—a spinning room—with purple and gray clouds consistently storming above, clouds so vast and dense that they were everything and all; no sign of a world below.

Similar to how her aunt's white dress had earlier, the tattered ends of the figure in black's cloak peeked out from around the curve far ahead, blowing in a wind that Sharon couldn't feel at her present point along the wall.

Digging her heels into the floor, she charged ahead and when she came to where her father should be defending himself against the figure in black, he instead lay in a pool of blood at the figure's feet, the hem of the black cloak drenched in wet, dark crimson.

The figure in black raised its arm, a gun protruding slowly from its sleeve.

A loud bang shook her from within.

She had done this more than five or six times, now. Maybe it was eight or nine? A wave of nausea swept through Sharon's stomach and intestines even before she started running.

There had to be a way to save time. Avoiding Aunt Clora, helping her mom, *then* getting to her dad . . . too many precious moments wasted.

If I could get to him first then maybe—She turned and ran the other way, not sure how far she had to go before . . . before she'd be forced to start all over again. Aunt Clora would be last. *If it isn't a super long run to Dad, then maybe . . .*

There was no telling how big the disc that encircled the gigantic marble pillar was. For all she knew, her aunt, her parents, and their assailants were only at the *beginning* of the circle. There was no set concept of time here. Moments sped, moments slowed; time was not steady like in the outside world.

She played over her run from the previous—Six? Seven? Ten?—times she tried to save her parents. She'd been so preoccupied with surviving and saving their lives it was hard to tell how many minutes passed between each encounter. She glanced at her wrist. No watch.

Figures, she thought.

It was weird running with the wall on her left instead of her right this time. More than once she noticed herself drifting off course toward the railing, her right side needing something solid beside it.

As with the previous times she'd done this, sharp, zig-zagging lightning crackled in the sky and thunder boomed low and full.

Out of habit, she prepared herself for Aunt Clora's attack. A wonderful relief followed when she reminded herself that Aunt Clora would not be showing up this time. At least not until later. She checked over her shoulder for Clora just in case.

The sound of wet cloth slapping polished stone came from up ahead.

No, not yet. Not ever! Dad! Sharon's heart kicked up its speed.

Tendrils of black material snaked out from around the curve in the wall.

Sharon ran faster.

The thick ribbons of dark fabric swam through the air in smooth waves, flowing inwards to a large figure in a black cloak. Sharon could not see its face. Around twenty feet away, she stopped, still beneath the figure's notice.

She couldn't be one-hundred percent sure, but the being in the huge black cloak seemed bigger. It might have seemed that way because she had previously come in from the other side, but yet the more she thought of it, the more she was certain the figure *had* grown since last time.

It doesn't want me to pass. That's why it's bigger, she assumed. She didn't know what she needed to do first: try and get her father out of the way, then face the cloaked figure, or go after the figure first, then help her father escape?

Maybe Dad could help me save Mom if we survive this? she thought.

Charging toward the figure, arms out, she grabbed hold of the cloak's thick, prickly fabric. The dark abyss of its face turned her way, the sheer blackness of its gaze she *felt* instead of saw; eyeless wonder pierced her through and through. She stumbled back, pulling the black cloak with her. Her father shouted something, but she couldn't hear him from beneath the figure's cloak. The material was dense, like a heavy sponge or carpet. It smelled of poison mushrooms and rotting wood.

Click-clack. Thok! Click-clack. Thok! The creature's steps were like horse hooves on a cobbled street, but with more weight behind them, more force.

Click-clack. Thok!

Hands shaking, she slowly pushed the heavy material off her face, eyes squeezed shut.

You must face him, it, whatever it is. You have to. Dad's gonna die and even if you save Mom and avoid Aunt Clora, you're gonna hafta do this all over again, face this stupid thing—man—thing again. Gah! Her thoughts were too loud for comfort.

Sharon's eyes opened to a gray-boned skeleton, the bones as thick as a pair of flesh-covered arms or legs. Behind the figure's ribcage, a heart beat amidst a mess of stringy veins, muscle and fat, appearing more like red spider webs thatched to the bone, crisscrossing from rib to rib, covering them like something out of an anatomy book.

She had been right about the hooves. At the bottom of the creature's shin bones, dirty gray hooves were cracked down the center, giving the impression of toes. The creature's fingers ran off jointed wrists like gangly branches off a tree. Its heart caught her attention again. It was vibrant red. Wiry veins snaked upward and coiled around vertebrae that appeared broken or cracked in a few places. Sharon expected the creature's head to be a skull; instead, the black abyss was still there, no longer the once-thought endless shadow created by the creature's large hood. The *black nothingness* was oval-like, the same as a person's head.

Looking closer, she saw there was a skull of a kind—the back portion of one, a cranial cavity that was from about the middle of the creature's forehead, running up and over and down the back, connecting to the vertebrae with stringy veins.

Lightning flashed as the creature neared her, a soft, echoey moan coming from a mouth she could not see. The lightning lit up its face for a moment and, for the briefest of instances, a pale dead face appeared beneath the murky darkness.

The creature grabbed her, and moaned again. She shrieked as she was hoisted up.

"Hey!" her father shouted behind her.

She strained to look over her shoulder. He stood on top of the heap of discarded cloak, holding the creature's rifle.

"Put my girl down!" he said and cocked the gun.

Click-clack. Thok! The creature took one step forward, its long, bony fingers tightening around Sharon's neck, each finger a spike that felt as if it was being forced through her windpipe. Tears leaked from her eyes and fluid filled her nose, giving her a headache.

In a swirl of darkness, the creature's cloak took on a life of its own, wrapping itself around her father, covering him up to his armpits. His arms were still free.

So was the gun.

The extra fabric, around his feet like a puddle, slowly slid toward her. Her father took aim.

It an ear-splitting shriek, like a thousand children screaming, the creature threw Sharon off to the side. She slid across the floor and crashed hard against the railing. Something crunched in her lower back and a burst of aching pain flared up in her tailbone.

The creature had her father's wrist in one skeletal hand, its other moving toward the gun.

"Sharon, here!" her dad shouted and flicked his wrists forward.

The rifle hit the ground butt-end first, and a yellow flash sparked from the end of the barrel as it went off. The creature, keeping watch on the gun, twisted its torso in a powerful jerk, the living cloak throwing her father against the wall. He lay there, his limbs twisted as if his arms and legs had been broken.

Each movement excruciating, Sharon forced herself toward the gun, her fingers clawing the floor as she pulled her body along. The pain in her lower back forbade her to stand.

The dark cloak rose up like a tornado and covered the skeletal creature, forming to its master like food-wrap to a dish.

A blur of black darted toward her and a chunk of the cloak knocked her back. Dazed, she tried to remember where she was and what she had been trying to do.

The gun.

Dad.

"Get away, you freak!" she yelled, emptying her lungs.

Adrenaline pumping, she frantically pulled herself along the floor. The creature's cloak shot out again, the tips of thick fabric whipping a fiery slash across her shoulder blades. She heard her T-shirt—a green one now—tear; the sudden wetness of blood from at least three slashes dampened the fabric and the skin beneath. Wincing, setting the fiery pain aside, she forced herself to move quickly. Anger and murderous rage ran through her. In a burst of energy, her legs came alive and though she could not stand, she used her knees to help her along the floor. The moment her fingertips touched the warm barrel of the rifle, the creature threw its cloak out once more, the fabric wrapping around the rifle's butt-end.

The fabric, like a hand, yanked backward.

She hung on.

It snapped its cloak back a second time, dragged her forward, her fingers clamping on the rifle.

Her kneecaps felt as though they were going to pop off as she tried to bend her legs. Painfully, she managed to get her legs under her, squatting as she struggled to maintain her grip on the gun.

The creature pulled.

Sharon slid along the floor, the soles of her feet burning as her skin skidded on marble. It was only then she realized she wasn't wearing any shoes.

The moment she felt the creature's pull ease some, she yanked the barrel as hard as she could and, her knees now at an angle, got her feet beneath her, and pressed backward against the floor as hard as she could. She fell, her tailbone smashing a second time from her weight. The rifle landed on an angle and whacked her in the shoulder where it was more bone than flesh.

Wasting no time as the creature moved toward her, Sharon cocked the rifle and pulled the trigger.

Her father was still out when she checked on him right after the creature fell. She was surprised she killed it. The bullet disappeared into the black deep of its face and, like smoke sucked into a fan, the black nothingness funneled inward, toward the back of its skull. It dropped dead and all that was left of its face was the lower half of a head, the top now missing thanks to the bullet, and thin lips. Pus-filled sores dotted the powdery-gray skin. The rifle in her hands dissolved into thin air as if the creature's demise triggered its own.

Her dad was unconscious. She rearranged his limbs so he was in a more comfortable position and hoped he'd be safe. It was only after she did that she realized she shouldn't have moved him if indeed his limbs had been broken.

I'm so . . . "I'm so sorry, Dad."

There weren't any other threats roaming the Spinning Room that she knew of. Any that had been directed specifically their way, at least.

Mom. The thought was like a hot needle driven into her brain.

Keeping her guard up, her sense of awareness in a heightened state, she charged alongside the wall, racing to save her mother. She had time. The distance—from what she could remember—between Aunt Clora and her mother was a long one. Between her father and her mother, it was shorter. Those few extra minutes could be enough to finally get to her in time.

A few moments later, no more than a couple feet away, there was a ridge in the wall she hadn't noticed before. The ridge ran the wall's height, nearly blending completely into its counterpart that was an inch higher—if you turned your head on its side—as it was an inch or so in thickness. She checked the wall's smooth texture, suddenly captivated by its polished surface.

Can't stop to look at this. No time, she thought. She broke back into a run. Her fingers were still on the *ridge* in the wall and had pushed against it. The wall slid forward like a gigantic drawer.

She went in. The hallway inside was painted a dull, light blue, the paint's finish marred by scratches and dirty fingerprints. The hallway ran to the right, the same way she was headed. It did not extend to the left. Small, dim lamps lit the hallway, but not nearly enough to be called bright or *just right*. The floor was tiled in that grungy grayish-beige that reminded her of elementary school.

Sharon took a few steps in. Up ahead on the right side, a shadow ran floor to ceiling. A room, perhaps?

The markings and smudges on the wall remained consistent as she ran toward the room.

Mom's in there, she thought with conviction. The room was where the large, rectangular window would be if she was outside.

If all occurred as before—and she had no reason to believe that it wouldn't; of her attempted rescues, there had been no alterations to her mother's, unlike her dad who had been killed in a different manner each time by the cloaked skeleton man—then the tall man in blue would have his back to her, a gun on her mom. If her mother didn't see her sneak in or didn't display any form of change in her facial expression or body language, indicating she was aware of her daughter's presence, that was.

She slowed to a brisk walk; her feet trotting along the tiled floor made too much noise.

Back against the wall, she peered inside the room. The man in the blue suit—Blue, she'd called him once before—yelled at her mom in a language she didn't understand; all spits and garbles and a dialect that sounded something like Pig Latin.

If I just had a rock or something to throw at him or break that window with, she thought. There was nothing except for an empty hallway. The guy in red would be along soon. He'd have his weapon with him, but she wasn't sure if she could wrestle it free from him without getting killed.

She wasn't wearing shoes so even throwing those at him wasn't possible.

Time was running out.

Sharon gathered her courage and entered the room. Holding her breath, keeping silent, she heel-toed toward the man as slow as she was able, unsure whether Mom had seen her or not.

Please don't say anything, please don't look at me. Keep watching him, Mom. Don't throw him off—The toes on her right foot rolled under her, pulling her instep along with them. Quickly recovering her balance, she cursed herself when Blue turned around.

Moving swiftly, she grabbed the gun with both hands, tugging with jerky pulls, trying to free it from Blue's steel-like grip.

"Hatwsh rea ouys oingdsh!" he said.

"Sharon!" her mom called. She hesitated for a moment then said, "I'll get help."

"Mom, don't!" Putting her shoulder into the man's sternum, Sharon twisted his arms to the front of her body, putting them in to some kind of lock. "Another . . . guy's . . . coming . . . he's . . . he's in red!"

Blue's foot hooked around her ankle from behind, locking in just above it. He pulled forward; she toppled onto him. The man's bony fingers and the hard metal handle of the gun stabbed her gut on impact.

The air shot out of her in a short wheeze, a sudden pang of sharp pain plowing into her ribs. It didn't take a chiropractor to know something was out of place.

"Sharon!" her mother screamed.

"Ivegsh tish otsh ems!" He pressed into her, his fingers squirming beneath her, trying to get a better grip on the pistol.

Forcing her weight downward to forbid any further movement, she caught a glimpse of her mother coming toward them.

"Mom . . . help . . . the guy . . . watching . . . red . . . coming . . ." Her air was gone and there was too much weight being pressed into her ribcage to inhale.

His lips to Sharon's ear, Blue grunted and something snapped like a pencil. The man's body went limp and the two dropped to the floor.

Rolling the two over as far as able, giving her some breathing room, her mother said, "Sharon, did you . . . are you . . . come . . . come here." She helped her off the floor.

"Go slow," Sharon said. Having the corpse's weight lifted from her was both relieving and painful. The gun's curved handle had been pressed so tight into her solar plexus it had nearly made a home there.

"Mom." Sharon's voice was barely a whisper.

Her mother embraced her. Blue's corpse lay there, his eyes still open, staring at them.

"What did you do?" Sharon asked.

"Kicked him. Meant to get him in the jaw, but I think I missed. I guess I kicked too hard because his head shot back at an odd angle and his neck bent outward in front. Broken." She squeezed Sharon tighter. "I don't care. He would have killed y—"

The short fellow in the red suit—Red—entered the room, rifle drawn. Without word or confirmation that his comrade was dead, he cocked the gun, brought it eye-level and stared down the barrel.

A loud popping-crack echoed throughout the room. The rifle flew from his hands, his first two fingers nothing more than bleeding, fleshy stumps, a gush of red spewing out their ends.

"Now!" Sharon grabbed her mom by the hand and reloaded the pistol's firing chamber. She fired, the window leading outside shattered, fell, and the two escaped. The anguished howling of the man in the red suit followed them.

"Aunt Clora's just around the corner," Sharon said. "She's got a gun, too, and she's trying to kill me. *Was* trying to kill me. Gah! Never mind."

"What does Clora have to do with—What?"

"Just like . . . what I said was . . . never mind." *If Aunt Clora gets Mom, I'd have to start over again, wouldn't I? No way. This is the last time,* she thought. Enough repetition. The thought of running in circles again made her head and stomach swim. The thought of being in that place at the beginning of the . . . challenge? Never again. The sores on her feet—she shuddered to think of the hard, pus-filled, yellowy-orange bumps on the balls of her feet and heels. But her body renewed itself with each cycle, didn't it? The bullet wound from Aunt Clora's gun was no longer present on her shoulder.

It doesn't matter, she thought. *It'll all be over soon.*

The pain-filled howls began to fade, and was soon lost behind them.

Yet when Sharon looked over her shoulder, she saw a red speck in the distance.

Extending her right arm behind her, Sharon motioned for her mother to keep back.

"How far do we have to go?" her mom asked.

"Shouldn't be too much farther, I don't think," she said. "Aunt Clora—" What could she say? That her mom's sister was waiting around the corner with a gun?

"Aunt Clora—?"

I have to tell her. She's gonna see her soon enough anyway, Sharon thought. "She's up ahead, Mom. She's got a gun and she's going to try and kill me. You, too, maybe."

"What are you talking about?" Her mother came to an abrupt halt, hands on hips. "I am not impressed."

Sharon slowed, turned around, and walked over to her. "It's true. I don't know why she's so upset or what happened that she's bent on killing me more times than I can count." She put her hands on her mother's shoulders. "We have to get past her."

Her mother's glare had the infamous look of, *Sharon, you did something wrong again. I'm disappointed in you, young lady.*

"Look, Mom, we have to get moving. We can talk about this after, 'kay?" In the distance, the speck of red was larger, now a red and tanned blur of the man in the jumpsuit.

"No, we talk about this now!"

The fellow picked up speed. In a few minutes he'll have caught up to them.

"Crap! Look, I'm going ahead. You can stay here if you wa—" But she needed her mom, didn't she? If her mom got killed, she'd have to do this all over again. It ended now even if she had to kill Clora in front of her mother, if only to end this. If she had to repeat running around trying to save her parents again, she'd do away with herself and hope that by doing so would end the cycle once and for all. But, it seemed, she had an equally good chance the cycle would begin again anyway and she'd forever be held prisoner to the hands of Repetitive Time.

Her mother's eyes were still fixated on hers.

"Turn around and you'll see that guy who almost killed you, Mom. You can stay here and wait for him or you can come with me and have a chance of getting out of here alive. It's up to you," Sharon said.

Mouthing the words, "I love you," she turned and jogged toward Aunt Clora's gun, soon to show at any moment. Her neck ached to turn and look back, to see if her mom was going to follow or not. *Show her you're serious and she'll follow*, she thought. *I will not look back.*

"Come on, Mom, let's go. Put your pride aside for once. You don't always need to have the last word," Sharon muttered to herself then added in a whisper, "Can't leave her here."

She glanced over her shoulder and was relieved when she saw her mom running behind her. She slowed down just enough for her to catch up before they continued on at full speed.

Less than a minute later, the stark white of Aunt Clora's dress appeared up ahead.

Maybe she won't take a shot at me since Mom's here? Sharon thought. *Mom could talk to her, right? Find out what the heck's going on.*

Doing her best to keep the sound of her footfalls to a minimum, she warned her mom to be ready to split up and for her mom to stay near the wall while she ran toward the railing in the hopes of distracting Clora long enough for her to get away.

"If she has a gun, I'm going to talk to her," her mother said.

"No, you can't. She might kill you."

"She's not going to—"

"Yes, she will!" Sharon didn't mean to scream, but couldn't control the suppressed frustration any longer. Behind them, Red gained even more ground, and quickly.

The white dress up ahead moved and was gone for a moment before returning to view. Clora must have heard them because she was moving toward them like a ghost, her feet *gliding* along the ground rather than stepping.

"'Kay, Mom, get ready," Sharon said.

"There's a guy following us," she said, seemingly surprised.

"Of course there is. He's going to kill you if Aunt Clora doesn't." *Come on!* She eyed the railing. "Okay, here's the plan—"

"But you already told me what you're going to do . . ."

"I know, but forget that. I have a better idea. Listen."

After sharing her plan, the two headed toward the railing. At first they kept in line with each other, Sharon in the lead. Aunt Clora moved toward them. Splitting up, Sharon and her mother ran opposite each other near then far, crisscrossing in a figure eight-like pattern. Clora moved first toward Sharon then to Sharon's mother.

Smoothly, Clora's baggy white sleeve moved upward, the black metallic pistol peeking out from the loose-fitting cuff.

Letting her aunt get closer, Sharon kept her zig-zagging pattern; her mother did the same. Suddenly Sharon stopped and, as planned, her mother ran past her far ahead. When Clora kept moving toward Sharon, her mother stopped along the railing and crossed over to the wall before running back.

To the left, Red charged toward them. She'd almost forgotten about him. At first it wasn't clear who he'd attack first—Sharon or her mother—but his intentions were made obvious when he pushed off the wall and cut in at an angle, heading toward her. Sharon wished they had taken Blue's pistol with them for protection. Neither of them had been thinking.

The man in the red jumpsuit and Aunt Clora closed in. Sharon stopped, gathered her breath and did her best not to panic.

Her mother was still a good twenty or so feet away. Not too close, but not too far either.

Sharon ran toward Red; Clora immediately adjusted her course. The crackling of lightning and the boom of thunder drowned out all sound. She couldn't hear herself breathe.

The man in red sped up his charge. Sharon stopped in front of him and prepared for impact. Within an instant he had his arms around her, bringing her to the ground. The back of her head smacked hard against the stone flooring; bursts of red, white and black grew to fuzzy stars before her eyes. The stars quickly blinked out in a flash of white when the man's bony fist landed between her eyes. Pain shot from somewhere in front, through her head and to somewhere far behind.

Thunder crashed.

She wasn't sure if the next flash of light was the lightning or another blow. All she cared about was the annoying buzzing in her ears and if it would stop.

"Sharon . . ." Her mother's voice was faint, coming from far away.

White fabric flowed along the floor over to the right.

Lightning flared up on all sides.

Aunt Clora's white dress was gone. Red's fist came crashing down again.

Thunder crashed like a shot from a gun.

————

Soft leather wrapped around Sharon's feet and something harder rose beneath her soles. She couldn't see anything in the syrupy darkness around her.

Shoes?

Her shaking hands held tightly to iron railings on either side as she made her way toward the white slit up ahead. The bright, thin bar of light was ground level and with each step forward, the bar grew to the outline of a door.

The sound of her shoes clunking along a metallic grate was foreign. She expected to hear skin on marble, slapping down with each footfall. Knees aching, she had to stop to rest and was surprised that it took a few minutes to catch her breath.

I'm never going to try this again, she thought. *I don't know why I talked myself into it. The guy by the door was clearly a freak.* She couldn't remember the fellow's name, but only a face, skull-like with a clown's smile and a floppy orange hat with a bushy yellow feather sticking out of the headband.

Keeping one hand on the rail, she set the other out in front of her, pawing at the air, searching for the door. Once she found it, she felt along its bumpy, metal surface for a handle. It was about waist height, right side, like a van door. She jiggled it first to see which way it was supposed to turn, then pressed it all the way down, moving the handle from a horizontal to a vertical position. The latch clicked with a loud *kla-clink!*

She pulled the door open and was blinded by yellow light. Instinctively her hand went to her eyes, shielding them from the sun straight ahead. The railing and walkway continued from the door and wound down six feet before blending into the cracked, weathered concrete outside.

Eyes slowly adjusting, she made her way down the ramp, the heat already causing her to sweat.

"What the—" she started. There really wasn't a word to describe it. She was in a compound of some sort, a—no, an old fairground. A rusted, long-forgotten Ferris wheel lay on its side some fifteen feet away, sand having blown in from the surrounding desert covering most of the crisscrossing bars at the bottom. At the far corner of the chain-linked fenced-in area, a wooden rollercoaster sat devoid of life, the white paint peeling and old, the absence of a rollercoaster car putting finality to what the coaster once stood for. An orange circus-like tent stood in the middle of the fairground, three of its posts still standing, one of the corners having collapsed inward who knew when.

As Sharon's eyes adjusted, more of the fairground became clear. She eyed the ramp she'd just been on, following its path up to the long white trailer she had just come out of. Plastered along the trailer's side in faded paint was the words SPINNING ROOM, and below that A HORROR HOUSE MADE FOR YOU. The sign's red and blue lettering—lightened to a pink and pale blue with age—brought back memories of what happened the night she came to the fair. It had been Halloween, sixteen years old, her parents in their mid forties. She had wanted to go into the SPINNING ROOM, the man with the face paint telling her that once she went in, there was no coming out, and if you did manage to escape, it would still take you a lifetime to do so. Of course, she didn't believe him. She handed the guy her ticket and . . . she began running.

How long has it been? she wondered. She moved to wipe her eyes and cried out when she saw her hands. Her fingertips were like raisins, the skin on her palms thin and paper-like.

"Oh no! What happened?" she said. Her breath caught in her throat at the sound of her own voice. It wasn't hers. It was no longer smooth and feminine, the kind of voice that drove the boys wild at school. She was speaking more from the back of her throat than up front by her tongue. Her voice reminded her of her grandmother's.

Misty-eyed, Sharon roamed the fairground for nearly an hour, stepping past old snack sheds and outhouses, a dried-up wading pool, a merry-go-round with small ceramic ponies with big teeth and wide grins. Some of their eyes were missing, lost somewhere to the ages.

The funhouse mirrors were all broken save one, the kind that made you look short and fat. Sharon took a good look at herself in the dirty, scratched-up surface, past the intended distortions and to the woman staring back at her.

Her hair was white, almost ankle-length, brittle-looking, and hanging over long, heavy breasts that appeared more like half-empty hot water bottles than the smooth firm breasts she was used to. Fine, wrinkly lines dented her skin, cheeks, arms, hands—everything. Legs giving way beneath her, she fell and screamed when her old bones landed hard against the wooden slat at the mirror's base.

She stayed there for a long while. When she finally gathered the strength to stand, a hard wind blew sand and litter at her feet. A yellowed piece of paper, crinkled and ripped, caught her eye.

It was her!

At least, it *was* her, how she looked when she was sixteen. Beneath her smiling face was one word—

MISSING.

IN THE REARVIEW MIRROR

Of course it had to happen. Nothing ever works out when you want it to.

The 1999 black Saturn came to halt along the shoulder of the Transcanada Highway just after 6 P.M. It was Friday night and Jimmy Griffith was going to be late for his getaway with his friends, Joey, Randall and Steve. It was snowing, the flakes coming down in clumps, but lightly enough so it didn't pose a road hazard. Not yet, anyway. It should ease up within the hour, Jimmy assumed, if not sooner.

The Saturn was on empty, but it was really impossible to tell with this car. Last year the fuel gauge began giving him trouble and its needle stayed at the three-quarter-tank mark after trips to the gas station, as if filling it hadn't made a difference. Some months passed and the needle began to dip until eventually it sat on E and it was impossible to tell how much fuel was actually in the car. Jimmy would watch the odometer, remembering on average how many kilometers he got to a full tank, but with work being hectic as of late, and trouble at home, he couldn't remember the number of kilometers on the odometer when he filled up last. Now, he was on empty. For real. Now, he was screwed.

The sky was already dark with deep gray clouds, evening having set in an hour ago.

He put the car in park, turned the key back in the ignition and popped the trunk.

There's a gas can in the back, he thought.

With a huff, he got out of the car, the fat flakes of cold landing on the tips of his ears and neck. He rounded to the rear of the vehicle and opened the trunk. There was a spare tire, some blankets, beer and hotdogs for the cabin trip this weekend, chips and some DVDs. But no gas can.

"Perfect," he said, remembering it was sitting in his garage at home. He had removed the clunky canister to make room for all the junk he was bringing to the cabin.

He glanced up and down the road. The white blanket of snow drifting down seemed thicker the further down the road he looked, the white flakes defined in clear white blotches in the yellow light of the street lamps of the highway. There were no cars coming.

Jimmy went back to the car and sat in the driver's seat, cursing himself for being unprepared.

"It's okay," he told himself. He wriggled his wrist, the cuff of his shirt sliding back, and checked his watch. "It's about ten after six. You don't have to be there until around eight. Plenty of time."

His head was so busy after a full day at the office looking over insurance policies that he forgot about his cell phone in his glove compartment. He snapped his fingers, remembering, and opened the glove compartment and removed his cell. The battery was down to one bar. He pulled out the antenna and dialed up Steve. He knew Steve was going to be leaving around 6:30. If Steve hadn't left early, and with a little luck, he might be able to catch him before he headed out and get some assistance. He dialed Steve's number and after four rings the phone cut out.

"Aw, come on." He pressed END and tried again. Same thing, this time there was only three rings before being cut off by a click and the line went dead.

Jimmy dug in the glove compartment for the cigarette lighter adapter and once he found it he plugged one end into the lighter, the other into the phone. He tried the number again. After five rings Steve picked up.

"Hello?"

"Steve, it's Jimmy. Got a little prob—" The phone cut out. "Oh, come on!" Jimmy shook the phone, as if it would help.

He tried Steve's number again. After only one ring it cut out.

Frustrated, he threw the phone against the dashboard. "Piece of junk." He crossed his arms, furrowed his brow, and thought of his options. His thoughts were interrupted when he heard a voice, low and smooth, calm and reassuring, as if it knew something he didn't. The voice came from the back seat.

Hello, Jimmy, it said. *You're in a bit of a rut, aren't you?*

"Who's there?" Jimmy spun around, glancing into the back seat. No one was there, nothing except a few McDonald's wrappers and some papers from work.

Swallowing the lump in his throat, he turned back around and tried the cell phone again. This time it didn't even ring. The snow started to come down heavier. His heartbeat picked up a bit, worried he wouldn't get to the cabin by eight.

A flush of heat came over him and he got out of the car for some air. He looked up and down the road. There was pair of headlights off in the distance, a good two kilometers away, if not more. He'd wait until the car came by, flag them down, and see if they had a phone so he could call a friend and a tow. Money wasn't an issue so a tow wouldn't be a problem. He just wanted to get to the cabin, away from the city, away from his job—just needed a break.

He stuck out his tongue and caught a few snowflakes, a habit since he was a kid. The flakes were cool and refreshing. Despite it snowing, it wasn't too cold and he didn't need his gloves. But, given Winnipeg winters, he knew that come eight or nine o'clock, the temperature would drop considerably and he'd need a pair of gloves and a toque. He didn't have either.

The car down the road drew nearer. Jimmy took a few steps onto the road, ready to start waving his hands. *Let's hope they stop.*

When the car was about a hundred feet away, Jimmy began waving his arms back and forth in an X, high above his head. The car sped past, as if he wasn't there. He suddenly had the taste of smoke in his mouth. He spat and the taste went away as quickly as it came.

"Jerks," he muttered.

He checked up and down the road again. No one was coming. The snow was falling even thicker and the wind was picking up. "Just my luck this'll turn into a storm." He went back to the car.

Sitting down, he tried the ignition again, hoping that by some miracle the car had been mistaken it was out of gas and it would start. Of course, it didn't, and Jimmy put his head against the wheel. He had a slight headache.

He always spoke aloud when things got rough and he was alone. It was actually more of a mix of thoughts drifting into speech then drifting into thoughts again then drifting into speech . . .

"Okay," he said, *Just think of your options . . .* ". . . you're on the side of the road . . . alone . . ." *. . . phone doesn't work . . . no gas in the . . .* ". . . trunk . . ." He checked his watch. It was 6:23. "Steve's left by now . . ." *. . . if he takes this route, I can wait and hope he passes by and sees me . . .* ". . . then again, with the snow . . ." *. . . he might not know it's me . . .* "Crap."

Jimmy. The voice. It was back.

"I'm not hearing this," he said.

But I'm here, Jimmy. Where else would I be? I'm always here with you.

He knew who was speaking to him. Jamie. He'd known Jamie since he was a kid. Jamie first came to him when he was seven years old, one day in the playground at school. A kid had pushed Jimmy over the edge of the sandbox and he'd hit his head on the box's edge.

It's okay, Jimmy. I'm here, Jamie had said that day long ago.

Jimmy first thought it was another kid trying to help him. When he looked around, he saw he was alone in the playground, the bell to go back inside having rung some time before. Jamie never came back after that day, not until Jimmy was fourteen and was trying pot for the first time. Jimmy didn't know if it was the light-headedness from the weed or the feeling of detachment from the world that triggered it, but Jamie returned, this time older, fourteen, like Jimmy.

Then Jamie left and didn't return until Jimmy was twenty-one, while on a trip to Europe, backpacking it on his own. It was seven years between visits. Perhaps because Jimmy had been seven years old when Jamie first came to him inside his head.

Here, in the car, Jamie was back. Jimmy was twenty-eight.

I see you, Jamie said.

"Go away, Jamie," Jimmy said. "You're not real. You're not here."

But I am. I've been here awhile, Jimmy. How was your smoke?

Jimmy furrowed his brow. "Smoke?"

A flashback to standing at the side of the road and the taste of cigarette smoke that suddenly filled his mouth. Jamie. Jamie had been smoking. Jimmy didn't remember doing it. Feeling his pockets, he pulled out a pack of Players Lights.

"Where did you get these?" Jimmy asked. He didn't smoke. But Jamie did.

Lunch hour, when you ran to Second Cup for a coffee. Don't you recall stopping at the drugstore along the way? Jamie chuckled.

Swallowing, Jimmy glanced again to the back seat. Jamie was back there. He just couldn't see him.

He paused. Then, "Why are you behind me?"

What do you mean?

"You're always behind me. On the playground, while I was lying down, your voice seemed to come from behind me, behind my head. Smoking dope in Joey's garage. I was sitting on a lawn chair. You spoke to me from behind, near Joey's dad's truck. You're in the back seat of my car."

Well, maybe you're always just one step ahead of me. Get it?

The windshield of the car was covered in white, the snow coming down in sheets. Jimmy's breath faintly fogged when he exhaled. The inside of the car was cooling down. Putting Jamie out of his mind, Jimmy got out of the car and slammed the door behind him.

The snowflakes licked the tips of his ears; refreshing, like before. Much needed.

Not long after, it really began to come down. No cars, just snow, falling heavily. He stuffed his hands in his pockets and felt the cigarette package. He didn't recall replacing the pack in his pocket.

"Creepy," he muttered and tossed the pack on the road.

He got back in the car.

Cold out?

"A little. Where are you?"

Look up.

He glanced in the rearview mirror and, there, sitting in the back seat, was Jamie. Jimmy spun in his seat. Jamie wasn't there, but he was in the mirror when Jimmy looked again.

"You should be gone by now," Jimmy said.

Maybe. Maybe not. I've never really gone anywhere, Jimbo. I was there with you today at Second Cup, there with you when you popped into the drugstore for some cigarettes. When I popped in for some cigarettes.

In the rearview mirror, Jamie smiled at him. His teeth were white against a tanned face, like he spent most of his days under a Florida sun. Jimmy didn't have a tanned face. Jamie's hair was dark like Jimmy's, but instead of combed from left to right, Jamie's was parted in the middle. He wore the same clothes as Jimmy: blue jeans, a red sweatshirt and a navy blue parka.

Getting cold, Jimmy rubbed his hands together then blew on them.

"What do you want?"

Remember Joey's girlfriend back when you were fourteen?

Jimmy didn't.

Her name was Sarah Daley. Beautiful girl, blonde hair, blue eyes; your regular Barbie-doll. Even at her age she had curves that would slight even some of the Playboy *bunnies. Anyway, that dope you smoked—she was smoking it, too—it loosened you guys up. Or were you so high you don't remember?*

Jimmy didn't remember. He wished he could. Wished he knew what Jamie was talking about.

Regardless, you two got friendly behind Joey's dad's truck when Joey went into the house to use the bathroom. He got sick off the dope and was in there for a while. He even said so and said he was going to throw up. He was new to it. But Sarah . . . Sarah, Sarah, Sarah . . . now that was a fine girl. I loved her. When you guys hung out at school, you, Joey and Sarah, I watched her as she moved, as she smiled, reveled in the way she sounded when she talked and how she sometimes squinted her left eye when making a point about something she was saying. Kissing her behind the truck was like kissing your girl at the time, Pam. But Sarah's lips were softer, more delicate, like kissing a flower, yet damp as though with dew. I poured myself into her.

"I . . . no . . . that didn't happen," Jimmy said. He put his head against the steering wheel again. Suddenly, he slammed his palms against the wheel with a *thwack!* and sat up straight in his seat, glaring into the rearview mirror.

Jamie only looked back at him, calm. *She and I never got together again after that. Joey came back into the garage, healthier, but still sick. Every time I tried talking to Sarah, she always shrugged me off. She would say, "Jimmy, you're different." She was talking about me when she said that, of course, but how was she to know that you and I shared the same body?*

"You only come every seven years," Jimmy said. "Seven years. Seven years old, fourteen, twenty-one, and now. Same date, too, March Twenty-third. I can't believe I forgot about today. Wasn't thinking. Too much on my mind."

My mind, you mean. Ours? Doesn't matter. Back to Sarah. Do you remember me taking her out back behind the school, leading her by the hand, promising her that Joey was there and that he had a big surprise for her?

Jimmy put his face in his hands. He didn't want to hear what Jamie was going to say next, but couldn't help but listen.

Behind the dumpster, I took her and made her stand against the wall. I tried to explain to her all that I felt and how it drove me crazy to see her with Joey. She didn't understand. I said my name was Jamie. She said no, my name was Jimmy. I told her again my name was Jamie and she got scared and wanted to get out from behind the dumpster. I wouldn't let her, couldn't. I pushed her up against the wall, tried to kiss her. She scratched my face. Your *face.*

Jimmy touched his right cheek. That's where those faint scars had come from—Sarah.

I hit her. Then I hit her again. And again. And again. She slumped against the wall, crying, begging me to stop. I didn't. I couldn't. I don't know why, but it felt so good to hit her, felt so good to come out of you and release all the emotions that you suppress when you keep me down. She tried to crawl away. I picked her up by the shoulders and slammed her into the wall, her head bouncing off the bricks with a dull thud. There was a small spot of red on the brick. Blood. Hers. I pushed her into the wall again, her head bouncing the same way. That dull thud was soothing.

"Then the snow came down," Jimmy finished.

Yes. You remember.

"I wasn't there when they found her body. I was home by then. Joey was devastated. He's never been the same since. Even to this day he still talks about her, but never mentions her by name, but we all know who he means when he does. You killed her. You killed Sarah." Jimmy turned to an empty back seat then glanced back up at the rearview mirror. Jamie grinned at him.

Jimmy bolted out of the car and ran as far ahead of it as he could until he was winded and had to stop to put his head between his legs. He could barely make out the car's black blur between the heavily falling snow. The wind bit at his skin. He spat on the ground, strangely captivated by the pale yellow glob of phlegm against a dull quilt of white. He took a deep breath, icy and sharp.

A car door slammed. Jimmy glanced up, hands still on his knees. Behind the sheet of snow was the silhouette of a man coming toward him.

Jamie.

Jimmy's heart sped up. So did Jamie's pace as he moved toward him. He stood, ready to fight. Appearing out of the rain of thick snowflakes, Jamie charged him and tackled him to the ground. Helpless on his back, Jimmy took it as Jamie delivered blow after blow to his chin—to *their* chin.

"You're . . . you're only . . . hurting . . . yourself," Jimmy told him.

No, Jamie said, *you're hurting yourself.*

It didn't make sense. None of it did. Jimmy swung out, but when his fist struck Jamie, it was no different than striking air. It was as if Jamie wasn't there.

"But you're not there, are you?" he said quietly.

Of course I'm here, Jimbo. Always have been. I've been here all along.

"Y-you killed Sarah . . . it was you," Jimmy said.

Jamie struck him hard in the throat, causing him to sputter. Snow got in his eyes.

No! Jamie said. *You killed Sarah, Jimmy. It was all you. All of it. I'm just an echo of what you truly want, truly are. Think about it.*

Jamie stopped hitting him. *Think about it, Jimbo. Think about the black dot.*

Jimmy coughed. "Th-the black . . . black dot . . . ?"

Yes, the black dot. Think harder.

The black dot. Jimmy knew what it was. It was that dark place that he stuffed all his anger, all his fear, all his shameful thoughts into. He always envisioned it as a black dot, a dark circle, a deep void that held all the negative things he controlled himself not to think or do. It was the black dot that created Jamie, a shadow version of himself. The most shameful part of him.

He thought back to Sarah and that day behind the dumpster. Though he wasn't in control of his actions, he remembered seeing everything as though looking through the bottom of a beer bottle, a dark lens. The black dot. He should have had control. He should have stopped Jamie. He could have . . . but didn't.

Tears ran down his cheeks.

Oh, stop your crying.

Jamie's weight on top of his chest was crushing. The snow surrounding his ears and cheeks turned bitingly cold. He had to get up or he'd get frostbite.

"G-get off," he told Jamie.

No.

"Please?"

No.

"Please, get off me."

No.

"Jamie!"

There had to be a way to get Jamie off him. He certainly couldn't push him off. Every time he hit him it was like hitting air. Touching Jamie was impossible. But knowing that wasn't enough. There had to be a way. Jamie must have a weakness.

Jamie struck Jimmy on the chin again.

"Stop it!" Jimmy shouted and tried to push Jamie off him instinctively. His hands passed through Jamie just as easily as they passed through the snow that was coming down.

I wonder if Jamie shares my thoughts? Jimmy wondered. *Can he hear me? Can you?* He waited for a response, waited for Jamie to mock him and say how he can hear everything that he was thinking. But no response came. Either Jamie was playing with him, letting him find hope in keeping his thoughts separate, or Jamie really couldn't hear his thoughts. Either way, it was a chance he had to take to get out of this.

Freezing, the snow around his ears and cheeks having numbed the skin, Jimmy thought of the black dot.

Then it all became clear. Jamie *was* the black dot. Jimmy closed his eyes and pictured it in his mind, setting the black dot on a mat of deep green, his favorite color. He could see the circle's edges, see its shaded-in center, a complete and utter void of darkness.

Jamie struck him again, this time so hard his head bounced against the snow. Jimmy blocked out the pain, but could still taste the blood on his tongue. He focused on the black dot. The image clear in his mind, he forced the green upon it, washing over it like waves over sand, washing it, rinsing it, covering it. The black dot began fading into the green as if sinking in a pool of quicksand. It tried to surface again, tried to rise out of the liquid green . . . but Jimmy submerged it. Soon the black dot was gone and only the green remained.

Jimmy opened his eyes. Jamie was gone.

He was panting, his heart racing. For a moment the black dot tried to surface again. He pushed it away once more and covered it with green. Legs rubbery, he stood and brushed the snow off his chest and legs, his fingers quickly freezing. Ambling over to the car, he covered his ears with his hands, warming them. It might have been his imagination, but the falling snow seemed to be thinning.

Is it because Jamie's gone? he wondered. He didn't want to dwell on it too much just in case Jamie returned at the thought of his name.

Jimmy got back into the car. He rubbed his hands together, blew on them, then rubbed them together again.

The keys dangled in the ignition. "I wonder . . ."

He turned the key and the engine started. Jimmy couldn't help but laugh with joy when he heard the engine purr.

"Don't want to risk it," he said. *Better get to the next gas station before I run out for real. I wonder if Jamie made me think the car wouldn't start?* Then another voice, his *own* voice, rose in protest. *Stop it, you idiot. Don't think about him or he might come back.* Then, *Sorry. I'll stop thinking about him.*

"Good," he agreed with himself.

He took another deep breath, thankful that the whole ordeal was over. He rolled down the window, clearing it of snow, and checked the road behind him. The road was empty. He swished the windshield wipers, pushing off the snow.

The black dot danced before his vision. The snow came down thick.

As he glanced in the rearview mirror, he saw Jamie grinning at him.

You killed her, Jimbo. It was all you.

A PERFECT DATE

It was going to be perfect. It had to be. Brian had been planning it for weeks.

It was a quarter after six when he jumped into the shower, shampooed his hair and let the conditioner sit for an extra minute just to make sure it worked. On a small rack in the shower was an assortment of body washes that he and his girlfriend Carolyn—Carrie—used. Having used her body wash instead of his own, he now smelled like freshly-picked strawberries.

When Brian first began dating her, he took special care when preparing to see her, in turn causing him to be consistently late for their dates. Now, that wasn't the case. They had been living together for the past two years. And tonight, he would be able to take his time getting ready. Carrie wouldn't be coming home before seeing him this evening.

She once asked him what his secret method was for smelling so good. He would never tell her, never say he used *her* body wash instead of his own. Sometimes, she would even hang around outside the bathroom after he showered, peeking in through a crack in the bathroom door, just to get a glimpse of anything that might hint at what made him smell so, as she put it, delicious. Every time she tried it, she was caught. He would come out of the bathroom wearing only a towel and scoop her up in his arms and carry her to the bed, where they would spend most of their evening.

The recipe for his smelling so good was simple. Three dabs of Ocean Perfect across the neck, one dab of Evergreen just under the chin, and a dab of Berry-blue on each wrist. When Carrie first asked him what kind of cologne he was wearing he would always reply by saying it was Fresh Water Fruit, a name he had given his private mixture. It wasn't until later she learned that such a cologne didn't exist. He eventually had to let her in on his secret. It was either that or spend the night alone on the couch in the living room. But she never knew it was also the scent of her body wash mixed in with the cologne that made the smell extra unique.

Now, alone in the master bedroom's en suite bathroom, Brian applied his cologne mix carefully, brushed on his underarm deodorant, and looked at himself in the mirror. Stunning. Red hair, blue eyes, the right amount of color in his cheeks. Perfect.

He went out into the bedroom and over to the closet. A picture of Carrie sat on the mahogany dresser beside it. He turned to it.

"What do you think, hon'?" he asked. "Light blue with a black shirt, or something gray with black? Your choice, of course."

Her picture gave him a considering look. Her blonde hair hung loosely over her shoulders, her blue eyes telling him she loved him.

Feeling she would choose the gray with black, he picked the suit out of the closet and laid it on the bed. A black leather belt with a brass buckle was selected, as well as an off-white tie. He knew the tie would be a tad flashy but, after all, being original was what he was all about.

He dressed with his back to the picture, not wanting her to see him until he was completely ready. As he pulled up his pants he made a wry smile, and discovered he must have put on an extra pound or two since the last time he wore them. The button on the waistline took a few moments to fasten into place before his body settled into them. These were the pants he reserved for special occasions, not his work pants. The pair he now wore used to belong to his father before he died.

Stepping over to the mirror that hung above the dresser, he opened the top drawer and pulled out a black comb.

He parted his wet hair and frowned—like he always did—when the teeth of the comb ran over the bald spot that was forming at the top of his head. He set the comb down and pressed his hair along the sides with his palms. It was perfect, not a strand out of place.

The tie was next. When he got his job at Maxwell and Davis, an accounting firm at the other end of town, Carrie would have to get up in the morning with him to help him tie it. Finally, one morning, she made him sit on the edge of the bed, her sitting behind him, and instructed him step-by-step on how to do it properly. And now tying a tie was as easy as tying a shoe.

Bending down to the bottom drawer, he pulled out a pair of black socks. Unfortunately, like all his socks, this pair had a hole near the big toe. He figured Carrie would let it slide. She would know that his heart was in the right place.

After the socks came a pair of black slip-on dress shoes. He batted the toes of them with the end of his tie to remove the little bit of dust that had formed there since the last time he wore them.

Brian donned the suit jacket.

"Almost there," he said, tugging on the lapels.

Returning to the mirror, he straightened his clothes and picked up the picture of Carrie to get her opinion.

"What do you think, Carrie?" he asked.

Her image didn't respond, but judging by the way she was smiling in it, Brian thought she decided he looked spiffy enough for the evening.

Brian set the picture down and opened up the jewelry box next to it. Before taking his shower he would set his gold watch and high school ring in there. Ever since losing a necklace while swimming in Lake Winnipeg as a boy one summer, going near water with any form of jewelry had always been a bad idea.

He put on his watch and ring and smiled.

She's going to like this, he thought.

Beneath Carrie's pillow on her side of the bed, Brian had hidden a love note for her. He took out the tiny envelope from beneath the pillow, opened it, and read the letter to himself.

"Carrie, I guess tonight's going to be it. I'm finally going to be with you forever. I've loved you since always, and tonight I'm going to prove it to you. I can't wait to see the expression on your face. Love, Brian."

He smiled again, the beat of his heart quickening. The clock above the bed said 6:45. He figured he had a few minutes before seeing her.

He went over to his side of the bed and sat on its edge and propped up his pillows. He lied down and set the love note neatly on his chest. The clock read 6:46.

A few more minutes, he thought, needing some more time to get used to the idea that life as he knew it was about to change.

When the clock read exactly 6:50, Brian opened up the night table drawer next to the bed and pulled out a blue, velvet case. Time to get moving. He didn't want to be *too* late this evening.

The lid creaked when he opened it. Inside was something smooth, silver and shiny. He took the object out and held it in his hands. After feeling it carefully, he set it on the mattress next to him, got up from the bed, picked up Carrie's picture and kissed it. He envisioned her kissing him back.

Bringing the picture with him, he returned to the bed, lay down again and replaced the love note on his chest. He picked up the object and studied it one more time. He had bought it earlier that day. For the one-hundred-and-sixty-dollar price tag, he hoped it worked, hoped it would ensure he and his sweetie would be together forever.

Carrie would agree I got a good deal, he thought. *I can't wait to see the look on her face when she sees me.*

He closed his eyes then put the object near his mouth, kissing it. His mind wandered to Carrie and he envisioned her the way he always did when he thought of her: running through a playground wearing the white dress she had picked out for their wedding day. A smile on her face and a glimmer of joy in her blue eyes.

It won't be long now, he thought. A tear ran down his cheek.

He pulled the trigger.

THE MAN IN THE WOODS

Bernie Calhoun wasn't too upset the night his wife sentenced him to sleep on the couch in the living room of their small home on Maple Tree Drive. It was quite understandable, actually. *Besides,* Bernie thought, *if I caught her moaning in her sleep night after night, I'd probably do the same to her. Ah well, no matter. Can't take much of her own heavy breathing myself, anyway.* And that was true. It was as if his wife, Elizabeth, made a conscious effort to counter each moan he emitted with an equally loud exhale of her own. The funny thing was, though Bernie was sound asleep when she exhaled so audibly, he was still able to *hear* her.

Bernie set his blanket and pillow down on the first of the three cushions that made up the seat of the couch. There was a hide-a-bed inside, but he was too lazy to pull it out. Besides, if he did, then it would show Elizabeth, when she came down for coffee in the morning, that he was able to make the best out of any situation that confronted him. Tonight, however, he wanted her to feel sorry for him. He would rough-it on the couch, without the bed, and when she came down in the morning, she would feel bad she made him sleep on worn cushions with nothing but a thin, knit blanket and a feather pillow.

Still, her actions were understandable. But the fact of the matter was, Bernie couldn't help his moaning in his sleep. He wanted to help it—but couldn't. Each morning Elizabeth would tell him he was groaning and muttering something as he slept, and each time he would reply by saying, "Yeah, maybe. But there would be no reason for it. I slept fine." Or so he would think because, when he was able to recall them, his dreams the night before had been pleasant ones. He hadn't had any bad dreams for thirty years. But he had plenty before then. And there had been one in particular that had topped them all. Deep down inside, he knew it was *that* dream that was responsible for all the moaning in his sleep, as if that dream still occurred somewhere underneath the normal dreams he dreamed now.

Though not one to give into any outlandish ideas or any hoodoo, Bernie did believe that something came through into this world the night he dreamt about the Man in the Woods.

—

Bernie had been ten years old, the oldest of the two sons of Jon and Dhelia Calhoun. His brother, Brent, was three years younger, placing him at seven at the time. They were the "Bee Brothers" to the kids down the street and in the schoolyard. Bernard and Brenton Calhoun to their parents. To each other they were Berno and Brento.

It was often a tradition on weekends for Bernie and Brent to have "sleepovers," not so much in the traditional sense since they lived under the same roof, but on either Friday or Saturday night, Bernie would drag his bedding up to his brother's room and set up camp on the floor. After lights-out the farting contests would begin and, after that, the air smelling of a poignant version of that night's dinner, quiet mutterings of dirty words they weren't allowed to say along with the giggles to compliment them. Words like "poop-butt" and "dinkus" seemed all the more funnier with the lights off. Then, after the profanities were exhausted and the boob-talk done, the Bee Brothers would call it a night, seldom waking, and if one of them did, the other knew about it by a glass of water splashed in their face when the other came back from the bathroom from a middle-of-the-night pee.

But there was that one night that scared Bernie, and it was then he swore never to sleep in his brother's room again.

———

"Catch!" Brent yelled across the field. He let the baseball rip toward Bernie.

"You putz! It's higher than it was the last time!" Bernie yelled back and followed the ball with his eyes as it came down from high in the blue sky like a falling meteorite before landing in his beat-up old baseball mitt. He looked back at Brent. His brother spun in circles in the dirt patch that seemed both out of—and in—place, in the grass before the trees.

They were out camping, playing catch before dinner, with Mom and Dad back at camp about ten minutes away.

Bernie hurled the ball at his brother, throwing a little slower than he would to his friends because Brent was younger and couldn't catch the fast ones. Brent soured his face, like he always did, as the ball came toward him. The ball smacked into his glove with a dull *thwack* when he caught it.

Brent stood up proudly, and with the ball still hidden in his glove, wriggled his ball hand above his head as if saying, "Hey, I caught it and I'm gonna throw it back at you, but even higher than the last time." He lowered his arm and added, "Hang on a sec." Then bent down to tie his shoe.

Bernie watched him, the sun glaring in his eyes from just above the trees. He turned away when the brightness caused a dull ache behind his eyes. When he looked back, Brent was gone.

The forest was uncharacteristically dark for during the day. The green around Bernie was that dark green, so dark it looked almost black. The only thing that told him it was still daytime was the light green highlights on some of the leaves from the sunlight streaking in through the holes in the canopy of treetops high above him.

Bernie looked around. He stood no more than four feet from the forest's edge, and if he took a couple of steps back, he would be able to see into the field where he and Brent had just been playing catch. But he wouldn't be turning around this afternoon. He had to find his brother. And wasn't it just like Brent to go and run off into the middle of a woods he didn't know. He had done the same thing a year ago while at the park near their house. They had been in a field there, too—doing what, Bernie couldn't remember—when, suddenly, his brother was gone, swallowed by a cluster of shrubbery and trees.

"Brento?" Bernie called out, quietly at first.

No answer.

"Brento!" he called out again, this time louder.

Still nothing. The leaves rustled in the breeze.

"BRENTO!" His imagination immediately stepped in and he could almost hear Brent call back to him. But Bernie knew the difference between his imagination and real life, and this was real life. Brent hadn't responded.

He stepped further into the dense woods, his footfalls slow at first, but quickly increasing from the panic of knowing his brother could be lost.

"Stupid Brento," Bernie muttered. He thought briefly about running back out of the woods and to tell his parents Brent might have gotten himself lost, but he knew that if he did, his father would no doubt scold him for losing track of his brother and leaving him all alone in the forest. "Dinkus."

The thickness of the brush eased up a little and Bernie soon found himself in a sparsely vegetated clearing inside the woods. He would have thought it would make a cool fort was he not so worried for his brother.

Off to his right he heard a branch snap and he immediately spun in that direction.

"Brento?" he said, his voice catching in his throat. "Is that you?"

The leaves rustled in the wind again; his only answer.

Bernie trudged toward where he heard the branch snap. He silently swore to himself that when he found his brother, he would noogie the heck out of him.

The twigs and kindling crunched under his sneakers. He came up to some taller shrubbery and trudged through that, too. He parted the branches, some of them slapping back at him. One hit him in the eye.

"Ow," he said, mostly to himself, but secretly hoping Brent was nearby and could hear that he hurt himself trying to find him.

More thin branches, more crunching of shrubbery, more light and dark green. The patch of bushes came to an end and now there was only tree after tree after tree. Bernie looked around, trying to get his bearings. Aside from the bushes behind him, everything else looked the same. This scared him. He had always been good at finding his way around places he was a stranger to, but they had all been malls or neighborhood streets. This was his first forest and he feared he might be lost.

"Great," he said. "I tell ya, Brento, if I get lost because of you, I'm gonna feed you your cojones."

He kept walking, the trees around him seeming to multiply like rabbits. Five minutes later he stopped and looked around again. This time he knew he had done it. Everything looked the same, and what was worse, he couldn't see that patch of bush he cleared a few minutes ago. His path hadn't been straight. He had to avoid trees, roots and other smaller shrubbery.

He was lost.

—————

Realizing you're lost comes in stages. At first the "oh-crap-I'm-lost" sensation hits you in the chest with a sharp and thick *whumpf*. Then that's followed with the rapid beating of your heart, pulsing, "What-am-I-going-to-do-What-am-I-go-ing-to-do." You think of how you got to be lost in a fast replay of everything that transpired up until the present, then you look at your surroundings once more and re-acknowledge that you're clueless as to your location.

Finally, you analyze your options.

And this is what Bernie did. He analyzed his options of where his brother could be. Except he couldn't arrive at any conclusions. His idiot brother had run into the woods, perhaps thinking a game of hide-and-seek would be fun, then not realizing that foreign woods was a bad place to do it in.

"BRENTO!" Bernie called. No one answered.

The air stilled, the rustling of the leaves quieted, the streaks of sun poking through the canopy of the forest ceiling muted.

That's when Bernie saw him. That's when he saw the Man in the Woods.

The Man, standing slightly hunched behind a thin veil of leaves and branches, was of average height and average weight. If Bernie were interested in specifics, he would have guessed around five and a half feet tall, one hundred and sixty-five to one hundred-seventy pounds. The Man's face was round—not fat-round—but round like a baby's. He was bald, too, and there were shallow indents in his skull, making his head look more skeleton-like than normal. He wore a long black coat and his eyes had no pupils or irises, at least none that Bernie could see. Was the Man blind? Maybe. But then why did it seem like he was looking right at him?

Bernie, his knees shaking, wanted to call out to the Man, but he didn't, and Bernie knew something right then. He knew if this wasn't a dream, he wouldn't have known that the Man knew where Brent was.

There was an awkward exchange of glances. The Man knew Bernie knew that he knew where Brent was. Bernie knew the Man knew that he knew that the Man knew where Brent was. And this cycle continued, the cycle of them knowing the other knew, until finally, after much he knew that he knew that he knews, the Man in the woods winked at Bernie then disappeared behind the leaves.

Bernie stepped forward slowly and approached the branches and leaves where the Man had just been. He was sure, just as he stepped up to the branches, the Man was hiding somewhere in the leaves and at any moment he would jump out and strangle him. But the Man didn't and he was safe. Except Bernie knew his brother wasn't. Somewhere, out there ahead of him, lost in the woods, Brent was being held captive by the

Man. Bernie could sense it, almost as evidently as if someone had told him so. He didn't call out his brother's name, despite his inclination to do just that. Instead, he walked on, carefully, and with each patch of leaves and branches he passed, grew all the more comfortable the Man wouldn't be jumping out from behind any of them, because, simply, the Man hadn't so far.

There was another clearing ahead of him, this one not nearly as big as the one he had first encountered when coming into the woods. But it was big enough to hold a small house with a round roof.

The Man lives here, Bernie knew. *And Brento's here, too.*

The house was something out of a storybook. Its walls were white, its roof a light brown with smooth shingles that looked to be more *impressed* on the structure rather than laid on it. There was a door, its edges round, with a window on each side, about head height, their edges round as well. What was *off* about the house were two things. No smoke came from the chimney. Bernie thought this strange simply because if someone lived in a house, like in all storybooks, smoke came from the chimney. That's just how it was. And no path led to the two steps that went up to the front door. All storybook houses had a path leading up to them. That's just the way things were.

Bernie approached the house, images of Brent filling his mind. He could almost see his brother inside the house, standing there in the center of the room, watching the Man wait for their visitor to arrive. The Man would pace back and forth, occasionally grumbling something about how Bernie was taking so long in getting here, and Brent, too scared to move, could only nod at the Man, his bizarre obligation to agree with the Man taking him over completely.

A shudder raced up and down Bernie's spine. A knot formed in his stomach. He started toward the house, his steps shaky. With each footfall—though he consciously knew he *should* be getting closer—the house seemed to be distancing itself from him, apprehension of what might come making his trek up to the house longer and longer.

The two windows at the front of the house were like eyes staring at him; the door a long, drooping nose, the two rows of steps the teeth in a haunting smile.

Step. Step. Step.

The house was three footfalls closer, but seeming to move two footfalls back.

Step. Step. Step.

Three footfalls nearer. Two footfalls further.

Step. Step.

Two paces. Then one away.

Step. *SNAP!* The sound echoed in his legs. Bernie yelped in surprise. A branch had broken in half beneath his right foot. He looked down, shook his head. His wobbling legs continued forward again.

Closer came the house. Further away the house moved.

After what felt like forever, Bernie was only two paces away from the steps to the door.

The house was menacing this close, its size seeming to have doubled in just a few short paces. There was dead silence from behind the door, no sign of anything living inside.

Bernie tried to call out Brento's name, but only a dry, pinching rasp rose from his throat.

He moved closer to the house. He raised his foot above the first step. It landed on the concrete foothold with a *thwack*, as if his shoe had slapped the stone instead of merely stepped on it. Bernie stepped onto the stair, paused, and found balance on his rubbery legs before stepping up to the next. He was face to face with the door. The sharp smell of pine filled his nostrils. There was that blasted silence within the home.

Bernie knocked, the sound hollow, the door that had just seemed so large and thick suddenly seeming so thin and weak. There was no answer, as expected. Why would there be? Bernie knew who lived behind the door. The Man wouldn't be inviting him in. The Man would want Bernie to *walk* in. He knocked again, just to be sure. Same hollow sound. Same silence responding. The door handle was a shiny, golden knob that Bernie could see his reflection in. He reached for it, grabbed it, its cool surface sending a shrill up his arm. He ignored it and turned the knob, the door unlatching itself effortlessly. He pushed and the door swung open.

What he saw took his breath away.

But not in that good way, like how Mary had taken his breath away when she entered his fourth grade classroom after she moved here from Ontario at the beginning of the school year.

What Bernie saw held his chest in an iron grip, his lungs refusing to inhale the thick, foul air of the house.

The interior was a simple room, rounded at the corners, with a straw bed over to one side. The walls, lower down, were covered with animal heads—deer, mostly, with a couple of dog and fox heads, rabbits, even a squirrel's. Higher up on the wall, however, human heads were mounted on dark, oak plaques, like prize trophies, which, Bernie supposed, was what these heads were to the Man. The heads were of all kinds: white people, black people, Native people. Males, females, both young and old. Even a baby's head, as if a match to the odd-ball squirrel head lower down.

Inexplicably drawn toward them, Bernie studied the faces of each dead person, his mouth agape at the slack-jawed mouths of the heads, their open eyes, the whites in them faded to an awful gray. Their cheeks were caved in slightly, their lips pallid and thin. Their hair sat unnaturally, as if the Man had taken the time to style and comb each mop atop all of them. The baby didn't have any hair, Bernie noticed. Upon further inspection, he realized his assessment of the hair on the top of the heads wasn't entirely accurate. On the tops of each of them the hair was crusty, tainted a deep red, almost a maroon, the tops of the head a mess of skin, hair and bone, as if something had sanded away the flesh on top. Bernie shuddered at the sight.

A semi-transparent, beige tarp stretched from about the middle of the room to the wall on the right. The silhouette of the Man danced behind it, his feet hopping from one to the other to a tune only he could hear. He danced around a table with a lump in the middle of it, the sound of scraping filling the silence of the cabin. Bernie knew what that lump was, though he wouldn't acknowledge it. How could he? The very thought of it made him cringe.

He took a step closer, the Man starting to whistle now. The raspy, scraping sound continued, droning in and out—*jsh jsh JSH JSH jsh jsh JSH JSH*—over and over. The Man held a large file, rubbing it back and forth along the lump, quickly in some places, slower in others. *Jsh jsh JSH JSH jsh jsh JSH JSH.* Bernie paused to look again, his breathing noticeably getting louder. He swallowed hard, the wad of spit in his mouth going down his throat like a pebble into his stomach.

The Man paused suddenly in his work, his head cocked, as if hearing something.

Bernie froze. The Man cocked his head a little further to the left, listening. Once it was determined all was at peace, he resumed his filing: *jsh jsh JSH JSH jsh jsh JSH JSH.*

Bernie, with legs like noodles and a rock in his stomach, approached the beige tarp. The fabric was inches from his nose. The Man kept working furtively on whatever project it was that occupied the table. However, Bernie knew *what* that project was. Again, he just wouldn't acknowledge it.

Just then, spittle caught in the back of his throat and he involuntarily coughed to clear it. The hacking sound was louder than it should have been in the silent cabin, the rough scraping inside his throat from the cough feeling a lot harsher as well.

The Man stopped, and though still concealed by the tarp, Bernie could swear he saw a grin spread across the Man's face. The Man set the file down, but Bernie could still hear—still feel—that awful scraping sound.

jsh jsh JSH JSH.

Bernie closed his eyes as he shuddered, the cold tingle taking him fully, the hairs on his skin standing on end. When he opened his eyes, he saw the Man wasn't behind the tarp anymore.

Afraid to move but compelled to do so anyway, Bernie lifted his right hand, reached across himself, and grabbed the corner of the beige tarp on his left. He squeezed the fabric into a bunch, his arm daring to pull it back. He had to see what that lump was. Had to. Had to make sure it wasn't—or *was*—what he thought it was. He held the edge of the tarp tight, the material already becoming damp with the sweat from inside his palm.

He squeezed his eyes shut.

He pulled the tarp back.

He didn't open his eyes.

The scraping went on, but more to the right and behind him—*jsh jsh JSH JSH.*

Bernie opened his eyes.

His brother's head sat on a wooden workbench, held in place by a small vice built into the tabletop's center. Brent's—Brento's—eyes were open, glazed over, and lifeless. Brento looked at his brother, his gaze filled with longing, asking—begging—for Bernie to take him home safe and sound to their parents. But Brent was dead, Bernie knew, and there was nothing he could do to save him.

jsh jsh JSH JSH jsh jsh JSH JSH—from off behind Bernie.

Why weren't you there, Berno? Brent's eyes pleaded.

Bernie didn't have an answer. This was already too much. The top of his brother's head was bald, the hair having been rubbed away by the file in a scalping. Wet and messy patches of hair smeared in blood was all that was left of Brent's scalp. That was what the scraping sound had been. The Man had been preparing Brent to be a part of his collection of heads on the wall.

Brento.

A part of Bernie was glad he found his brother. He was glad he could see his brother one last time before—

The Man came up behind Bernie, his callused hand spinning him around. Bernie looked up at the Man through watery vision. The Man's head was very round, but very square all the same. It was as if it had been carved from a cube of ice, the edges softened and rounded to take on a more human appearance. His eyes were big—as big as they come, Bernie thought—the blank whites of his eyes now replaced with irises bluer than the ocean on the most beautiful of days. His skin was beige like the tarp in the room, however slightly more tanned. His skin was rough with large pores. He had on a long, deep black smock that swallowed the light, and was rather clean and neat in appearance against the more rough-and-tumble atmosphere of the small cabin.

"You killed my brother," Bernie said. "You killed Brento."

The Man only smiled a kind smile, as if killing Brent had been the right thing to do. Bernie took notice of the Man's extraordinarily crooked teeth, black gaps having taken the place of some of them.

A welt of heated loathing brewed up inside him. "I hate you!" he screamed and started pounding his small fists against the Man.

The Man, not retaliating, only took Bernie into his arms, holding him like a father would a son. Bernie sobbed and sobbed, the hurtful knowledge of his brother's death rampaging through him. His skin rubbed against the rough material of the Man's cloak, making near the same sound as the scraping he'd heard earlier. Almost, but not quite. The Man smelled like warm orange juice.

Jsh jsh jsh.

The Man pushed Bernie away so he could look at him. Bernie kept crying. Brent's head looked on.

"Why did you kill Brento?" Bernie asked, his voice thick with tears.

The Man didn't reply. He only stared at Bernie.

"Why did you—" Bernie began but couldn't finish. *Why did you? Why did you? Why did you have to run off, Brento? Why did you? Why did you? Why did you have to run off?*

———

There were no answers that night. The Man didn't have any to give Bernie. He just simply did what he knew how to do.

And Bernie. Poor Bernie. His head, too, sat on a shelf along with his brother's, their eyes peering out into the rest of the musty cabin. What drove Bernie nuts, though, wasn't that he was forced to stare at the same interior day in and day out. No, sir. It was the draft. The draft that cooled the worn-away bald spot on the top of his head.

And the tickling. There was the tickling of the matted strands of hair that hung just above his ears, just touching their tops, that drove him crazy.

He couldn't speak. His voice box was gone. He wanted to ask Brent if he was being tickled, too, and if he felt that draft all the time or if the torment was only his.

———

That night, out here, in the real world, ten-year-old Bernie woke up with a start, his body jerking itself free from the quilts that covered him. He was in Brent's room, on the floor, with Brent fast asleep in his bed.

It was a bad dream. That's all. It was over. It was—

A voice echoed from the basement of the house, two floors below Brent's room.

See you tomorrow night, it said.

———

Bernie's wife was sleeping upstairs. Bernie knew that she was because he heard her breathing. That blasted breathing.

He pulled the knit blanket up close under his chin and closed his eyes again. Thinking about the Man in Woods had exhausted him. Long ago, the Man had warned him he would see Bernie *tomorrow night.* And he did. There had been many *tomorrows* since that first night, and on each of them, the Man had visited Bernie. Bernie couldn't prove this, but he *knew* it was true. There were nightmares beneath the pleasant dreams, nightmares about the Man, but, when recalling his dreams from the night before, he could only remember happy ones . . . but with a darker edge. Maybe Brent had these same strange good-bad dreams, too? But Bernie didn't know if Brent knew anything about the Man, as he didn't have the heart to ask his brother if he was having the same recurring dream. How could Brent be having those dreams, anyway? Brent was only *in* the dream. He hadn't dreamed it.

But the Man came back, just like he said he would.

Bernie's wife was breathing more loudly now. Bernie opened his eyes; the sound of her breathing eased, but not completely. He closed his eyes again. The breathing resumed.

jsh jsh jsh.

He dreamed of being on the shelf, dreamed of the draft that would constantly pester the top of his head. Sitting on the shelf, his eyes staring out into the cabin, his brother beside him, Bernie thought maybe this was how the Man got inside his head in the first place: through the filing down of skin and bone and hair. Through the filing down of all the heads in his prized collection and that somehow all the people in the room, even the animals, now dreamed of the Man and his cabin all the time. But if that was true, that would mean maybe his brother *did* dream of the Man.

Maybe.

Bernie awoke again; his wife's breathing eased once more. He recalled his realization in his dream. If Brent dreamed of the Man, maybe he could talk to his brother about it? Maybe, together, they can put to bed a nightmare that started over thirty years ago.

Maybe.

His heart sped up with hope. This was a good thing. Too excited to sleep, Bernie threw the blanket back, sat up on the couch, stretched, and stood. He went upstairs. As he approached the door to the master bedroom, he half-expected to hear his wife's breathing. But the bedroom door was closed. Bernie paused, just outside the door, his hand wanting to embrace the knob and enter.

Elizabeth was sleeping soundly. It didn't add up. All those years of marriage, all those nights of laying awake, his eyes closed, listening to his wife's labored breathing. All the times he told her she breathed loudly in her sleep and she said she didn't. All those mornings of her complaining of his moaning in his sleep, his retaliating by saying she breathed too loud. All those—

Then it hit him. His mind, perhaps because he was focusing on the subject, replayed that breathing: *Jsh jsh jsh.* It was then Bernie realized what he had taken back with him from the woods. It was so clear the shock of it sent his heart racing.

He knew his knowing would be the death of him.

———

Elizabeth woke the following morning, sad and slightly upset at herself for making her husband sleep on the couch in the living room. She knew she had been hard on him, but she couldn't take any more of that moaning in his sleep. But there was more to it than that. More to the moaning that she hadn't told him. There was also the breathing, the raspy breathing that sounded as if something was being sanded and filed down. That awful *jsh jsh jsh* sound that kept her awake most nights. But he was her husband and marriage was about putting up with the other's more annoying habits. If Bernie breathed loud in his sleep, she had to accept that.

She got out of bed and, yawning, made for the bedroom door, almost tasting her morning coffee. When she opened the door, her breath caught in her throat. Her hand slid off the doorknob.

No one needed to confirm for her what she saw. She knew.

Bernie was dead.

He lay just outside the bedroom door.

BOOTH 2

Intensity. That's what it was.

Every afternoon they came in between one and three. Every day exactly one hour after midmorning mass. Today, it wasn't supposed to be any different. It's what assured Father Haldo Mr. Thompson would come into St. Mary's Cathedral for confession that afternoon, come to Booth 2, his confessional.

The confessional door creaked open, the number 2 swinging loosely on the nail that held it in place on the door, and Mr. Thompson—Gerad, was his first name—came in and kneeled behind that black mesh, crossed himself and began his confession the same way he had every week for the past twenty years.

"Forgive me, Father, for I have sinned. It has been one week since my last confession," Gerad said in a flat tone, the one that stated things never changed for him.

As usual, Father Haldo leaned on the armrest of his chair and ran a palm over the bald spot atop his head. He wiped a thin film of sweat on his black robe. Sweat still ran down his dark sideburns, trailing along his jaw. He hated the stuffiness of Booth 2. Hated the scent of the wood and the smell of his own sweat mixing with the warm air.

Gerad began going on again about his wife and how he thought she was sleeping with their neighbor, "Mr. Smith." Gerad called his neighbor that, but Father Haldo always thought the name sounded too *made up* to be the truth. He didn't appreciate lying while confessing. It defeated the purpose. So, thinking his wife was having an affair— "Not her first one, mind you," Gerad added—Gerad started venturing off on his own at night, searching for any woman who might give him company. He wasn't a bad looking man. He was in his mid fifties, his dark hair already heavily streaked with gray. He had this jaw that looked as hard as an anvil and a weathered-yet-kind expression was always in his soft gaze. He was slim and seemed to be in good shape from his many years as a construction worker.

Father Haldo was in good shape, too. Lately, he'd taken up jogging in the mornings and doing push-ups before bed. He found the exercise helped him deal with the monotony of sitting day in and day out in a small booth, listening to people go on and on about their secret sins and how he was somehow expected to forgive them when, in truth, it was not his place to forgive them, contrary to popular Catholic belief. And giving sermons was no Wonderland either. Saying the same thing each day for an hour in the mornings, an hour in the afternoons, an hour in the evenings—it weighed on him. Turned his mind to jelly.

Father Haldo supposed he first noticed the change four years earlier when he listened to Mrs. Snyder explain her sick habit of touching each of her six cats between their legs at least four times a week. It was then, he later realized, he discovered that a life of serving hadn't been the correct choice. But he stuck it out anyway, seeking council with the other priests in the church, especially those late night talks with Father Reynolds in the rectory.

Before Gerad even got into the thick of it, Father Haldo had—*What? What was it I'd done? What* have *I done?* He ran his fingers along the black wire mesh and felt moisture on his fingertips. There, in the bottom right corner, was a hole, a weakness in the wooden frame holding the mesh in place. Gerad had begun speaking about something but . . . Father Haldo knew about the hole and the next thing he realized, he was reaching into it, Gerad not paying attention, too lost in his confession about his night out with Daisy. Or was it Trixy? What was her name, again? Father Haldo had suddenly grabbed him by the collar of his winter coat and, with a violent tug, pulled him into the mesh, Gerad's head denting the wire, a startled scream filling the tiny space that was the confessional booth.

Again. Again. Again. Father Haldo kept pulling, kept putting his body into it. He was a big man and outweighed Gerad by at least seventy pounds. But he didn't want to hear of Gerad's adultery anymore. Didn't want to be the one to say, "I forgive your sins, my son. For penance—"

For penance . . . I kill . . . I killed him. He ran a callused palm over his face, wiping at the splashes of blood that had got on his cheeks.

"Oh Lord, what have I done? I—" *He deserved it, didn't he? Coming in here, telling me about all he's done wrong but . . . but what about me? What about me hating these last four years, not wanting to give another sermon, not wanting to stuff one more flake of bread into someone else's mouth? Oh God, help me!*

Father Haldo put his face in his hands and wept, all the while envisioning poor Gerad and the expression on the man's face each time his head crunched against the mesh and the hard oak frame surrounding it. He remembered hearing a bone crush and the popping of flesh as one of the sharp corners of the frame punctured a hole just above Gerad's left eye.

The light, a small lamp in the ceiling of the confessional booth—he dared not turn it on. The orange glow would mix with the red that was no doubt all over the little meshed-covered window and in blotches on the wall surrounding it. As for Gerad's side of Booth 2—Father Haldo couldn't bear to think of it, yet he was tempted to sneak a peek. He wanted to check and see exactly how much damage he had done.

"Don't. No. Stay," he told himself. He folded his hands, fingers entwining together. *Don't. But—*

The digital ring of a cell phone startled him out of his weighted thoughts and heavy heart. It came from the other side of the booth. From Gerad.

Must be in one of his pockets.

The phone rang persistently, each techno-drone of its ring seeming to grow all the more louder in the quiet church.

Grunting, Father Haldo stood up, straightened his robe, and opened the door to his side of Booth 2, purposefully avoiding looking back into it, not wanting to see the blood.

His hand paused above the door handle of Gerad's side. When he opened the door he'd see a dea—*No. Don't think of it.* The phone kept ringing. *Why am I doing this? Why answer the phone? What's wrong with me? You want help, that's what. I just wanted him to be quiet. Just wanted peace. Just wanted silence.* The rings never gave up and it was a wonder Gerad didn't have voice mail. *Screw it!*

Father Haldo opened the door and pawed at the bloody body inside. Gerad's head lolled back when he moved it so he could get into the inner pocket of the man's parka. After much fumbling and squinting through watery vision, trying not to gag on the scent of blood, Father Haldo finally found the cell phone.

He straightened himself and pulled up the thin radial antenna. Blood from the receiver wet his skin when he put his ear to it, the blood from Gerad's head having run down the inside of the parka, settling in his inner pocket in a syrupy pool.

Father Haldo pressed the SEND button. "Hell" —he cleared his throat. Gerad's blood-soaked head lay tucked up against his chest, still on his knees, slumping forward a little. "Hello?"

"Hello. Who's this?" came a girl's soft voice.

Swallowing, Father Haldo didn't know what to say. Was it Gerad's wife calling? A friend? Daisy? Trixy?

Have to say something. Anything.

"I have a confession to make," he said.

WOODCHIPS STIRRING

Daniel had bought Shelly the gerbil for two reasons. One, it was their six-month anniversary. And, secondly, he felt sorry for it. No one wanted it because of how ugly it was.

Shelly had named the gerbil Befriend because that's what she and Daniel had been before they started dating: best friends.

Befriend was small, fitting into the palm of your hand perfectly, with light tufts of beige fur around her neck, nearly hiding her tiny face. Her body, however, looked as if it had been doused in oil, its golden fur matted in clumps, a deep tan color.

Daniel had also bought Befriend a cage but, when assembling it, he accidentally broke the door. He told Shelly not to worry as he would replace it when he came by tomorrow.

It was night and Shelly was in bed. Eyes closed, the last thing she heard before falling asleep was Befriend squeaking in her cage and moving amongst the woodchips.

Shelly dreamed she was in Befriend's cage with the gerbil, wandering along the woodchips like a child in an amusement park. Befriend was nowhere to be seen.

Hiding in the woodchips, Shelly assumed.

Just then her mouth filled with the sensation of fur, her tongue rubbing against the roof of her mouth, trying to work the hair off. She gagged, then spat, and thought it was nothing. She knew she was dreaming and strange things happened in dreams.

A sharp pang hit her throat, a lump somewhere in her esophagus, soft and spongy. It was working its way down. Shelly swallowed, forcing the lump down.

She cleared her throat. "Befriend? Where are you, girl?"

There was a stirring in the woodchips. Then there was a stirring in her stomach.

A prick, like a needle puncturing the inside of her stomach, suddenly caused her to stop moving.

"Ooie," she said. *Ouch.*

The prick came again and so did a sharp scraping, something tearing at the interior lining of her stomach. And it wasn't just one sharp scrape—it was two, like two tiny nail heads scratching her internally.

Shelly fell to her knees, the pain red in her imagination, her eyes blurring over with tears. "Ooie."

She put her hands to her stomach and felt something moving within. The coppery taste of blood filled her mouth. The scratching increased. She could hear her stomach tearing inside her head.

Then it stopped.

She breathed a sigh of relief and fell to her side.

The scratching resumed and soon the movement in her stomach spread, the lump moving deeper into her, in between the muscles and organs, poking and pricking, ripping her insides to lace. Blood bubbled from her mouth.

The woodchips stirred and her mind quickly focused on Befriend. The woodchips ruffled and Befriend poked her tiny head out of the woodchips while at the same time, in the real world, the gerbil tore through Shelly's stomach and crawled down her belly, descending lower.

NOT THERE

Dear Terrance,

My wife Judy and I are pleased to inform you that we accept your invitation to your tenth-year anniversary party on March 17.

Your brother,

John

Ps. There's something I have to tell you.

I

The cars rolled up the drive just after nine as Terrance Michaels specified in his invitation. Today marked his tenth wedding anniversary to his wife, Elizabeth. Watching from the living room window, Terrance eyed Judy as she stepped out of the passenger side of his brother's new Bentley. Though Terrance was successful himself, a part of him was upset that John could now afford an automobile as well. The "automobile" had been on the market for a short time and up until tonight, every time there had been a party at the Michaels's Estate, John had ridden up in horse and carriage, their driver George opening the door for him and Judy the same way he had for the past eight years. John was a surgeon, one with a stellar reputation, so suddenly deciding to get an automobile was no surprise. Especially a Bentley, one of the most prestigious automobiles on the market. John had a flare for the dramatic and always tried to upstage Terrance in everything. John saved lives whereas Terrance ruined them as president of the Wind City First National Bank, complete with the power to deny loans and mortgages on a whim. As for John "saving lives" —it was butchery yet Terrance found John's fascination with cutting open the human body intriguing. To dedicate one's life to cutting people up . . . . Even as a child, John was always dissecting things: dragonflies, toads—the neighbor's dog.

Blast, but no matter, thought Terrance. "Come as they will."

"Sir, your guests are arriving," Clara, the housemaid, said. She stood at the entrance where the living room met the hall.

"I'll be there in a moment."

The little woman in her traditional black dress and brown hair tied up in a taut bun scurried off to greet her employer's company.

In the next room, the front hall filled with voices, several more than just the two that belonged to John and Judy.

If you only knew what she and I've been through, John, Terrance thought as he turned from the window. Adjusting his bowtie in the wall-length mirror over the ornately-carved stone fireplace, he gathered himself and vowed to show no sign of the secret he'd been keeping from John. Oddly enough, John implied in his reply letter he was keeping something from him as well.

Hands clasped behind his back, he made his way to the front hall.

"Stanley, James, Carl," he greeted with outstretched arms.

James, a stout man in his early forties, removed his top hat and stuffed it under his arm so he could shake Terrance's hand.

"Congratulations, old boy. Ten years, my, how time flies."

Terrance smiled then dipped slightly at the waist when James's wife, Rita, appeared from behind her husband.

"Congratulations, Terry," she said, giving him a peck on the cheek. "Where's Elizabeth?"

"Upstairs. You know my wife: she takes all the time in the world. Plus, she complained of a headache so she might still be resting before coming down."

Rita smiled sweetly. She and Elizabeth were close friends.

"Gentleman, please," said Terrance, "this way. Clara, if you please, let Charles know our guests have arrived. It's only a small gathering. Can't have him hiding away in the kitchen all night."

Charles, the Michaels's butler, was known for staying away from the guests during parties, only emerging from the kitchen to serve hors d'oeuvres, the meal, and dessert.

"Yes, sir," Clara said and hurried off to the other room.

As they made their way to the dining hall, Stanley and Carl also offered Terrance their well wishes.

"I'm surprised you hung on as long as you did," Carl said.

"Women like Elizabeth are special," Stanley added.

I know, he thought. *But you can't always trust them completely.*

"And where are the children?" asked Stanley's wife, Christine.

"Tucked away as usual, when we have guests," Terrance replied.

"I love children. I would very much have liked to have seen them."

"Perhaps I'll bring the sleepyheads down later to say hello."

He didn't have to survey his guests to know their eyes darted about the white, marble walls of the front hall, taking in the spiraling banister off to the side, the paintings of his ancestors starting with Frederik Michaels, his great grandfather at the top, straight down to him and his wife and two boys, Terrance Junior, seven, and David, four.

When they entered the mahogany-paneled dining hall, Charles stood at one end, a bottle of merlot at the ready. Clara stood at the other, wiping her hands on her apron.

As Terrance sat down at the head of the table, he saw John waiting by the entrance, Judy at his side.

Terrance arched his eyebrows, signaling to his brother: "Are you joining us?"

"In a minute," he said and took Judy aside, out of view.

I hope she doesn't say anything, Terrance thought. *He might then say something he shouldn't. Or he might tell her what he wants to tell me. No matter. I already—*

"Terrance?"

"Yes, Elisa?" Elisa was Carl's wife.

"It simply wouldn't be right for Charles to serve us without Elizabeth here. Why don't you see what's taking her?"

He considered for a moment. "Very well." He slid his chair back and stood. "Ladies, gentlemen, one moment, please."

A few nodded his way while others chatted.

"Charles?" he said.

"Yes, sir." Charles stepped up to him, his slim form a solid four inches taller. Terrance was pleased Charles wore his black suit tonight instead of his usual gray.

"Retrieve the '89 from the cellar and give everyone here a healthy glass." The "'89" was the 1889 Scotch he'd been saving since he bought it at auction two years prior. "It is much better than the merlot."

"Very good, sir." He turned to leave, then, "Sir?"

"Yes?"

"I'm sorry to ask, but have you seen the hammer? There's a nail in the floor that I noticed sticking up earlier. I wish to bang it down before someone snags their foot."

"No, Charles, I have not. Now, about that Scotch . . ."

Charles left the room.

Terrance exited the dining hall, crossed the front hall and went up the orange-and-black-patterned carpeted stairwell. Even after living in the large home for the past eight years, he still reveled in the way his fingertips glided across the smooth surface of the polished oak railing.

The hallway at the top of the stairs was dim, the only light coming from the medium-sized chandelier in the front hall below.

The master bedroom was yet another floor up and could only be accessed by the staircase at the end of the hallway. Doors lined the hallway though he couldn't remember the last time he'd been in them. The rooms were fully furnished; the inside contents remained hidden beneath white sheets, only inspected once every few months by Clara for anything that might need tending to. The children hadn't need for the rooms and neither did him or Elizabeth. If there were guests, they would stay in the guesthouse across the yard.

The boys' bedroom ran off the east wing, accessed by an opposite stairwell across from the one that led up to the master bedroom. Their playroom was on the main level, as was the servants' quarters. He had considered building small residences for Charles and Clara at the back of the property, but landscaping a garden and having a story hut built for Elizabeth and the boys made more sense.

Terrance considered himself an excellent family man.

He ascended the stairwell and turned right once at the top. He opened the master bedroom door. The lights were out. Elizabeth lay in bed, her headache not having left.

The bed was in the middle of the room, a large oak dresser with carved-in cherubs up against the wall on either side; one his, the other hers. Above the headboard was a painting of the back garden, their little place reserved for quiet evening walks when the kids were in bed and the butler and maid were off for the night. After the walks he and Elizabeth checked on the boys together then returned to their bedroom, occasionally made love then went to sleep.

If love was what it was, he thought.

Terrance sat on the edge of his side of the bed, the starched sheets crunching beneath the comforter. Elizabeth lay on her side, facing away from him, silent.

"Our guests are waiting for you," he said. "John is here. Judy, as well." *I can only imagine what Elizabeth might say right now. Does she know I know?* "How is your headache?"

No answer.

"I realize you don't want to talk to me. I'm sorry about earlier." He sighed. "I got upset and I apologize. But you got upset, too. It's both our faults. The boys . . ." They should never had heard him raise his voice at her. Ever since becoming a father, he swore he would never let his children see the two of them fighting. All couples fought, Terrance understood. It happened and, to a degree, it was expected. Growing up, watching his parents fight nearly every evening, exceeding the boundaries of simple tiffs regularly—the way his father treated his mother; the way his mother would leave for days, too scared to face his father—Terrance would not have his boys witness the same. He vowed to protect them from the ugliness of family life and give them nothing but peace.

"What am I supposed to tell everyone?" He set a hand to her shoulder. "You can't stay here all night. It's our ten-year anniversary. We should be celebrating it."

He waited a moment longer then stood from the bed.

John was at the door. "How is she?"

"You know you're not supposed to be up here. This is *our* bedroom."

"Terrance, I've been up here many times before."

"I know."

Judy appeared behind John. The look on her face said something was wrong.

If he said anything to her . . .

"What?" John asked.

"Nothing," he said. "Elizabeth is fine. Now, let us leave her."

"As you wish," John said.

The three returned downstairs.

II

"Tell me, how is it you bought out the *Wind City Gazette?*" Stanley asked in between mouthfuls of sautéed salmon.

Elizabeth hadn't come down for dinner in spite of everyone waiting an extra hour for her. Though no one said anything, any outsider looking on could tell you something was wrong. Adding to matters, John and Judy kept their conversations to themselves and didn't mingle with the other guests. Terrance planned to have words with him afterwards regarding his manners. He would speak to Judy, as well.

Come up here in that automobile of yours and suddenly you're better than everyone, huh? he thought. He paused a moment, took a deep breath, calming himself. *Keep control.*

"Terrance?" Stanley said.

"I'm sorry. What was the question?"

"How did you manage the *Wind City Gazette* buyout?"

Terrance took a sip of his wine. It was a little too dry for his taste, but what wasn't these days? *Why does she have to be in the bedroom? Why did I let myself get—I wish the boys were here. To see everyone together . . .*

"The former owner wasn't paying attention," Terrance said. "He had a soft spot for . . . women? It's not surprising what happens when you lose your footing. Simply put: he fell."

Stanley wiped his mouth with the cloth napkin from the same set he had given Terrance and Elizabeth for their fifth wedding anniversary.

"Well, I'm proud of you for taking advantage when you did."

"Thank you."

Clara appeared from behind the kitchen door with a silver-plated pot of coffee and an equally lavish serving tray with porcelain cups and saucers.

As she began setting the dishware in front of the guests, Terrance noticed John's facing pinching at its center, Judy's eyes wide just beyond.

"What did he tell her?" he grumbled. *She knows, and you know that. You did it to yourself. No. He did it first.*

He eyed the two coldly. They didn't eat their meal. Those two never ate. Not even on him and Elizabeth's wedding day.

After the meal, while all sat back, cigarettes lit, drinking their coffee, Terrance excused himself from the table, stating he wanted to check in on the boys.

When he entered their bedroom, he was greeted with the fond memories of early mornings waking them for school, encouraging them for the new day ahead. He was greeted with the nightmare of them seeing him and Elizabeth fight. The words the boys heard.

What they saw.

Never again.

He went over to David, the little one, whose bed was on the right. The boy was just as he left him, tucked beneath the covers, warm and snug. Terrance Junior's bed was on the left, against the opposite wall. He, too, was just as he had been when Terrance sent him to sleep.

"Only to dream . . ." Terrance said quietly.

Hands in his pockets, he watched over them a moment more then left the room, closing the door behind him.

John stopped Terrance as he descended the stairwell to the front hall.

"Are they asleep?" he asked.

"Resting peacefully."

"I'm sorry, Terrance." John's dark eyes seemed earnest.

"For what?" He knew, though, what his brother was talking about.

"Judy's sorry, too."

"Why? She didn't do anything."

John slouched, his posture sagging so his tummy stuck out more than a gentleman ought to let it.

"Let's just try to have a good time," Terrance said.

"Okay." John straightened and the two returned to the dining hall.

The evening wore on, James, Carl, Stanley, their wives—all seemed to be having a good time.

Except for John and Judy.

III

"Clara, if you will, mind the house while I'm gone. John and I have things to . . . discuss," Terrance said.

She stood in the doorway, peering out at her master who was on the front step.

"John?" she said softly.

"My brother. Now, if you please."

"But sir—"

"Now, Clara."

Pulling his gloves over his fingers, Terrance marched down the front steps to where his brother stood by his new Bentley, Judy in the passenger seat.

Clara crossed her hands across her apron, unsure what to tell her master.

Glancing over his shoulder, he waved her to go back into the house and do what he asked.

With a slight dip of the chin, she obeyed and closed the front door.

Alone in the front hall, the house suddenly felt much bigger than it was, the room that much wider, the ceiling that much higher.

Mind the house while I'm gone, her master had said.

The first thing she would do is check on the misses. Elizabeth hadn't been out of her bedroom all night.

"I hope she's all right," Clara said. "Headaches are nasty things especially when they grab you unexpected. And on her anniversary, too. Pity." But with the way Terrance had been treating the help lately, with the way he dictated orders without feeling in his voice and the way he wanted things done *now* —a part her was glad Elizabeth hadn't joined him for dinner. *He doesn't deserve her,* she thought. *He doesn't deserve anybody.*

She made her way up the winding staircase, left down the hallway and to the next set of stairs that led up to the master bedroom. Before she opened the bedroom door, a chill swept through her and she adjusted the short sleeves of her dress so they covered her upper arms completely.

It was more than just a chill. There was no heat at all. It was as if the master had closed all the vents in this wing of the house. The brass doorknob was like ice when she turned it, the wooden door cool when she pressed against it.

The door opened; the room was dark. In the shadows, Elizabeth's sleeping form was barely visible; the outline of the white sheets were a blurry gray against the dark dresser beyond.

I shouldn't wake her, Clara thought. *Yet perhaps she thinks it's still evening and is waiting for someone to come for her so she could visit with her guests?* She didn't know if she should be the one to let her down, that her husband had left her there all evening and into the night, missing her own wedding anniversary.

No, I'd best not, she thought. *Let her sleep.* As she turned to leave, something moved on the pillow: the waves of Elizabeth's long brown hair.

Seeing the misses was awake, Clara went into the room and gently approached her.

"Ma'am?"

The hair stirred against the pillow again.

"Would it be all right if I switched on the lamp?" Clara asked. *I don't want to burden your eyes, but if I could see you . . .*

No answer.

"The guests—" *No, don't, just wait. The master will be back soon and he could tell her her friends have gone. Let him face her and see what happens.*

Clara knew that Elizabeth, as sweet as she was, could be as cold as a frosted window if needed be.

Elizabeth lay still. Clara drew nearer and placed a hand on her shoulder.

"Ma'am," she said.

Elizabeth's skin was cool beneath her evening dress.

The poor thing. She must have froze while she slept, Clara thought. As she leaned over her and gripped the corner of the blanket to cover her up, she caught sight of what was moving on the pillow.

Her scream echoed off the walls, piercing her own ears.

IV

Charles's tall, lanky form burst into the room, his weight shoving the door into the adjacent wall as he swung it open. It smacked against the wall with a woody *thud!*

"Clara!" he said.

His friend and fellow servant stood pressed up against the dresser, palms at its edge, eyes wide and as hard as stone, staring at Elizabeth. Her mouth was drawn so tight it appeared that if she did speak, any words that broke through would shatter her lips. The lamp was on, Clara's face white compared to its light yellow glow.

"Clara," he said again and went over to her. When he touched her arm, it was as ridged as a clothes hanger and just as hard.

Elizabeth lay facing them, eyes open, mouth slightly agape. Above her left eye was a large dark blotch of brownish-red, shining and wet. Blood still oozed from the wound, pooling on the pillow then dripping off as it ran down its edges, coating and matting her hair.

"She's-she's—" Clara started.

Carefully, Charles reached across her and cupped her cheek, turning her head toward him. Even as he did so, it wasn't until she fully faced him did her eyes leave Elizabeth's body. He pulled her into him, hiding her from their employer's departed wife.

The stone-like gaze that held Clara in check gave way and she burst into tears, crying into his shoulder.

"She's-she's—He killed her!" she said.

"Who?"

"The master. Mr. Michaels. He killed her!"

She shook beneath him.

"Lord, have mercy," he said calmly. "First things first. Let's leave the room, get the boys and ring the police." *Madam,* he thought.

Elizabeth, the queen to a king, was dead.

"He could be back any moment!" She shook again.

"Where did he go?"

"He—"

Instead of letting her finish, he took her from the room, eyed the body of Elizabeth Michaels one more time, then closed the door.

———

Clara was to meet Charles in the kitchen after he got the boys. The four would then exit through the back and go to the police station in town using the master's old horse-and-carriage. Hooking up the two horses to the carriage wouldn't take long and it was the only option lest they walk; the Michaels's Estate was outside town and far from any neighboring homes.

Charles rushed to the boys' room on the third floor. He entered. The room was dark, the boys beneath their covers. Moonlight from the large window in the middle of the room cast a pale glow on the boys' white sheets, turning them a bluish-gray. Their chests didn't seem to rise and fall as they breathed.

If they were breathing.

Darting first to Terrance Junior on the left, Charles flung back the covers. His legs buckled beneath them when Junior's sleepy stare and slightly open mouth greeted him. Dark liquid encompassed his head like a murky halo around the pillow. "Ter—"

David!

He ran to the other boy and tossed the sheets back. David lay with eyes closed, his forehead a mess of hair and flesh, blood and—

Charles fell to his knees and slammed his fists against the hardwood floor. "No. They-they . . . not them, too."

"Charles?" called Clara from the foot of the stairs, distant and almost *not there.* "Are you all right? What happened?"

They're-they're— "They're dead," he whispered.

Hands shaking, innards shaking worse, he stood, swayed on his feet, then debated if he should cover the bodies or just leave them be.

Leave them be, he thought. "Clara," he said softly. How could he tell her of the boys' demise without sending her into a panic?

They had to leave, get out of the house and get hold of the police straight away before the master returned.

"Where did he go?" Charles said through gritted teeth. When he exited the room, he left the door open thinking that if he closed it—for why, he did not know—he would somehow be abandoning the children, really *allowing* them to be dead.

The decent down the stairs never took so long.

———

"We're leaving," Charles said the moment he entered the kitchen.

Clara was not there.

Where the—? he thought.

"Clara?" he said again, thinking maybe she was behind the rack of pots that hung over the large, tiled counter in the middle of the kitchen.

He was alone.

Mind racing, he ran out the back door and into the yard, moving straight for the stable.

Maybe Clara was already with the horses.

———

Clara heard shouting and cursing and—weeping?

On her hands and knees by the living room window that overlooked the front lot, she kept herself from view, only peeling back the curtains just enough to see outside. Fortunately, there was a large shrub in front of the six-foot-tall window, its tops coming up about a foot above the windowpane.

Outside, Terrance paced back and forth, shaking a fist at—

———

"I can't believe you told him!" Terrance shouted at Judy. "I confided in you!" He gripped the vehicle's door where the window met metal, and shook it. The automobile rocked from his force.

John lay on the cobbled-stone unconscious, his breathing slow, his breath visible in the cool night air.

———

What is he doing? Clara thought.

Terrance stood there, his hands latched onto—

———

Judy wouldn't leave the vehicle. She held onto the inner handle for sweet life.

John lay at his brother's feet.

Just . . .

. . . laying there.

"You're killing him!" she screamed.

"He drove me to it! It was him. All him!" Terrance said. "He was sleeping with Elizabeth!"

"No, he wasn't!"

You lying b— "He slept with her! I saw them together. I heard her call his name. She even spoke of him while she slept."

Terrance pivoted on his heel and kicked John in the head.

———

When Terrance's foot came back down, Clara yelped and covered her mouth.

———

"Come here!" Terrance growled, balling his fist. He punched the car's window, a spider web spiraling outward over the glass.

Judy jumped back in her seat, releasing the door handle.

On the second strike, the glass shattered. He reached through the window; Judy turned to go out the other door. He grabbed her from behind and hauled her out.

Squirming, screaming, she beat against him . . . but it was useless. Throwing her to the cobbled-stone drive, Terrance pounced on her, slamming first his right fist then his left into her face. His bony knuckles reveled in the softness of her flesh when he struck her cheeks; recoiled when they hit her cheekbones. She screamed for help but somewhere inside, Terrance knew no one would come. No one would challenge him.

No one *knew* to come.

He eyed John, making sure his brother was watching him beat her into the nothing that she was.

"You stole my wife, my life, my family," he said. He didn't know if he uttered the words aloud or if they were in his head.

Screams turning to whimpers, Judy stopped struggling.

He hit her, beat her, coated her face with her own blood and mangled flesh.

Within moments, her face a mess of pink and red, distorted and torn, he finally stopped.

Panting, brow coated with sweat, his shirt untucked from his trousers, he stood and kicked his brother in the head once more.

———

Even from her low position, the blood and ripped skin and muscle on Terrance's fingers caused Clara's stomach to churn. She had to leave. Had to get out of there.

Had to get help.

But she couldn't turn away.

Terrance's mouth moved furiously though what he was saying was muted by the window's glass.

She turned away and covered her eyes. She didn't know how much time had passed until there was a hand on her shoulder.

———

He spat upon him, a murky wad of phlegm upon his brother's face.

"Elizabeth was mine!" Terrance said. "She was everything."

I am everything.

———

"Clara?" It was Charles.

She peered up at him. When she spoke, her voice wavered. "He's killing himse—" The words were too painful to speak.

Charles peered out the window. "Killing who?"

Clara got to her feet and flung upon the curtains.

The front drive was empty.

"There's no one there, Clara," he said. "The horses are re—"

"The master was just there! He was just—" Her heart caught in her throat when she realized she and Charles were not alone.

"I'm here," Terrance said.

He pulled the hammer out from his jacket's inner pocket and took a step toward them.

LIKE A WORM

The sweat that coated his skin was thick, like oil. Each lungful of air was like breathing deeply on a muggy night, after the rain. The air was warm inside his lungs.

Gary Smith couldn't see anything. Darkness and isolation hung on the air almost as thick as the humidity. He didn't know where he was, but one thing was certain: it was a cramped space, tight, weighing in from all sides. He lay on his stomach and the ground beneath his belly was like a moist sponge covered in breadcrumbs. This *sponge* pressed against him, left, right, top and bottom, even above at the top of his head and below at the soles of his feet. He soon realized he was buried alive, deep beneath the earth's surface. He felt like a giant worm burrowing through a gardener's bed.

There was something else on his skin, too. Steam, or, at least, what felt like the moist warmth left on your skin after you take a hot shower and stand before the mirror shaving.

I'm not supposed to be here, Gary thought, knew. *But yet I am, aren't I? After all, I deserve it.* His heart sank at the notion.

He felt along the bread-crumbed ground with his fingertips. Some places in the sponge were weaker than others. He dug his fingernails into it and, with barely any room to move, slowly pawed at the sponge, scraping it away bit by bit. The crud got beneath his nails and more oily sweat dripped off his brow. A drop leaked into his eye. It stung. But he kept digging, pawing like a dog, hoping that because the sponge felt weaker where his fingers pried, so would he find a hope for escape from this confined place.

I'm not supposed to be here, he thought again. There was nothing worse than being where you didn't belong.

Each time he grabbed a handful of sponge, he scooped it to the side, beside his palms. Soon there was no more room to push the sponge aside and the hole he was creating began to fill quickly. As he dug, as if the sponge around him knew he was trying to get out, the more it pressed on him, collapsed on him.

"Oh . . ." he said and spat out a bit of sponge that got in his mouth. He wished he could see. Anything would be better than this darkness. Just knowing where you were always helped, always brought comfort.

The sponge beneath his fingertips gave way to an open space. He probed the hot air with his fingers. Hope. He pressed his palms where he had dug and the sponge gave way completely and his arms hung down into a hot room below, his arms bent at the elbows, dangling.

Gary tried digging his feet into the sponge, but it was too thick. There was, however, a light down in the room. The light was dim, a golden yellow. It reminded him of his living room back home on cold winter evenings. The light was inviting.

Wriggling his body between the mash of sponge, he managed to free himself a little more. The sponge began to break apart beneath his upper torso and, finally, broke apart completely. Gary hung at the waist from the ceiling of a dimly lit room, the source of the light concealed. The light was just *there*. He could now see what was around him. Dirt, damp soil, bathed in yellow warmth.

He arched his back as hard as he could, his muscles straining, so his torso was parallel to the floor. Quickly he stuck out his arms, pushed his palms against the inner edge of the hole. It was hard for his fingers to find purchase in the soil, but he found enough to hold himself up parallel to the floor momentarily. His back gave way before he could twist his legs and wriggle them free. He grabbed the inner edge of the soil and tried again. Twisting his hips and kicking his feet, his legs broke free and he fell to the ground of the dimly lit room. It was like landing face first hard into a mattress. Gary lay on his stomach, catching his breath. He spat out more soil, a bitter taste on the tongue. Sweat dripped off his dark hair and ran along behind his ears before trickling down and off his jaw.

Face first in the dirt, there was only one thought: *I'm not supposed to be here . . . . But it all makes sense. I do* belong here. I'd give anything for home.

He didn't know how much time had passed before he sat up, one leg out before him, the other bent at the knee and brought up to his chest. And he didn't know how much time had passed until he realized what he was wearing. Black, liquid rags covered his body, with only his neck and head, hands and wrists exposed. The inside layer of the fabric was wet against his skin but when he felt the material, it was dry, like crusty, dirty cloth.

I deserve this, he thought. *Where am I?*

Just then a voice off to the side startled him.

"You got out?" it said. The voice was raspy, like an old man who'd spent the better part of his life smoking.

Gary looked around. His eyes must have gotten used to the light because it wasn't as dim now and the walls weren't as blackish-yellow as they first were. They were grayer, like dry dirt, but the occasional sparkle in the dim light told him the soil around him was damp. Damp from what? Just damp.

"I can't believe you got out," the voice said.

"Who's there?" Gary said. "Where am I?"

"Oh, calm down, now, won't you? This isn't so bad. You and I probably would have met in a hundred years or so, once the dirt around you wore away over time and your head could peek in."

Gary's heart leapt into his throat when he saw a face on the ground in the corner of the room, looking up, as if whomever it was had been buried alive and only his face was left out in the open like a doormat. The brown eyes of the face didn't look at him when it spoke but instead stared up at the ceiling.

Backing himself away, Gary brought both his knees to his chest. The oily sweat still sat on his face. His hands were sweaty, too. It was very muggy in here, the air fuzzy, like that of a steam room but not nearly as thick. Just a fine haze over what would normally be a clear image.

"And now you recoil in disgust, hiding away from a face on the floor. No wonder you're dead, friend. You probably got offed up there by some bugger who wanted your wallet and instead of trying to defend yourself, you let him kill you when, after you gave him your wallet, it wasn't enough and he wanted more. Your watch, perhaps? Your ring? Hey, even the jacket off your back. You didn't put up a fight because you're a coward."

Gary thought again about his clothes. He held his arms out before him.

"What—What is this?" he asked.

"I don't know. I can't bloody see you. Come closer."

Hesitantly, Gary came over to the face and showed it the clothes that bled off his skin, as though he had cut his arms, body, legs, and the blood was oozing off him.

I don't belong here. Sure I do. You do, Gary, and you know it. Tears pricked at the corners of his eyes.

The face on the floor studied the clothes. "There's no telling what precisely that is. I've only seen faces about this room, those like me who don't know where their body is. There was one on the wall just over there." The face's eyes cast down, pointing to the wall of soil ahead of Gary. "There was another above, too, like yourself, before you fell through. They were all over this room at one point or another. Then the Benders came. That's my name for them, Benders. In all truth, I don't think they have a name, at least not in any language we would know." He paused, then, "My name's James, by the way."

"Gary," he replied. "Wait. You said . . . you said I was . . . I was dead."

"What else would you be? You found yourself buried alive up there, right?" The eyes stared at the ceiling again.

The clothes on Gary's skin felt like a heavy wet towel.

"I don't belong here," Gary finally said. He felt a little bit better after saying it, too.

"Neither do I," James said. "That's all our stories. But it's our fault we're here. We didn't believe in Him and so we're here."

"Believe in who?"

Before James could answer, a low howl was heard behind one of the soil walls.

"Benders," James said. "They do that from time to time. They're hungry." James's pale gray face looked up at him. His red lips spread thin into a smile. "They'll come for me one day, just like they did the others. They eat us, you see, wait until we're nice and ripe and then remove us from the dirt like potatoes or carrots. They're saving me for last. I was the first one here and, like aged wine, I'll be the last to leave because I'll taste the best. I reckon I would have been gone before you showed up. You were probably the new me, come to think of it. I was told I'd be eaten shortly, but they were waiting for someone to replace me—a new stock, as it were—first. Now you're free. I couldn't get out when I found myself buried alive. I didn't know what to do. I slept most of the time. Now I don't know where my body is and all I have is this face and a window into the same room for the past two thousand years, give or take a century."

Two thousand years! Is he crazy? Then Gary realized James wasn't. He finally realized where he was.

He was in Hell.

Hell. The reality of it wouldn't set in.

"I still can't believe you got out," James said.

"Why are they called Benders?" Gary asked.

James sniffed. "Because they can make a person do whatever they want them to—bend their will. I've seen it before, when they come to eat you. The screams, Gary, the screams. They pull you out of the dirt and, with just one look, you succumb to them and stop struggling. Even when they take their first bite, you have a smile on your face, as if what they're doing is normal. As if you *want* them to eat you."

Gary shivered despite the damp heat of the place around him. *Benders.*

A low rumble filled the room and bits of dirt sprinkled down from the ceiling and off the walls.

"They're coming," James said. "If they see you loose . . ."

When Gary looked around for a way out, he couldn't find any, just four walls made of damp soil, nothing more. "How do I get out of here?"

"You can't. We're in a sealed room, in case you haven't noticed."

"The ceiling. Can I get back in there?"

"How am I supposed to know? You're the first one who has fallen through. You haven't aged properly. They might not even want to eat you. The again, they probably don't care. They eat a lot. This room was full of faces a short while ago. Wait a sec, that was six years ago, that's when it was. Man, time flies."

"But . . ."

The rumbling grew louder. Then all was still. The dirt of the wall to Gary's right burst open in a black spray and a Bender stepped through. It stood less than four feet tall, its shoulders wide, its waist small. The Bender's body was humanoid. Sort of. It was naked, sexless, the skin appearing tanned in the dimly lit room. Its muscles rippled even though it stood still. Its arms hung to the floor like an ape's and it had only two toes, two fat toes as thick as three fingers each with dull gray nails at their ends. Its jaw was long and it reached its chest. It had no neck. Long hair draped down to its shoulders, parted in the middle, revealing a flat face with a hooked nose. The Bender snarled, big, block-like teeth as fat as Chiclets that looked to be as hard as stone.

Immediately the Bender set its gaze on Gary. The creature stalked toward him, slow at first, as if in disbelief that Gary had ripened before his time. Soon the Bender's pace picked up. Gary darted to the side and rounded the creature and went for the hole in the wall. On the other side of the hole was a long tunnel with soil walls just like the room James was in. The lighting in the tunnel was dim, too, and, like the room, its source could not be seen.

I don't belong here. Then, another voice in his head: *Sure you do. You stopped going to church when you were eighteen. Did you forget? If you don't believe in the big J.C. then you wind up here. You're in Hell, Gary! There's no getting out.*

Gary ran down the tunnel. Groans filled his ears, seeming to come from all around. He heard someone say "Ow!" and realized he must have stepped on a face on the floor.

He glanced over his shoulder as often as he could while finding his way down the tunnel. To where it would take him, he didn't know. A low rumbling far behind him sporadically grew louder before dying off again. He rounded a bend in the tunnel.

There was a muffled "Hey!" from somewhere above him. It didn't sound like a Bender. But Gary also didn't know what a Bender sounded like. *But it's human, isn't it, the one who just shouted? No rumbling.*

Gary stopped running. He looked up and spittle caught in the back of his throat. He swallowed hard. Up against the soil ceiling was a man, shirtless, only his upper torso showing, and only his forehead and eyes. The rest of his face and the rest of his body were concealed in the dirt.

He's breaking through, Gary thought absentmindedly. *Like me. Maybe he, like me,* knows *he doesn't belong here.*

"Leth mphe dowmph . . ." the man said through the layer of dirt.

The rumbling grew louder and a bead of sweat stung Gary's eyes. He wiped it away. He shook his head. The rumbling grew louder yet. He had to get moving. He looked at the man. "I can't. I'm sorry."

Gary glanced over his shoulder. Against the golden-gray soil wall of the tunnel was the Bender's shadow. "They're coming. I'm sorry." He took off down the tunnel.

The further he ran, the more he saw people and faces partially covered in dirt in the walls and floor and ceiling. *So many,* he thought. The rumbling died off again. Then it picked up immediately and a loud grunt echoed behind him. The Bender. The moment Gary turned around to check how far behind him the Bender was, the creature was already on him and wrestled him to the ground. There were more Benders behind this one.

Don't look at the eyes, Gary reminded himself.

"No . . ." he said. He struggled with the creature, keeping his eyes closed. The Bender's fat fingers pawed at Gary's eyelids, trying to get them open. The Bender was heavy and sat on Gary's lungs. It was difficult to breathe.

Gary swung madly at the creature, his fists connecting as if pounding a slab of raw meat. They didn't have an effect on the Bender. Soon his arms felt like they were filled with lead and each swing at the creature grew more and more futile.

The Bender forced Gary's eyes open. Gary tried to squeeze them shut but it was too late. The Bender already had him.

The creature's gaze was soft and reassuring, reaffirming in Gary's mind that eating him was the right thing to do.

"But . . ." Gary began. "But I don't belong here. I don't . . . please put me back. I'm not ready yet. Let me age. Jesus, I'm sorry."

He thought of James, there, alone in the room down the tunnel.

The Bender's gaze continued to turn Gary's mind to jelly.

"Okay, you're right," Gary said. "I deserve this. Eat me. It's okay. Please?"

I belong here.

The moment the hot pain from the Bender's bite stung his shoulder, Gary woke up.

Thank God. It was just a dream. Sweat dripped off his brow. *I'm so sorry, Lord. I believe in you, Jesus.*

Heat flowed over his skin.

His heart jumped when he spat out what felt like sponge coated in breadcrumbs.

His fingers dug at the soil.

BELOW

"Did you find what you were looking for?"

"No, not yet."

"Why not?"

"Because it isn't there."

"Then you haven't looked hard enough."

———

If only they would bite. The fish were out there, Carry knew. He caught hundreds since he began fishing at the newly-named Bedright Lake each evening ten years ago. But tonight . . . tonight they all seemed to be asleep.

The sky was gray and there was a chill on the air. The wind, which seemed to pick up speed about an hour ago, folded the brownish-gray water over itself as it rolled into shore. He wouldn't mind if it rained. He'd stay out all evening and into tomorrow if he had to, if only to catch one fish.

When he and his wife, Fae, took up residence in their cabin on a fulltime basis twenty-three years ago instead of keeping their small home in town, she told him she'd lose him to Bedright Lake (then, Lake Marman) and that he'd spend all his time there like he did when he was young.

But he never did. Not until she died ten years ago last April. And he didn't fish because he loved it or because he found it relaxing. He just needed to pass the time. He was seventy-one when she died, eighty-one now, and death wasn't that far off. Carry thought fishing to kill the hours might speed up getting to the end and he'd see her sooner because of it. Even still, that wasn't the real reason he dragged his old lawn chair to the shore each evening, baited a hook and flung a line out onto the lake.

Philip was the reason—his son, dead long before in a life he could barely recall.

The two had gone out on canoe one fall, long before him and Fae bought the cabin. Carry had wanted to show Philip the lake, take him across to the other side and along the foresty-shore where the branches hung over the water like fingers dipping into a pot. You could canoe under those fingers and for a moment believe you were in a secret tunnel of wood and bark and darkness.

Philip had been seven at the time. Carry had been twenty-nine, and the sky had been overcast like it was this evening, all cool and gray.

The water had been calm.

They paddled beneath the branches, Carry all the while enjoying the look on his young son's face as he knew his boy was feeling the same sense of security he felt when traveling beneath the branches. In there, you were safe from the world and from a mother who was always telling you to clean up your room.

"Can we go back, Dad?" Philip asked once they emerged from the wood-like tunnel.

"Back through?" Carry said.

"Yeah." Philip's wide eyes never left the branches.

"Sure." Carry turned the canoe around; they entered the tunnel once more.

Not near a quarter of the way in, Philip got on his haunches.

"Careful," Carry said as he felt the canoe start to rock.

Philip slowly sat back down. "How did you find this place, Dad?"

"By accident. I found it when I was a kid, actually. Bobby, um, I can't remember his last name—anyway, his dad took us out here but, see, the tunnel wasn't here then. At least not like it is now. It was starting up a little though. The branches were already leaning toward the water. I just liked the forest."

Philip seemed to have lost interest and stood up in the canoe, reaching for the middle of one of the branches hanging over them.

"Phil, I said sit down," Carry said calmly. The boy got enough "stern talk" from his mother.

The boy didn't listen and grabbed hold of the branch. For some reason, he didn't let go and as the canoe continued moving forward, his body stayed where it was and was soon in his father's lap.

Carry dropped the paddle in the water.

Was that a bite? There had been a tug at the end of line, Carry was sure. He reeled his line in. The line came in slower now that he was an old man, he noticed. When it finally reached the end of the pole, he brought its tip close to his face so he could see it more clearly. A glistening brown lump of rolled-up worm remained on the hook.

No fish.

"Darn," he said quietly.

The breeze picked up and swept between the buttons of his flannel shirt. He shivered and considered calling it quits.

I won't give them the pleasure, he thought and, not bothering to adjust his shirt so it covered his chest more evenly, he stood, his knees cracking, and made his way to the shore. He hated this part. Ever since getting arthritis in his joints a few years before Fae died, anything that involved moving his elbows was torture. He took a breath, rotated his hips, and extended the rod behind him. A dull, achy pain shot through his elbow and wrist. He made a face and cast his line out. Back slightly aching, he went near his chair and tightened the line. When he sat back down, the weight being lifted off his bones felt like Heaven.

"They'll bite," he said.

Carry waited.

Carry never came home the night Philip and him had gone canoeing. He didn't come home the following morning either. It wasn't until early afternoon when Fae drove to meet them at Bill's—a small hamburger joint on the edge of town—and Carry and Philip weren't there, that she had gone to the lake to look for them.

Carry sat on the shore, legs crossed, staring out onto the lake.

Fae came up behind him. "Carry?"

He didn't answer. Instead, he bowed his head, steepled his fingers, and pinched the bridge of his nose. He knew that she knew he had tears in his eyes.

"Carry!" she said and came down beside him, holding him.

"He . . . he fell," was all he said.

The two stayed there by the shore, the sun glimmering off the waves.

For the second time Carry's head dipped toward his chest. He checked his watch. It was 2:13 A.M. Not a single fish had nibbled on his hook.

Not wanting to give in but not wanting to stay and catch a chill either, he reluctantly stood, reeled in his line, packed up his tackle and grabbed his chair.

"Tomorrow," he said. *Tomorrow. If I don't die first.*

He headed for the cabin.

The key stuck in the lock like it always did and, like always, took four quick jiggles to pry it loose. He entered, kept one hand on the doorknob, leaned his pole up against the corner behind the door, and set his tackle down.

Though he'd done it thousands of times, he relished in taking off his cap and flannel over-shirt and hanging them on the coat hooks by the door. There was something "I'm home" about removing your outerwear when entering your place. It was as though you were stripping away the person everyone saw and revealing the person you truly were to a place where you could genuinely be yourself.

He closed the door, locked it, and flicked on the light. He went in to the kitchen that ran off the landing and also opened up onto the living room. The inside smelled musty, like most cabins, and Carry liked it just fine. It was old like him and he blended right in, thank you. The previous owners of the cabin had sold it to him and Fae after an episode there involving their son. They never said what occurred.

He squinted after he opened the refrigerator door, the bright interior light making everything seem white for a moment.

"Ah, I see you," he said and removed a jar of pickles.

He set the jar on the counter, popped it open and, not bothering to use a fork—the utensil drawer was all the way over on the other side of the kitchen—pulled out a pickle. As he chewed, he looked out the front window over the sink. Outside the night was as black as pitch. You couldn't even see the road not twenty-five feet away. The street lamp across the property had burnt out long before and no one ever bothered to come by and fix it.

One more, he thought and grabbed another pickle. Its sourness sent a shiver down his back. Just how he liked it.

He replaced the lid on the jar and set it back in the fridge. When he straightened, there was a knock at the door. His insides jumped as the hollow wooden sound filled his flesh. Carry peered out the window. He made a face when he realized the small lamp hanging outside the front door, like the one across the way, had burnt out long ago. He kept meaning to get around to replacing the bulb but a drive into town seemed like too much of a chore.

He couldn't see anyone.

Running his hand over his bald head, he placed a hand on his hip. The moments ticked away. The knock hadn't occurred again. It was time for bed. Tomorrow he could think about what that "knock" had been. Maybe some kids had thrown a few rocks at the door? Nah. There hadn't been any kids around here for a long time.

About to pass through the landing to the bedroom just on the other side, he stopped his steps when the knock returned. Two raps and that was all.

"Okay," he breathed. "Could be some poor soul who's lost." *Didn't see a car in the drive, though, but then again, can't see anything out there.*

Two more knocks.

Just go to bed. They'll go away. And he moved toward the bedroom.

There was another knock, this time only one.

"Okay," he said quietly.

When he looked down, he saw his hand was already on the doorknob though he couldn't remember walking toward the front door.

Two more knocks.

"Yes, yes," he said, unlocking the bolt and pulling the door open.

Carry's jaw went slack when he saw the silhouette of a man in a suit, wearing a fedora with a feather sticking out from it.

———

Years ago, Carry sat in the living room of their home. Fae would never forgive him. How could she? *He* had been responsible for their son. It had been *his* job to make sure their boy was safe. And he had made sure, hadn't he? He had told Philip to sit down, told him even before they crossed the lake that standing up in a canoe while on the water was dangerous, had said . . .

Shouldn't have gone without lifejackets, he thought. But they did anyway instead of waiting for his neighbor to return them. He had been too excited to take Philip out on the lake.

"But I still should have watched out for him," Carry said.

Fae was upstairs. She hadn't spoken to him for nearly two weeks. After Philip's funeral, communication just kind of stopped. It wouldn't be till four months later when the regular everyday talking started again.

In the end, Carry supposed, it had been for the best. Fae needed time to deal with what happened. You couldn't just get over it. What parent could? The four months were what it took to just speak to him never mind trying to look into the eyes of the man who let her son die. But they did get past it. Eventually. It took years, long talks, longer arguments, sleepless nights and even some outside help before everything went back to normal. They considered having other children but both knew they could never parent another child after losing the first.

What parent could?

———

Carry's heart felt like it sunk into his stomach; his fingertips began to tingle. A moment later, his pulse sped and he didn't know how much time had passed before he realized his shirt was clinging to the sweaty skin of his back.

His elbows still ached from flinging his line out on the lake. His mouth was dry.

"Can I come in?" the shadow said.

Carry quickly closed the door and welcomed the sudden relief of shielding himself from who was on his doorstep. Safe and alone in his home. Wait—he didn't close the door. He was still staring at the shadow. The outside light didn't have to be on for him to know what color suit the man was wearing, didn't have to be on to know who—Why couldn't he close the door?

"I'd like to come in, Carry, if I could," the man said.

Carry was shocked the man knew his name but yet he wasn't all that surprised either.

"No, you . . . . No, you can't come in," Carry managed to say.

There was silence between them. Shame bathed Carry's heart because he still hadn't closed the door.

"Why not?" the man asked

"I know who you are," Carry said. He had heard the stories before, campfire tales about the Magic Man and his ability to make the pain—the heartache—go away.

"Then you know what I can do for you."

"No," he said and, gripping the doorknob tight, closed the door. He stared at the door's wooden paneling a long while, repeatedly reassuring himself that, yes, the door was closed and he hadn't just imagined it.

He turned and headed for the bedroom.

Two knocks on the door.

Don't debate with yourself, Carry thought. *Just go to bed. He'll be gone by morning. If you ignore him he'll go away.* But Carry didn't want him to go away because he knew why the Magic Man had come to see him.

Philip.

Philip was the reason. Was always the reason. Philip was why Carry didn't like getting out of bed in the morning. Philip was the reason each breath was sometimes an effort, as if the built-in need to breathe—to stay alive—was a curse rather than a gift.

Philip. Always Philip. It was always hi—

Carry was at the door again and he watched his old, wrinkled hand move toward the doorknob as though watching a movie. He felt the coolness of the brass in his palm, but still refused to believe he was the one in control. It would be much easier to believe the Magic Man was controlling his actions, *forcing* him to open the door and finish the conversation.

Just a talk, Carry figured. *I can hear his side of things then tell him no. If I don't listen, if I don't hear him out . . . .* His thought finished with a twist in his stomach. Regret. That's what would happen if he didn't at least hear what the Magic Man had to say. The chance might never come again.

Carry opened the door.

The man was gone.

<hr>

That night Carry lay in bed, watching the moonlight brighten then fade against his ceiling. The only sound was the wheezing of his breaths as he tried to relax.

Philip.

He should have said yes. Should have at least listened to the man with the dark long hair and beard. Should have—

Two knocks on the door. A smile creased Carry's lips. He was about to leap from bed—as quick as any old man could—and go to the front door, but when the two knocks came again, he realized they were against his bedroom door.

His heart sped up. *Just breathe. Just—* "It's open," Carry said. The moonlight against the ceiling stopped fading and remained there, bright against the stucco, as if Time's passage had suddenly ceased.

His bedroom door creaked open and the Magic Man stepped in.

"I can bring him back, Carry," he said. "I can make the pain go away."

———

The water *glubbed* around him, the same sound you heard when jumping into the deep end of the pool, the same sound that rushed past your ears and disappeared to somewhere above. And for a moment, Carry thought it was the first time he had heard that sound, but then remembered he heard it at least a dozen times in the last hour, if not more.

If it had been an hour that passed.

He opened his eyes on reflex, his eyeballs suddenly met with the icy cold of dark lake water. He squeezed his eyelids shut and got a nose full of water when he tipped backward and slowly did a somersault.

Frantic, he tried swimming to the surface, his old arms carving through the water as hard and as fast as he was able. A rush of wave pushed him back down with each thrust upward. He kicked, his power generating in his hips and thighs, running down his legs and out through his feet.

Up, up . . .

Cold water pushed him back down.

Not like this! Should have said no, he thought. But thoughts were all they were. If only he could translate them into speech. If only he could *tell* somebody—but no one was down here beneath the water's surface. No one was with him in the lake.

He opened his eyes again and was greeted with the dark murk of dirty water. He squeezed his eyes shut. Shivers ran through him, starting at his fingertips then shooting straight through his arms, shoulders, his whole body. His muscles tensed.

Just relax, swim upward, he thought. *Arms up and out and push down and—*
The water pressed against him.

Carry jolted when his lungs instinctively tried to take in a breath.

No! Can't! His thoughts were lost to the pressure against his rib cage and the sudden headache forming above and beside his eyes. He clenched his jaw, fighting to keep the water from coming in. His chest muscles lurched and his lips opened—barely—just enough to let the metallic taste of lake water sit upon his tongue. He thought about spitting it out but didn't want to risk any more of the filthy water coming in.

How did he end up like this? Why had he given in and asked the Magic Man for help?

Philip. Just to see him again.

"I can bring him back," the Magic Man had told him. "I can make the pain go away."

"How?" Carry remembered asking. They were still in the bedroom, the Magic Man just inside the door, Carry in his bed.

At first it didn't seem as if the Magic Man would answer, but just as Carry was going to ask again, the Magic Man said, "Leave that to me. I've done it before, countless times. You said yourself you know who I am. That would mean you also know what I'm capable of."

"I also know that what you do comes with a price."

The Magic Man removed his purple fedora and ran a hand over his long, matted hair. He put the hat back on. "I only ask you do something for me in return, that's all and that's fair."

Carry closed his eyes. Though he had closed the door on the Magic Man before, he didn't know if he could do it again or if the Magic Man would return a third time. This could be the only chance he had to see Philip again, to have him brought back to life or to perhaps have the whole incident averted in the first place and have the memories of a life without his son replaced with new ones. But at what cost?

I can't say yes. If I do . . . "No," Carry said.

"Then you don't love him as much as you think you do."

Carry's heart fell to pieces. He loved his son, more than anything, more than even . . . Fae. Her death didn't hurt as much as Philip's had. Then again, he also hadn't been responsible for her death either. He loved him. Philip. He died with him that day on the lake.

Philip. He was everything and always.

"I-I love him," Carry said.

"No, you don't." The Magic Man turned toward the bedroom door and disappeared into the dark.

Philip. The name echoed in Carry's mind, but it wasn't his voice that put it there. It was the Magic Man's, that smooth, deep and melodic voice, one backed with confidence, compassion and the reassurance that his word was gold.

Carry got out of bed and went into the dark.

A pinch at the back of his throat and Carry was coughing. His limbs shook from stress and fear. He was drowning.

Just like Philip had.

The lake water rushed into his mouth and filled his windpipe with ice and doom. He reflexively coughed and inhaled a lungful of water. His lungs pounded from the pressure, from being over-filled. Shivers ran through him. His spine turned to steel.

Desperately trying to swim upward, Carry opened his eyes when he couldn't move his arms or legs.

There was nothing above him, only the dark of the lake.

———

It started again.

The water sped past him as Carry fell further and further into the dark, the sounds of air bubbles whisking by then bursting above, making him think he'd only sunk down a few feet. When he opened his eyes, the muddy brown of the lake above, so deep and dense, told him he was a lot further below than that. His old bones turned to cold rods of iron beneath his skin. He could barely move.

Push yourself, he thought. He raised his arms and tried to swim upward, the weight of his nightclothes pulling him back down.

Fingers fumbling for the buttons to his top, he kept kicking his legs, trying to move upward. The buttons wouldn't come undone. The cold water froze his fingertips and all he felt was vibrating, fatty numbness as his fingers tried to grasp the buttons.

Move! He kicked and swam several feet upward and, like before, a rush of water sent him back down, down, down—He landed on his bottom against something soft. Biting back his breath, he felt beside him. It felt like dead, rotting fish but he knew it was only the lake's floor. He took a scoop of mud in each hand and squeezed his fingers into a tight fist.

Should never have said yes to him, he thought. And for a brief moment, he thought Philip wasn't worth it. Wasn't worth dying for. *Stop it! He's everything. It's my fault, my responsibility. It was me, it was—*

His lungs filled with frigid water. He coughed, and bolted—floated— off the lake's floor, his scream muted by the water around him. Lungs bursting with pressure, pain and a sensation he couldn't put into words but only brutally feel, he opened his eyes and felt his life slip away.

———

"Did you find what you were looking for?" the boy asked.

"No, not yet," Carry said.

"Why not?"

"Because it isn't there."

"Then you haven't looked hard enough."

Philip.

His son was here with him beneath the water. It wasn't so cold anymore.

"I'm sorry," Carry said. He knew he shouldn't be able to speak under water, but he could.

Philip was in a seated position, floating in front of him, the boy's clothes moving loosely around him like some kind of sheet over a ghost. His dark hair floated upright in smooth, rhythmic waves, and though it was dark, Carry shuddered when he saw how gray Philip's skin was. Gray and pruned from spending too much time beneath the water.

What am I looking for? Carry thought. He'd been down here so many times before, more than he cared to recall. His lungs didn't hurt as much. Perhaps having to do this over and over was building up some kind of endurance and he could hold his breath for longer stretches at a time.

"Dad?" Philip said.

"Yeah?"

"I'm sorry."

Though there was water all around his face, Carry swore he felt tears creep up to then leak out of the corners of his eyes. "It's not your fault."

"I should have listened."

"And I should have caught you."

"Dad."

"Philip!" Carry reached out to grab him when he began floating away, slowly disappearing into the murk. No matter how hard he tried, he couldn't swim fast enough and before he was even able to propel himself forward, Philip was gone.

"No," he said, and the moment he opened his mouth, lake water rushed in. "No," he tried saying again, but this time only heard a muted grunt.

Don't give in, don't speak, don't breathe, he told himself. Stomach lurching, his innards filling with the metallic, filthy taste of lake water, he tried swimming toward the surface.

What just happened? Was Philip really there? Did the Magic Man come through? He wanted to cry because he knew the answer was no and that it was all in his mind.

Opening his eyes, he glanced upward, hoping to see the surface of the lake. Instead there were only the small bubbles dribbling from his lips, floating upward.

I want to go home, he thought. His lungs ignited and he thought that if he could figure out some way to swallow his tongue, at least for a short while, he could seal off his windpipe and stop the water from coming in. He even tried doing so but when he bent his tongue back, it pressed against the roof of his mouth, creating a small opening between his lips.

More water rushed in.

Ah, hell, he thought and inhaled. He choked, tried to cough, but nothing came of it and instead his throat felt like it was going to burst.

I want to die. I'm sorry, Philip, but I can't keep doing this. Not anymore. This has to stop.

Despite how much he knew it was going to hurt, Carry sucked in more water, filling his lungs to the brim. In less than a minute, he knew, he'd pass out. And, if what he had read about drowning was true, two or three minutes after that, he'd be dead. At least those were two to three minutes he wouldn't have to consciously experience.

Then I'll have to do it all over again, he thought.

He waited for the dark.

Carry's back hit the water with a hard slap and he tumbled downward, fast at first but as the water cradled him in its icy arms, his descent slowed and, soon after, his feet touched bottom. He shuddered when his toes curled around that sick, mushy gunk at the bottom of the lake. He knew it was mud but it still felt like dead fish.

As if I've ever stepped on dead fish, he thought. Making a joke in spite of his circumstance made him feel a little better.

What would Fae have done if the Magic Man approached her with the chance to see her son again? Would she have said yes? Could she have said yes if she knew she had to drown for a lifetime just to see him?

Carry's eyes shot wide when he remembered the Magic Man didn't say *how* he was going to bring Philip back. Would Philip even be alive? Would the Magic Man somehow find Philip's body at the bottom of the lake and present to him a bunch of bones covered in a boy's clothing?

Don't think about it. Just get this done, Carry thought. He didn't know how many more times he could do this or how many more times he even wanted to. How many times he *had* to. He didn't even know how many times he had already done this. His heart broke when he realized he *didn't* want to do this anymore. It was enough. He was tired of feeling warm then suddenly freezing when his body submerged in the lake and those stupid air bubbles rushed past his ears. He was sick of his lungs pounding after a minute of not having any air and pounding even harder—burning—as he tried to hold his breath a moment longer.

All for a boy who died over fifty years ago.

Philip wasn't worth it. No life was worth dying for. And though he'd never been a selfish man, Carry was proud for being one now.

He closed his eyes and gathered his strength. Maybe the Magic Man was listening.

When he spoke, his words were nothing but muted noise. Still, he knew what he was saying and he hoped the Magic Man could somehow make it out. "Please, I'm sorry. I was wrong. You win. I don't want to see my son anymore. No more. Just let me out. He isn't . . . . You're right. I don't love him as much as I—"

He waited to see if anything would happen.

Nothing did.

Fine, then I'll get myself out.

Carry breathed in.

———

Carry hit the water like before. How did he end up here? A moment ago he was in the canoe with his father and saw a branch and grabbed hold of it and—*Not* my *father. It was Philip who grabbed the branch. It was Philip who—Just to see him again.*

It all came back to him and he remembered why he was here. The Magic Man could not win.

Carry breathed in.

———

The moment his memory returned and he knew he had plunged into the lake hundreds—if not, thousands—of times before, Carry gulped back the water and waited for death to come.

———

The icy water shocked his system.
Carry welcomed it to his lungs.

———

Carry breathed in.

———

Carry drowned.

———

Carry wouldn't let him win.

———

He'd died countless times, each time willingly, but with each time, the Magic Man did not come.
Carry let the pain take him away.

———

I don't love my son, Carry thought and though the words pained him, he also knew them to be true. If he did love Philip—truly love him—he would be willing to die a thousand times for him, tens of thousands. After all, didn't Jesus say, "The greatest love comes from he who would lay his life down for his friends"? Philip was his friend. Best friend. But Jesus didn't say anything about laying your life down more than once. When you died, you died. There were no repeats.

How many times did he say he'd give anything for fill-in-the-blank? Carry realized those words were empty because when it came right down to it, people looked out for themselves despite good intentions.

Floating there in the dark, cold water around him, swirling up his clothes, cooling his wrinkly skin, he thought about Fae. Pictured her here with him and knew that she'd die for Philip.

Over and over.

He remembered the day Philip was born and the fourteen hours of labor she endured for him. He remembered the look on her face when the nurse told her she had to have eight more contractions before she'd be allowed to push. The look of longing—begging—she gave him, pleading with him to somehow step up Time and let her push their son out. To take her pain away . . . . Afterward, he felt small because he knew he couldn't have gone through what she had. That was one of the reasons why they never had another child. He couldn't put her through that again. Later, when Philip was asleep in her arms, she told Carry she'd do anything for their son, go through labor for a lifetime if it somehow meant their boy would be happy.

I'm not a man, Carry thought. He tried swimming upward but the water pushed him back down. *I'm so sorry, Phil. I'm sorry that you died. I'm sorry for not saving you. Sorry for just sitting there in the canoe, watching you fall into the lake like some kind of movie. If I could do it over again . . . . I just want to see you.*

His lungs burned, his limbs jittered. He was so cold that even beneath the water his teeth started to chatter. Water went up his nose, burning his nostrils, dripped down his throat. He tried swallowing but only gagged and inhaled Bedright Lake.

He sank toward the bottom.

———

The light pierced Carry's eyes, warm and welcoming. When he opened his eyes, he was in the canoe with Philip.

Philip was coming toward him and when he looked up, he saw Philip was hanging onto the branch.

Where am I? Wasn't I just—Those would have been the words in his head but they were more just *feelings* rather than thoughts. He was startled from them when he heard his paddle splash as it hit the water.

Philip came at him, back first, and bumped into him, landing in his lap. The canoe rocked and Philip tumbled into the water.

He disappeared into the darkness below; Carry watched as he sank.

Over and over.

THEATRE OF SKULLS

Driving through the streets of Winnipeg carried the same monotonous tone as a consistently busy phone line. Same streets. Same people. Same middle fingers. Gloria Riler hated it, but she didn't have a choice. She had to take her two boys to her mother's house on the other side of the city so she could go on a string of errands and meet up with a friend for coffee later on. And ever since construction season began, she hadn't been able take her usual route: over Chief Peguis Bridge, down Main Street, turning right to get to the suburbs.

Instead, she was forced to make a detour which, after driving over the Disraeli Bridge and getting onto Main Street, made her double back then turn left into the 'burbs. Despite all challenges and frustration—it had to be done.

Oma (German for grandmother), was always happy her two grandsons Keith, age four, and Alex, two, could come and visit. Sometimes Gloria caught herself wondering if Oma loved Keith and Alex more than she loved her when she was a child. It didn't matter. At least Oma was willing to sacrifice three evenings a week to watch the kids so Gloria could have some semblance of a real life. In fact, the three evenings Gloria did this were the highlights of her week. She also knew it was the highlight of her mother's as well.

Gloria's thoughts were interrupted when a horrible screech ripped throughout the car's interior. It was Keith. Gloria peeked into the rearview mirror.

"AAAEEEE!" Keith yelped, ripping Alex's hand from his golden curls.

"What's going on back there?" Gloria put her eyes back toward the road, returning the vehicle to center-lane.

"Alex keeps pulling my hair, Mom," Keith said.

"Alex, leave your brother alone."

Alex's hands snapped back to his lap. In the rearview mirror, Gloria saw him look at her, mouth drooped at the sides: his way of apologizing. She continued driving. After four years with kids and two of those years spent with Alex adding to the weight of parenthood, she had pretty much grown immune to frustration and impatience. But, like all mothers would tell you, one's shirt could only get stretched so thin.

Gloria turned on to Main and habitually locked the doors as she drove through the north end of town. *You can never be too safe, especially out here.*

The road was blocked up ahead with a barricade of orange and black signs, telling that construction hell was about to break loose. An arrow on one of those signs said to take a left and travel down the street that ran parallel to Main. With a sneer, Gloria turned and took yet another detour.

"Are we there yet?" came Keith.

"Er wee ther et?" Alex said.

"Almost, honey," she said.

Finding the street she needed, Gloria slumped her shoulders and gave herself a moment to relax. Traffic and bloody construction always got her worked up.

It suddenly grew dark inside the car. Nothing felt right. At first the outside world appeared the same, but when Gloria slowed to search out the source of the giant shadow, she saw everything around her had changed. She was still downtown, on the detour street, but she didn't know *where* she was. The buildings looked as if someone had dumped bags of sawdust and dirt on them. Blotches of what looked like melting tar were speckled against the bricks, the windows fogged with either smoke or steam

She stopped the car and noticed everyone else who had been driving beside her had disappeared.

"Why we stopped?" Keith asked.

"Mommy just wants to stop and look around," she said as comfortingly as possible. She wished someone would comfort *her.*

There was an alley adjacent to the street she was on. In it a swarming tribe of homeless people milled about. Some were sleeping on broken mattresses, others in rusted cars with half the parts missing, some just treating the muddy pavement as a bed. Gloria looked through the window on the passenger side and saw the same thing. More people. More debris. More hopelessness.

Straining her neck so she could see better out of her window, she noticed the sky had also changed, turning an ashen gray instead of the normal blue. The clouds seemed to be melting off the sky.

Alex began to cry.

"Shut up, you baby!" Keith told him and gave him repeated jabs with his elbow.

"Keith!" Gloria said and unbuckled her seatbelt. Keith immediately stopped. His head sank into his shoulders. Though only a boy, he, too, seemed to feel the shadows start to penetrate him.

Gloria paused and placed both palms on the steering wheel, trying to determine what she should do, and precisely where they were.

Okay, she thought, *we were driving along and BOOM! out of nowhere, a cloud of darkness settles and everything around us changed into some sort of slum.*

Alex cried louder.

"Shhh, honey. It's okay," she said, turning to Alex and patting him on the thigh.

"Mom—I'm scared," Keith said.

"I know, dear."

All three of them jumped when an awful banging thundered throughout the vehicle, causing all sides to vibrate. Gloria looked out the windshield. A disheveled man banged a squeegee against the hood of her car. Once. Twice. Three times. As if sensing her gaze, he jerked around and faced some of what she presumed to be his friends in the alley opposite to them. He pointed at the car and started shouting . . . something. Gloria couldn't make it out.

"What's he doing, Mom?" Keith asked.

"Uht's he doie, Mom," Alex said.

"I don't know." She tried to start the car again. The engine wouldn't turn over. She pumped the gas and again turned the key.

Nothing.

The squeegee man pressed his face against the driver's side window with a *thud*. Keith and Alex yelped. The squeegee man's filthy skin left a film of gray upon the glass. Then he smiled, displaying a mouth with only three crooked, yellow teeth. He let out a chuckle. There was another *thud*, this time coming from the roof of the car. Someone was on top of it. The boys kept yelling and crying. Gloria didn't know what to do. Should she leave the boys and try to ward off the pugs who were wreaking havoc on the car? Panic set in.

Like a bear protecting her cubs, Gloria thrust her door open, knocking the squeegee man off balance. She hit the power-locks and closed the door all within an instant. Her kids would be safe.

The squeegee man was on the pavement. For his size, he seemed to have the stability of a coat rack and couldn't hold himself up properly. Gloria remembered something had landed on the roof of the car. Turning around to see what or who it was, she saw a black man doing a tap dance on her roof.

"Get off!" she shouted, her fist banging against the roof. The man only sneered at her and looked down at his new dance floor, increasing the speed and aggression of his tap-tap-tapping.

Inside the car, Keith and Alex screamed as the whole vehicle began to wobble from side to side. The driver's side window smashed, catching Gloria off guard. A second later, the squeegee man grabbed her from behind, putting an arm across her throat. Her boys unbuckled and banged on the back seat glass in a seeming effort to somehow scare this stranger away from their mother. The squeegee man laughed.

The black man came down off the roof and rammed his elbow against the back seat window. The sound of his elbow against the glass sent a dull *clunk* through Gloria's chest as he did. The black man appeared to be much stronger than the squeegee man. *Oh no!* she thought, acknowledging the man was trying to get to her children.

"Staurp—" Gloria gasped, her voice a garbled mess. What she meant to say was "Stop!"

The black man continued his assault on the window. Keith and Alex backed up into the far door. Gloria stepped on the squeegee man's foot, causing him to lose his grip. She faced him and delivered a right hook that connected squarely with his jaw. The man fell to his knees then to his side, and lay on the pavement perfectly still.

Not slowing her attack, Gloria spun around to face the black man. The sound of shattering glass pierced her ears. The man had gotten through. The boys screeched in terror. Gloria ran toward her children's assailant and jumped onto his back. She hammered away at him with her fists, hitting the back of his neck and the top of his head. The man shrugged her off. She fell to the ground and bruised her tailbone. He swung open the car door and grabbed the boys: Keith by the arm, Alex by the neck of his shirt. More screaming. Gloria stood. A jolt of white hot pain pierced the back of her head.

She saw stars and fell back down.

———

She woke up to the sensation of water dripping across her forehead. Focusing her eyes, Gloria saw an old Native woman leaning over her, dabbing a cold, wet rag above her eyebrows. She sat up, immediately running her fingers along the back of her head. It was tender and sore. Luckily, a bump hadn't formed.

She looked at the woman. The woman smiled back, forming creases of skin in her cheeks. Gloria stared at her then took a moment to take in her surroundings.

Like recalling a dream, she remembered her fight with the squeegee man and the other fellow. The attack on her boys. Her bruised tailbone. The black man. Did he take Alex and Keith?

Gloria stood up with a start. "Where's my boys?" she exclaimed, grabbing the old woman by the shoulders.

The Native didn't respond.

"Tell me!"

The woman smiled again and pointed across the street to the alley opposite them. Deep within it, Gloria saw an old, abandoned movie theatre.

She ran toward it.

———

Gloria slowed her steps and cautiously proceeded toward the entrance marked by an old revolving door. She looked around and made sure she was alone. The last thing she needed was another run-in with the squeegee man or black man or anybody else for that matter. Fortunately, the coast was clear. There was nothing but the silence of a garbage bin, some cardboard boxes, and few shards of ragged clothing that littered the street.

She went to move toward the door when a short, stubby man jumped out of the garbage bin and landed on her shoulders, forcing her to the ground. The fella's weight was incredible! She assumed he weighed at least sixty to seventy more pounds than he was supposed to. Gloria pressed her palms to the gritty cement beneath her and pushed as if doing a push-up. The beggar, bum—whatever he was—jerked his weight and forced her down again. Her face slammed into the pavement, her nostrils getting a nose full of old, muddy water mixed with fresh spurts of blood.

In a fit of vengeance, she pushed up again, this time rolling onto her back, squashing her assailant. She freed herself from his grip and got to her feet. Turning around, she looked down at him. He stared back at her from beneath the hood of his filthy tan-colored coat. His eyes were washed with innocence, his lips pursed as if apologizing. As if to say, "I'm sorry. I didn't know any better." Yeah, right.

Giving no sympathy, Gloria gave him a swift kick between the legs, the sharp toe of her shoe landing decisively between privates and rectum. The short man yelped an awful shriek that sounded like an old bus screeching to a stop.

Leaving him to writhe in agony, Gloria bolted for the revolving door. She pressed into it, followed its spin, and fell to her knees from the momentum of her speed and the door pushing her from behind. It took her a moment to slow her breathing and heart rate down.

With a trembling hand, she wiped a slick film of sweat off her forehead. It was hard to put everything into words. Her motherly instinct banged on the door of her mind, as if having a voice all its own, repeating the same stanza over and over: *Alex and Keith. Alex and Keith. Alex and Keith. Alex and Keith,* except there were no words, only feelings and images of her kids. She stood up and stepped further into the theatre.

The lobby was dim with no other lights visible. The only illumination was a misty gray ray of light seeping through the fogged windows of the revolving door. A ticket booth was in front of her and a little beyond that, a concession stand. On either side of the concession stand were aisles, which she assumed led into the rest of the theatre. She slowly moved forward. "Alex? Keith?" Amazingly, her voice did not echo, instead seeming to be absorbed by darkness.

Just go slow, she told herself. She had been passing the ticket booth when it suddenly lit up. The scorching light pierced her eyes and once they had focused, Gloria screamed. Staring back at her was a grotesque, zombified man in a tuxedo, running his twig-like fingers along the smooth inside glass of the booth. Gloria tried to run but couldn't. Her shoes were stuck to the floor. Each struggle to pull her feet out only caused the laces to grow tighter until her feet were nothing but pins and needles.

"You cannot enter without a ticket," the zombie stated as-a-matter-of-factly. Gloria swallowed what felt like the pit of a plum. "Come closer. Buy a ticket. It's all right. You must have a ticket to enter. Please, we haven't had business in so long."

She looked toward the concession stand half expecting to see somebody like the zombie-man there, and was relieved when there was none. Her boys were somewhere inside and no one outside the theatre seemed to want to help. Anyone outside just wanted to hurt her and her kids.

Gloria faced the zombie and mustered up the strength to get a ticket. She approached the glass, expecting the monster to speak. There was silence for several moments. Then the zombie growled, "Aren't you going to say 'one, please'?"

What? was all Gloria could ask herself. Then she understood. It was only polite to ask for a ticket than to expect it. "One, please," she said.

Hoping not to be asked for any form of payment, Gloria watched as the zombie rang the ticket into an old cash register on the counter beside him, his decaying fingers crudely banging on the web-covered keys. The price of the ticket rang up. The cash register displayed: $XXX. Gloria furrowed her brow. The zombie printed out her ticket and slid it across an opening in the glass. When she went to grab it, he pulled it away.

Here it comes, she thought. *How much could this possibly be?*

"The ticket is on the house tonight, Life-girl. You have already made it up to us," he said, a grin sweeping across his face and displaying his shriveled gums.

Gloria snatched the ticket and pounded against the glass with her fists. "My boys! What have you done with them! What the—" The booth grew dark and the zombie was gone. She looked at the ticket in her hand. The top of it read: WELCOME TO THE THEATRE OF SKULLS! WE APPRECIATE YOUR BUSINESS. Then below that was a photograph of a skull with deep, foreboding eyes, and a pentagram carved into its forehead. Underneath the skull it said: ENJOY THE SHOW! YOU'RE IN THEATRE NO. 6, 6TH ROW, 6TH SEAT. THANK YOU ONCE AGAIN FOR COMING TO THE THEATRE OF SKULLS! BE SURE TO POP BY OUR CONCESSION STAND!

She dropped the ticket in disgust then picked it back up again. She scanned it once more and walked over to where, forming out of nothingness, a female ticket-taker stood. She was robed in an almost-transparent white gown, her eyes dark.

At this point Gloria was running on instinct. The instinct to save her boys. She walked to the ticket-taker, her hand outstretched, offering her ticket. The ticket was removed from her hand by white fingers with red-painted nails. Gloria noticed how stark white the ticket-taker was. Aside from her eyes, everything was white. The only hint of color was in her long, wavy hair: a pallid yellow.

The ticket-taker ripped the ticket in half and handed Gloria the stub. The other half was eaten. Gloria held the ticket in complete bewilderment. The ticket-taker smiled and pointed in the direction of theatre number six. Gloria dropped her half of the ticket and ran down the corridor.

From behind, a light from a concession stand flashed on. Thinking maybe her boys would be there, she turned toward it, acknowledging that, like the zombie before, the ticket-taker had also vanished.

The moment she approached the concession counter, Gloria lurched forward, head between her legs, and threw up. On display in the hot dog roaster, rotating smoothly as they cooked, were sizzling plump fingers, their nails charred and crisp. Beside that, the popcorn machine popped teeth. And beside that, was a 'smoothie' machine. Through the little circular windows where the slush turned and mixed, was a combination of blood and guts. A murky red soup with streaks of swirling beige.

Spitting out the remnants of throw up, Gloria wiped her mouth and stood. She was light-headed. She yelped again and went to throw up one more time. She couldn't. Her stomach was empty. She gagged a few times, her stomach finally settling.

Sitting on the counter, taking on the role of a concession employee, was a human head next to the cash register. It was the head of a bald little boy, his skin dark with dirt, his face partially decayed.

"Don't be sick. You should have a snack," he told her with an apparent sense of compassion. "The smoothies are especially nice. They are made from the fluid of life."

Gloria didn't say anything and ran back down the corridor, pretending the encounter with the boy never happened. Behind her she heard the boy laugh and tell her that the finger-dogs were ready. "Come on! Have some! Come on! Eat! Eat! Eat!"

Her stride didn't break and she didn't bother to look back to see if the concession stand, too, would shut down after she had visited there.

A few feet ahead of her, a sign lit up an ominous red.

THEATRE #6 -> NOW SHOWING:
THE DISMEMBERMENT OF ALEX AND KEITH.

Panicking, she threw the theatre door open and screamed her sons' names into the vast cinema. It was empty and surprisingly clean. The walls, seats, and curtains were all the color of brown brick. Everything was quiet.

Gloria looked around and was jolted back to the attention of the screen when the curtain began to open, sliding and squeaking along its rail. A bright beam of light hit the screen as the projector started rolling.

The screen counted down in Roman Numerals: X - XI - VIII - VII - VI - V - IV - III - II - I . . . and white text displayed against a black background.

HELLO, GLORIA RILER.
WELCOME TO
THE DISMEMBERMENT OF ALEX AND KEITH.

The letters then dripped with white blood and faded away.

The story began and was in black-and-white. She saw her children.

Both her boys were in a dark laboratory, lying side by side on an operating table. Their hands and feet were tied to a crudely-designed device of some sort at the foot of the table. Gloria turned toward the projection booth. It was nothing but shadows and the bright beam of light from the projector blasting forth and hitting the screen.

Her boys.

"Alex! Keith!" she yelled and ran up to the screen. She pressed against it, thinking her boys were on the other side. The canvas only rocked with each press.

"Stop!" she cried, sticking her hand out in protest. Nothing but the blinding white light of the projector replied back. It didn't appear anyone was running the machine.

She faced the screen again. A doctor entered the laboratory. Her gleaming white coat clashed with the black outfit she wore underneath. Her hair was dark with white streaked throughout. The doctor's eyes hid behind a pair of square bifocals.

Tears swelled in Gloria's eyes and she found herself helplessly watching the screen. She didn't know what to do or even what was happening anymore. The doctor on screen then tauntingly began rotating the handle that activated the device. A knowing grin beamed from the doctor's face. She would turn the handle a little, stop, then, with the sleeve of her lab coat, wipe the tears from each of the boys' eyes. Gloria saw her children screaming, but she couldn't hear them. A silent movie.

The doctor turned the handle some more, stopped, and this time stroked each of the boys' foreheads as if comforting them. She turned the handle again, then again, then again. Gloria could almost hear her boys screech in pain and terror despite the silence of the film. She cried out, but the evil doctor kept turning the handle, watching first as Alex and then Keith, began to be pulled apart. Their arms were the first to detach with a gush of black blood. Then their legs, the flesh tearing like wet cardboard. The doctor turned the handle in a frenzy. Torsos spurt with blood, their entrails hanging out like strands of a sopping and muddy mop. The blood rushed at first then slowed to a glossy ooze, bathing the table and dripping to the floor.

The doctor stopped and looked at Gloria. She motioned with her finger for Gloria to come closer. Speechless, Gloria ebbed herself away from the screen.

That's when the doctor stepped out of the film and grabbed her.

BENEATH THE SAND

Just *look at her,* Gerry thought. *She's got her face in her book, completely on purpose.* His wife, Maria, hated Danielle Steel, something about how Steel told the same story every book, just different characters. But today at Birds Hill Beach, Maria was reading the latest Steel romance. *Whatever.*

Gerry squinted when the sun shone in his eyes. Nothing worse than sitting on a sun-drenched beach after pulling a sixteen-hour shift. That was one of the reasons Maria was mad at him. Hey, it wasn't his fault the dishwasher broke. His daughter, Emily, was the one who put her Barbie in there. Barbie hit the blades and—BAM—snapped one of them.

"Barbie stays in the bathtub," Gerry had tried to explain to her. She was only four, but seemed to understand.

Now he had to work overtime because they needed a new dishwasher.

Shirt off, he sat with his feet dangling over the edge of a two-foot-wide hole in the sand. It was about two and a half feet deep; it seemed only barely started a few moments ago. His eight-year-old, Jordan, worked feverishly, trying to dig the hole deeper and deeper.

"Let's bury you, Dad!" he had said when they first got there. He immediately got to work building up a mound of sand that would be about two feet high in the end.

"Sure," Gerry had said. Seemed like a good idea. Why not. Kids buried their parents all the time. Usually once at the beach and once at the graveyard. He shook the thought from his head, but not without a wry grin.

Jordan had wanted to try something different and bury him standing "up and down." Good for him. He was thinking outside the norm. Such a practice would serve him later in life even if the boy didn't understand it now.

Maria. Crap. Gerry ran his hands through his brown hair then tugged his fingers back when he felt the bald spot forming at the top of his head. There was a time when there was nothing but thick hair up there.

Stupid stress.

Maria hadn't wanted him to work a double. They were going to the beach and she had wanted him rested. But he worked evenings and he could only pick up extra hours during the graveyard twelve-to-eight if he wanted overtime. Palliser made up the rules, not him. He packed furniture into boxes before they loaded them on the truck for order fulfillment. By logging hours in during the night, he would be helping the skeletal crew who worked the nightshift. Everyone benefited.

She was mad because he was tired and had yelled at her in the car when she told him she wanted to drive because she didn't trust a tired man behind the wheel. He'd been up for nineteen hours by then and was in go-mode, had his coffee, everything was fine. He knew if he did doze on the way to the beach, he'd wake up from the nap cranky, moody and wouldn't be any fun to hang around with. Besides, he hated waking up from a short nap when his body craved an actual full-night's sleep. That, and there had been a sudden lack of communication in their marriage as of late, making them feel like they didn't really know each other as well as they used to. They were working on it though. Kind of.

"What do you think, Dad?" Jordan said.

The hole was deeper now. Nearly four feet. How did Jordan dig so quickly? Ah, it was probably because he was tired and time seemed to go by faster.

"Looks good. Hit any clay yet?" Gerry asked.

"Not yet." Jordan dusted off the sand from his stomach, leaving a few light scratch marks on his skin. Emily sat at her mother's feet, filling a tiny green bucket with sand then dumping it over, then destroying the upside-down mound she'd just created and started all over again. She had done it three times before Gerry looked away.

Maria's eyes never left her book.

Gerry glanced around. The beach was packed. His family was about in the middle, roughly twelve feet from the water. A few blankets down to the left was another family, this one with four kids—two boys and two girls, all under the age of ten. The dad was on his back, sleeping, the kids burying his feet. The mother was returning to the blanket, dragging an air mattress behind her. But to the right—she could be no more than sixteen, smooth skin, a white bikini with pink flowers on it, long strawberry-blonde hair, and a body that would make any man look twice. For a brief moment, Maria disappeared until—

—his wife cleared her throat.

The look she gave him made his heart miss a beat and a rock fill his stomach. He cast his eyes downward, too ashamed to look up.

Way to go, Jackass, he thought. *Idiot.*

It could have been the tiredness, but he so badly wanted to look at the girl again and who cared what Maria thought. He wasn't her favorite person in the world right now anyway.

"Almost done," Jordan said. He was bent at the waist, his upper torso hidden as he hung over the sand's edge, digging.

"Jordan, be careful," Gerry said and, reaching over, tugged on the back of the boy's bathing suit, pulling him part way out of the hole.

"Don't!" Jordan said.

"What if you fall in head first?"

He didn't seem to hear him. Only a moment later did he slowly back out of the hole, dragging an armful of sand up the side. He pushed it away once the mound was clear from the hole's edge.

"Okay, that's enough," Gerry said. He looked over the edge.

The hole seemed to go on forever.

"Get in, Dad, get in," Jordan said, wiping away strands of blond hair off his forehead.

Gerry glanced over at his wife. Her eyes never left the page. For some reason a part of him wanted to show her, *Hey, look, I'm playing with our son. Ain't I a good father, now? See? I know what I'm doing. At least I don't sit there lost in a book instead of trying to resolve an issue. At least I'm making an effort!*

Gerry brought his heels up to the hole's edge, slid his backside between them, then dropped his legs in. It was weird when his heels didn't touch bottom. How deep was this thing?

Palms beside himself, he slowly lowered himself in, his shoulder muscles beginning to strain the lower he went. When a sharp burning sensation ripped through his front right deltoid, his mind flashed to the night before and how trying to maneuver a boxed-up dresser by himself instead of waiting for Stan resulted in pulling something in his shoulder.

Palms at his armpits, he lowered himself in so his forearms were on the sand, his weight resting on them. The tips of his toes finally touched clay.

Didn't look this deep when Jordan was hanging over the edge, he thought. Then again, he was half asleep so who knew what he really saw. Jordan could just have been pulling himself out of the hole, for all he knew, and that's why it was now deeper than he thought.

He set his heels down, the sticky cool of the clay sending a chill through him. He hoped his feet wouldn't freeze.

"Put your arms down beside you," Jordan said.

Emily came alongside him and was already pushing sand into the hole.

A few grains hit his eyes. He blinked them away. "Careful, Em," he said.

Jordan pushed sand into the hole. The sand filled in around him like a prickly rainfall. Another chill ran through him when he wiggled his toes against the clay. It felt kind of rubbery.

"Should have put some sand on the bottom," Gerry said. "My toes are cold."

"It's okay, Dad," Jordan said.

Gerry wiggled his toes some more, allowing some of the sand that had filled up beside his ankles beneath his feet. There. Much warmer.

The sand was up to his shins now. He was immobile from the knee down.

Emily pushed in more sand with her small hands. A few of the kids passing by with their parents stood and watched for a moment before continuing on.

Jordan filled Emily's bucket with sand and dumped it in.

"See what your kids are doing?" Gerry said to Maria.

She glanced up from her book.

Finally.

He gave her a smile.

Her eyes returned to the page.

Sheesh. "Cut me some slack already. You're being unreasonable."

She didn't say anything. Was she mad at him for something else and not just because he worked a double, or was this just what they had dubbed their Non-communication Syndrome? Everyone got grouchy. He also realized he was acting like a child.

He was too tired to care.

The sand was already at his elbows. How much time had passed?

"Are you stuck, Daddy?" Emily asked.

There was still some maneuverability in his hands and wrists, but he was useless from the waist down. He could still get out though, if he had to.

"No, honey, I'm fine," he said.

She kissed his forehead. Jordan kept piling the sand in.

Fatigue hit him. His arms felt weak; his legs relaxed in the sand. His shoulders sagged. The double shift had finally caught up. Eyes heavy, he yawned and got a spray of sand on his tongue.

"Yech," he said, spitting it out. "You did it again, Em."

She gave him a sweet smile and continued helping her brother shovel in the sand.

The sun found a blue patch between two clouds and seemed to have its rays singled in on Gerry's eyes. Tiredness pressed against his temples.

Maria was mad at him.

Jordan poured in the sand.

Emily helped.

Tiredness pushed on.

———

Gerry opened his eyes. He was alone.

It was night, the stars sharp points of light against a rich purple matte. A few dark gray clouds hung low in the sky. The moon was white and bright and right across from him.

Maria was gone. So was Jordan and Emily.

So was everyone else.

He turned his head as far to the right as his neck would allow, half expecting Maria to be there, sitting on her chair, reading her book. But there was nothing, only the light gray sand where she once was. Even Emily's little green bucket was gone.

"Hello?" he said. "Hello!"

The only sound was the waves rolling in to shore then receding back into the water.

He wriggled his arms. They were packed in with the sand. His legs. He wiggled them hard, pressed down where he thought his feet would be. Even if he could just stand on his tiptoes, elevate himself somehow, maybe he could set himself free.

"Anybody!" Louder. He could scream louder. "Anybody! Help!"

Nothing. No one.

"Hey! There's somebody here! Hello!" His voice scraped against the back of his throat. "Maria! Kids!"

Heart racing, he fought against the sand. He was in it right up to his chin and with each struggle, the sand seemed to press down harder on his shoulders, squeeze tighter against his neck. A small clump of sand landed on his tongue. After spitting it out, he clamped his mouth shut and wriggled then thrashed about as hard as he could.

"Gah!" he shouted.

Did his wife leave him here? How could he have been left alone? Wouldn't anybody have seen him? It wasn't hard to miss a sleeping man, his head poking out from the sand. There's no way anyone hadn't seen him.

For an instant, he thought he might be dreaming, that this was just some horrible nightmare and he'd wake up soon, look up into his kids' faces, his heart beating hard from such a terrible dream.

But he wasn't dreaming. Even during those dreams you swore were real—were the truth—there was still that faint underlying feeling of *this wasn't reality*.

Eyes watering, he sucked in a deep breath then screamed, "Heeellllppp!" Voice catching in his throat, his stomach lurched and tangy bile bubbled up onto his tongue. Coughing, he accidentally swallowed then spewed out a small pool of gooey bile that looked more like frothy orange juice.

He cleared his throat, blinked away the tears and closed his eyes. *Okay. Don't panic. If worse comes to worse, you'll be found in the morning. Folks always come to the beach on Sundays, so no big deal.* His pulse was in his neck. Despite his best effort to calm himself, he couldn't steady his heart. What if he had a heart attack and died? What if the wind picked up and blew the sand up and over his head, burying him?

"Lord, please . . ." he said. *I'm sorry, Maria. Did you do this? Did you leave me here?*

He looked up and down the beach again and suddenly realized what had been nagging at the back of his mind—the footprints were missing, both around him and up and along the whole length of the beach, as if no one had ever set foot here before.

This couldn't be real.

Focusing, he tried to slowly draw his arms up. Just raise the shoulders then pull up with the elbows; slide out of the sand as though out of a shirt. He tried moving his fingers, but couldn't.

His arms were asleep; the pressure from the sand against his body must be pressing against a vein or two, blocking off the blood. He felt the sand all around his skin, but couldn't for the life of him make his hands or arms work.

He tried focusing on his legs, tried raising his knees, perhaps by doing so allowing a certain amount of sand beneath his feet so that, once done, he was in a more seated position instead of standing straight up and down.

His legs wouldn't budge. The sand had him the same as his arms.

The waves rolled in to shore.

Listening intently, he searched the air for the sound of cars driving down the road that ran by the beach's parking lot.

Please let somebody be out there, he thought.

There was nothing. The sound of the waves even drowned out any rustling of the leaves the light breeze might have stirred as it blew through the tree tops about forty feet behind him.

He was in Bird's Hill Park. There was camping, a beach—surely somebody was around. Didn't they have park rangers or some such that patrolled the grounds either on foot or by car?

Someone had to be by soon.

He didn't know what time it was, but if he had to guess, it was probably around one in the morning. It was late, no doubt, but it didn't feel *too* late.

Then again, I could be way off, he thought. If he was off, that might be a good thing. Maybe it was around four or five and soon the early morning beach-goers would be along to set up their blankets.

A sharp pang of cold stabbed his feet and he remembered the clay. Was that why he couldn't feel anything beneath the sand? Was he frozen from the knees the down?

His thoughts stopped when something crawled along the sand toward him.

What was that? Looked like a shadow skittering across the ground. A leaf?

No, he thought. Though there were trees behind him, it was still far from fall and he couldn't see any other leaves on the sand.

The shadow—the thing that moved—was gone.

Dark circles rippled on the water's surface, the waves' crests sharp and white as they curled in. If it wasn't for his circumstance, Gerry would have called them beautiful.

"C'mon, Maria," he muttered. *I can't believe she left me here. Who does that? How could Jordan or Emily let her do that? Hey, they're young, but they know not to leave their father buried in the sand, only his bloody head sticking out. How could anyone not have seen me? Wouldn't someone say something?* "Wouldn't anybody do something?" Tears wet his eyes. "AARRGGHH!" His scream echoed on the air. Twisting, turning, he tried to rip himself free from his sandy imprisonment. What was going on?

How many times can I get mad over this? I'm stuck. He knew it was true. No matter what he did or how loud he shouted, there was nothing he could do about this. Nothing but wait.

Man, he was thirsty. If only the water would roll in as far from the shore as he was. Just to have a drink.

Don't look at it. It's funny how that worked—seeing water or the like when you were thirsty—you'd almost be willing to get down on your hands and knees and lap at a dirty puddle if you had to.

A chill swept through him and he wondered how much the temperature had dropped since he first got there that afternoon. Probably a good ten degrees. Maybe more. His arms and legs were still numb. He had an itch where the corner of his eye met the bridge of his nose. He twitched, wrinkled his cheeks, trying to scratch it or "move it away." It didn't work and for a moment thought he'd lose his mind if he couldn't scratch it.

His heart raced again. *I could die out here. It'd serve me right, too, for the jackass I'd been today.* Then, *I'm sorry, Maria, kids. Maybe I should die out here. They'd be better off without me, right? At least maybe happier.* He didn't know. Obviously his family needed him for financial support, but as of late, he hadn't really been *there* for them. He'd play with his kids, kiss his wife good night, help out with dinner (even do the blasted dishes)—but his heart was never in it. He was just being the good father, doing those things because that's what good fathers and husbands do.

Stomach flipping upside down, realizing his own selfishness, he tensed up when that dark something moved along the sand toward him. He squinted his eyes, focused, tried to take a closer look. For a second it looked like a scorpion.

"Couldn't be," he whispered. Scorpions didn't live in Manitoba, at least not on a provincial park's beach.

What was that thing?

It wasn't an animal or anything *warm blooded,* that was for sure. He couldn't make out fur or hair of any kind, and its body didn't appear soft or something that would indicate it was mammal or, as he always thought of mammals, friendly.

Before he could really see what it was, it zipped passed him and disappeared out of eyeshot.

Sharp cold tickled his toes then something wet and slippery, there, deep beneath the sand. Clay? Had his body heat somehow melted it and it was now oozing between his toes? What happened to the sand he allowed in earlier, between his feet and the clay? Maybe he pressed the sand into the clay and some of the clay came up. It didn't matter.

Come on, he thought, *don't be ridiculous. Body heat can't melt clay and even if it could, it wouldn't have taken this long to do it.*

Head feeling full of fog and weight, he realized his thoughts were nonsense. He had never been one to stay up late and not get crazy thoughts when the hours crept toward dawn. In bed by eleven, that was his motto, a habit since as far back as he could remember. He remembered being a kid and if he stayed up past twelve, his father would rain fire and brimstone on him for doing so. "People sleep at night," his dad always said.

Maybe I should just go to sleep and wait until morning? Maybe I'll wake up and someone'll be digging me out? he thought. *Then again, if I fall asleep and someone comes by, they'll never know I'm here.*

"Gah!" he grunted. He hated being trapped. Worse, he hated being helpless. Take charge, take control, do things your way. That's the way life had always been after he got married. Very seldom did he cave into someone else's way of doing things. Now . . .

Now I'm stuck, he thought. His heart ached at the thought. At the truth.

He closed his eyes, tried to calm himself. *Just relax. Take it easy. You'll think clearer if you slow down. There's got to be a way to*—His eyes shot open when a sickening feeling that he wasn't alone came over him.

The shadow—probably no more than a few inches long—was right across from him, near the water. It raced back and forth, out of sight then back into it again.

Then it came toward him.

He jerked his chin inward then pulled his head back; it was the most he could do since he couldn't move anything else.

The shadow sped toward him, weaving left then right in blurred figure eights, starting then stopping until . . . it was at his mouth. Gerry clamped his jaws tight, but not before getting a quick mental flash of this small dark thing hopping inside his mouth, resting on his tongue. His breathing shaky through his nose, he forced himself to look downward to get a closer look. The thing *was* like a shadow, smoky and dark, not having any real substance at all, but it was there all the same. It was roughly three inches long, maybe an inch wide, no legs or arms of any kind, just a body similar to a spider's: a thinner bulb attached to a slightly wider one behind. He couldn't see a face.

What do you want? he caught himself thinking. He knew full well it couldn't read his mind, but there was this unavoidable sensation that perhaps it could.

The creature just stayed there by his mouth. It didn't move.

Maybe it can't see me. There are a ton of animals out there with vision based on movement. Just. Stay. Still.

He took his eyes off the creature and looked out on the lake, hoping to see a boat despite knowing the lake was too small for boats. But what if . . .

He looked down again and briefly lost the creature against the shadows created by the curves and dips in the sand.

There it was.

It still hadn't moved. Instinctively, he curled his toes deep beneath the sand, a habit he had when his patience was wearing thin. If only this thing would move or do whatever it was it was going to do. He also wished it wouldn't do anything because what if whatever it was going to do had to do with him?

I'm going to die, he thought. *That's it. Over. Done. Bye-bye me.* Though he rarely prayed, he was praying now. *God, look, I know we don't get along, but if You take this thing away from me, I'll do anything You want. Anything.* Then, as an absentminded afterthought, *I'll get a new job so I won't miss going to the beach with my kids.* As if he'd ever go to the beach again if he survived tonight. *I'll talk to my wife. Anything. Just . . . anything.*

The thing didn't move. Didn't wiggle. Didn't dart away.

Could it only see him if he moved?

He curled his toes, scooping clay in between them and the balls of his feet. At least gripping onto the clay gave him something to do. The moment he squeezed the clay and pictured in his mind's eye the gray mush seeping out from between his toes, the shadow moved and circled around and sped past him, out of eyesight.

Gerry's breathing sped up, short and choppy. It was only when he saw a bit of sand dance in the lower part of his vision did he realize he opened his mouth. He snapped it back shut.

Where is it? But it was more a feeling than a thought. *God, help me. I don't deserve it, sure thing, but I'll do anything if You get me out of this. It's behind me. I know it.*

Gerry waited.

And waited.

And waited some more.

The waves rolled in to shore.

He released the clay from between his toes, and turned his head side to side.

Then the creature came back around and settled in front of him, just like before, staying perfectly still.

Slowly, carefully, Gerry leaned his head forward slightly, maybe only a millimeter or two. He sniffed, thinking that maybe if he knew what this thing smelled like, he might be able to identify it. It didn't smell like . . . anything. The only scent he picked up was the tinny, almost perfume-like smell of the sand.

What if this is all in my head? he thought. *Some paranoid delusion because I'm stuck out here all alone?* He swallowed. If only it was a hallucination.

Movement at the bottom of his line of sight.

The creature stirred and backed away, a short strip of black against the gray of the sand.

Please go away. Please go away. Please.

The creature remained.

Gerry curled his toes.

Something moved in the water. Whatever it was, it was about five or six feet from shore. At least that's what Gerry thought, the way the moonlight danced upon the water in horizontal swirls of white. Ovoid dark circles moved along the top of the water like black oil. For some reason it reminded Gerry of a painting he once saw. He couldn't recall which one.

Then, the sound of a fish jumping out of, then landing back in, the water. The water sprayed upward in a small splash, but he couldn't see what had come up then quickly ducked back beneath the lake's surface.

The movement stopped.

The inky liquid atop the water's surface disappeared.

Gerry felt his toes curl and again the clay smooshed between them. He hated the feeling. The clay was watery and solid at the same time, like wet dough.

He twisted and turned, tried again to free himself. He grimaced when the bottom of his chin scraped against the sand piled up high against it. Was it his imagination or, though he couldn't recall correctly, was the sand packed higher around his neck than when Jordan had buried him? Now that he was focusing on it, the sand was up near the bottoms of his ears than by the bottom of his neckline where he could have sworn it was before.

"Help!" he shouted. He waited, thinking again that maybe a car would come by the parking lot or that some park patrol fellow would hear him.

No car, and no one came.

That thing, he remembered. Frantically scanning the beach for any sign of that shadow-like slug, he braced himself for the creature to suddenly scurry back to him. Already in his mind's eye he could see it dart toward him, pause just below his chin and sit there, as though the two were waiting to see "who would blink first."

The creature didn't come.

I can't believe this is happening to me, he thought. *As if I did anything—I mean, really, anything—to deserve this.*

His heart ached, its beat quick and fast, to the point of discomfort. He didn't know how long he could stand the fast thump-thump-thumping beneath his chest and was sure that his heart would give out on him if it didn't slow down. Unfortunately, there wasn't much one could do to slow a fast-beating heart. Taking deep breaths didn't work. Not when you're buried from the neck down. Too much pressure against the lungs.

His eyes focused back on the water when he heard another splash, this one bigger.

The black oily substance not too far from shore had returned, like a dark shadow hovering along the water. It somehow looked *thicker* and less liquidy.

"I can't deal with this," he whispered.

Splash! Something black jumped up out of the water and came back down again.

The shadow-like slug was back on the beach, right in front of him, no more than ten feet away.

Gerry tried to swallow, but couldn't because his mouth was too dry.

I need a drink, he thought absentmindedly.

His heart raced and the numbness of his limbs set on full force.

The creature sped toward him, weaving left then right, back and forth.

It was dragging something behind it.

Enough! "You want a piece of me? Fine. Come and get it!" he screamed.

The creature was right before him in a heartbeat and instead of stopping just before his chin like the last time, it leaped into the air and latched on to his mouth. His lips were pressed tight, but he felt the creature trying to pry its way in between, pushing, wriggling, worming. Just below his nose he saw its black body lashing side to side as it tried to break the seal of his lips. The thing pressed so hard he wasn't sure just how much longer he could keep the creature out. Already he was revisiting that mental image from earlier, the image of that thing burrowing into his mouth and sitting on his tongue.

He clenched his jaw, tightened the muscles around his lips. He almost didn't notice the creature didn't really feel solid, but more like a tight beam of hot air constantly being blown against his lips. The hot pressure reminded him of the hard rush of air you felt when you stuck your head out of a car window going a hundred kilometers an hour.

His muffled grunts were suddenly muted when the water splashed . . .

. . . and splashed.

And splashed.

Looking past the creature to the water, the waves stopped rolling in to shore and for an instant the water near the shoreline was perfectly calm and flat. Then the waves started curling *away*. The water bubbled and popped and splashed and something began to emerge.

It rose quickly, bringing a wall of water with it like a sheet of gray-and-black-and-white-stained glass. Gerry's mouth fell open. Before he realized what he had done, the creature dove inside and sat on his tongue.

It didn't move.

The sheet of water went up and up and up, a hump of black at its peak. Then the hump hung at its apex a moment before coming back down in a rush and sending the wall of water outward in a violent spray, submerging Gerry. A sharp pang hit his nasal cavities as the water rushed inward. His head spun, and along with the metal-like taste of lake water that burst in through the corners of his mouth, he also tasted the creature. It tasted like cotton and . . . paint. He squeezed his eyes shut and forgot about the creatures, both large and small, and waited to die. The underwater current rushed toward him, plowing against his skin, icy and cold. His whole body shivered and when he clenched his toes, the clay spread around his skin then quickly receded and suddenly he wasn't clenching anything at all.

The water around him grew still for a moment before moving in the opposite direction, the sand up around his neck growing thinner. The water pushed his head forward into the sand. He thought his whole face would be plowed into the mound of sand built up around his neck, but instead found the sand gone. Soon he was able to feel the cold water against his shoulders. A sudden coolness touched the top of his head and the water continued to recede. When his head was finally above water, he instinctively took a deep breath and, in his lower peripheral, saw the tail of the creature inside his mouth hanging limply from his lips. He tried to spit the thing out, but it was latched onto his tongue like a leech. In spite of the water in his mouth, the creature still tasted like dry cotton.

He opened his eyes and blinked out the lake water.

The lake was a tumult of waves, gray and black and white, roiling and rolling; huge mounds of water. He tried to focus on the waves as they began to settle instead of looking at the hulk of black that had risen from the lake.

If it's going to kill me, I don't want to see it, he thought. But he couldn't help himself. He took his eyes from the water and watched as the large creature raised its black, slick, leather-like tentacles toward the sky. From what he could see, there were six of them, each tentacle about fifteen feet long, if not more. They spread out from a huge bulb of black nearly the size of a house, its skin—if that's what it was—dark and shiny and liquid-looking. A single eye, black and infinite, took up half its face, the eye so dark it paled the black latex-like skin of its body. Running from the center of the thing's face was a thin thread that reminded Gerry of a tar line in the road. The thread ran from the blackness to his mouth and he realized it was connected to the creature on his tongue. He spat and gagged and flicked his tongue, trying to get the thing out of his mouth.

It didn't move.

His heart pounded and his chest ached.

He noticed the sand-stained skin of his shoulders and saw he was free from mid chest up. He wriggled and twisted and pulled his arms up, tugging his still-asleep limbs away from the grip of the sand. Not looking up at the creature before him, he redoubled his efforts and was able to get his arms free up to the elbows before his shoulders and arms sagged from exhaustion. Panting, cold and alone, Gerry peered up at the creature. Its dark eye took him in, and he wished the moon hadn't hid behind a cloud so he could see his captor more fully.

Mind empty, he watched as the monster snapped the tar-like thread like a whip, yanking the thing off his tongue and ripping it out from his mouth.

Gerry spat out the tinny, paint-like taste. Blood ran from his tongue and in between his lips.

The tiny shadowy creature sped back toward its master and disappeared.

Dark patches, out of the corner of his eye. His son's body lay beside him, face down in the sand. Turning his head, he saw Emily lying on her side behind him, half-buried in the sand. Maria was on her back not far from Emily, a good part of her body buried as well. All up and down the beach were bodies, adults, kids, even a few elderly people, some completely revealed, others still partly covered with sand.

Tears mixed with the lake water running off his hair and over his eyes.

"Jordan! Emily! No! Maria . . ." He was already out of breath.

The beast on the lake grunted, low and guttural, its sound echoing inside him.

My kids . . . "It . . . they . . ." The words would not come and he didn't think they ever would.

The revelation of what might have happened hit him hard and it quickly explained why he hadn't noticed any footprints on the beach earlier. Not even a sign of any stirring of the sand. This thing had covered everything, probably had brought up the sand that was just beneath the shoreline when it rose from the depths the first time that afternoon.

It covered everything.

Except for him. He had been higher up.

"Jordan!" His son just lay there, still and waterlogged. "Emily," he whispered. "Wake up. My kids . . . . Maria!" Their bodies absorbed his voice and didn't react.

Though he knew they hadn't survived, it was at that moment he truly acknowledged they were dead. When it really hit home.

Everyone was dead.

Everyone . . . except for him.

The creature on the lake lifted its tentacles then brought them down with a hard slap, showering up a spray of water.

It began to move toward him.

Gerry's muscles locked and for an instant his heart stopped beating. At least he thought so until it started pounding inside his chest, his head, its pulse echoing in his throat.

The big, black hulk scrambled out of the water like a dog, its tentacles suddenly rigid, clawing at the sand, bringing its mass toward him. With each inch closer, the thing grew a foot taller, a foot wider.

Enormous.

His breaths came out fast through his nostrils; the creature's shining, liquid eye locked on with his.

Gerry tried to swallow, but his mouth was so dry that nothing would go down. He forgot where he was—forgot *who* he was—forgot what happened, forgot about being trapped. Nothing mattered, but the giant squid-like monster coming toward him.

The world disappeared in a flash of darkness and when it focused back into being again, the creature was right in front of him.

It stared at him, but like the shadowy slug, it didn't move.

A part of him just wanted it to be over. Just wanted the creature to *do* something. Anything. He hated playing this staring game and constantly wondering what was going to happen next.

Minutes passed, maybe hours, before the creature moved its girth, its huge body-head pushing the sand in a heap around it when it turned.

Without meaning to, Gerry tried once more to free himself and, with a hard pull, yanked his arms free from the sand. The second his arms came out, the creature shifted its weight and its eye was once again fixed on him.

Don't move. Don't even breathe, Gerry thought.

The two exchanged stares: the creature's soul-searching and evil; Gerry's wide-eyed with panic.

Again after a time, the creature shifted its weight.

Gerry tried to move and the second he did, the twenty-something-foot-tall behemoth stared down at him. He couldn't see a mouth on the creature, just a slick, oily face with a single eye.

Its vision is based on movement, Gerry thought. At least he hoped so. If he could just somehow stay still and wait it out. Surely there were others in Birds Hill Park near the beach or, at least, there would be shortly. It had to be nearly dawn, though he was still unsure what time it was.

And so he waited, forcing himself to remain still, forcing himself to breathe slow, methodic breaths, anything that would make him appear no less significant than a tree stump.

Don't think about where you are. Pretend you're at home with the kids, with . . . ". . . my kids," he accidentally whispered. Jordan and Emily were dead. Tears swelled in his eyes and as much as he tried not to cry, he couldn't stop himself from sniffling. A sharp pang filled his chest, pierced his heart.

He took in the creature, his field of vision following the liquid slick contours of the monster's form and he was awed by how perfectly round it was, how impossibly smooth.

The creature moved again and its mass pushed up a mound of sand that was quickly picked up by a light breeze that decided to come by. Some of the sand hit Gerry's face, tickling his skin. And, a moment later, an itch formed. It poked and pricked and begged to be scratched.

Gerry grimaced, bit his lips, tried to take his mind off it. *You're not itchy. Everything's fine. Relax. It's okay. You're at home. You're watching TV. You're at the park with the kids. You're sitting across from Maria at the dinner table, eating a turkey club.* The itch pinched and he could envision his skin curling from it. He tried to ignore it, but he couldn't. It hurt so bad and he—

His hand snapped back down to his side as the blessed relief of an itch scratched took over.

The monster grunted, faced him and, near its lower jowls, its face seem to split horizontally in two, revealing row upon row of sharp, jagged teeth, each at least six inches long, if not more, and almost nearly as wide. Its breath was hot and smelled of fish.

Its eye locked onto Gerry.

He couldn't help himself but scream.

THE BEAT

When Granddad called me up and invited me to the family cabin for the weekend, I was surprised. Well, it wasn't actually the *family* cabin. It was his, but he let all his kids and their children use it. He and Grandmama had purchased the lot up by Lake Winnipeg sometime in the early eighties. With the help of his two daughters and their husbands, over the course of a summer the cabin had been built.

The cabin's a fair size. It runs roughly fifty feet long, twenty-five feet wide, the ceiling starting at ten feet by the door, rising to sixteen in the middle, then descending back down to ten feet at the other end. I'm proud to say it had been my suggestion, when I was around sixteen or so, to make off with the ivory paneling on the outside and install artificial dark brown logs, giving it an old pioneer/early settler kind of feel.

I'm eighteen now. Granddad's seventy-four. Grandmama is only sixty-seven—if you consider such a number as "only" when it comes to an elderly person.

Someone once asked me while I was helping Grandmama loading groceries into her cart at a supermarket how old she was. The guy asking had guessed by her looks and zeal in her voice that she was in her mid-fifties. When I told him her real age, his eyes went wide, obviously not believing me.

She kept a positive attitude and that impressed me. Especially now since Granddad had fallen ill, lung cancer manifesting itself to its full extent as a result of his forty-some-odd years as a smoker. Granddad had been in the hospital twice, the second time being just two nights ago. Like I said before, I was surprised when he called me up today and asked in his raspy, gurgly voice (his throat burnt to a crisp from the years of hot smoke, no doubt), "I just got out of the hospital, Robby, and I was wondering if you wanted to come up to the lake with me this weekend?"

"Do you really want me to come," I said, "or do you only want me there because I always have a pack of Winstons with me?"

He chuckled, knowing I was on to him. Ever since he had come down with cancer, Grandmama had forbade him to buy any more cigarettes. "You're not going to help yourself to yer deathbed as long as I'm around!" she would scold him.

Of course Granddad, playing the sheepish innocent, obliged to her demands, only to secretly stash a cigarette here and there around the house. Knowing that he would do such a thing, Grandmama scoured the house top to bottom and found every one, yelling at him each time a cigarette was found. Granddad didn't learn his lesson and often came to me, always complaining of a nic' fit.

Grandmama would have a bird if she knew I was slipping Granddad smokes, but, I figure, who was she or I to deprive him of one of his favorite pleasures in life? In return for my supplying him with cigarettes, he treated me to different things: taking me out for breakfast, giving me gas money, buying me a lighter when mine conked out—things like that. So far, our secret trade had gone on beneath Grandmama's notice.

However, since Granddad's recent turn for the worse, I decided that I did not want to be responsible for his next visit to the I.C.U.

"I'll come along," I told him, "but I can't give you smokes anymore."

"Aw, come on, Robert. Ah, okay, you win. Just don't smoke in front of me, okay?" he said, sounding as if I had just broken his heart.

"You know I can't let you smoke because I care about you, right?"

He sighed. "I'll pick you up Friday night around eight. We'll be at the lake before eleven."

I told him that sounded fine. This should be an interesting weekend. Maybe I'll leave my cigarettes at home for the next two days, just to be safe?

———

The gravel seemed to crunch louder than usual when Granddad and I pulled into the cabin's driveway. It was more like a short, small stone-covered path than a real driveway, the path not far from the road. I watched the headlights from Granddad's Ford pickup bathe the cabin with a yellow glow, transforming the dark brown of the cabin into a deep tan.

In all my years of coming here I've never arrived at night. Usually family trips to the lake were either done Saturday morning or afternoon, plenty of daylight left when we arrived.

Granddad put the truck in park, idled it, and gazed at the cabin as if it was a lost relative. And, in a way, I suppose it was. The cabin was as much family as both of us.

After a few minutes he turned the motor off and got out of the truck. I got out, too, rounding to the rear and pulling my duffel bag off its bed.

Hoisting the bag's strap over my shoulder, Granddad, with a hard pat to my back, gave me the key to the front door. He told me he had to run to the outhouse at the left of the property and he didn't want me standing in the chilly night air waiting for him.

Granddad went off, disappearing into the night. I watched him dissolve into the darkness and waited a moment in case anything went wrong. I didn't know if he was able to manage himself as well as he used to since he had gotten sick. Once Granddad was out of view for a few seconds, I adjusted the bag's strap on my shoulder and made my way for the door.

A sudden gust of cool wind sent a shiver up my back and down my arms. Bad timing, too, because my eyes had been locked on to the three black windows of the cabin, one for the kitchen, one for a bedroom, the last for the living room. The windows seemed to draw my eyes into their void, only darkness emanating from them, extinguishing the pale moonlight that shone against them.

I walked up the two steps leading to the front patio landing. The screen door squeaked on its hinges as I opened it, revealing the door I had the key to. I stole a glance at the window to my left before entering, then perked an ear for Granddad. Blackness glanced back and silence hung on the air. I didn't know why I was so afraid. Actually, I *did* know why: too many scary movies and violent comic books. Disregarding the thought of an ogre with a cloak made from human skin waiting inside for me, I put the key into the lock, heard it click, and went in.

I turned on the light. The cabin lit up. There was only two light switches other than those for the two bedrooms and bathroom—one for the front door and main living area, the other for the back porch.

I slid my shoulder out of the strap, my bag falling to the always-dirty welcome mat beneath me.

Any childish fears I had when standing outside vanished. It felt good to finally be back here. Startling me out my lamentation, the screen door behind me screeched open.

"So, are ya comin' in all the way or are ya jus' gonna stand there like a bellhop?" Granddad asked, putting a hand on my shoulder.

"All the way," I breathed, feeling as if I just did something wrong.

He appeared all right. His leathery skin was a bit paler than usual but he looked healthy enough. He lovingly smiled at me, the crow's-feet by his eyes rising up. The gray hair on top of his head was slicked back, as if he had just got out of the shower.

Picking up my bag, I shuffled off into the room where I'd be staying. The room was across from his.

I turned on the light and tossed my bag on the bed. The coils of the mattress squeaked from the weight. My room was plain: pale yellow walls, a curtain-less window, a small closet and an oak dresser with a mirror, all blending in nicely with the worn dark brown carpet of the floor. The carpets. That was another thing I enjoyed about this place. Each room had a different colored carpet, most of them similar to the brown one in my room (but different shades of brown nonetheless), except for the floor of the kitchen (the floor sharing the floor of the living room), which was covered in light tan tiles. The inside of the family cabin was a perfect testimony to the earth-tone theme of the seventies and early eighties.

Taking a few of my things out of my bag, I heard Granddad clanking around in the kitchen. He was probably preparing us a snack of some sort and a couple of beers. (He had come up here last weekend to stock the fridge and pantry, he said.)

Putting a sweatshirt on a hanger, I watched myself in my peripheral in the mirror to my left. It took a moment after hanging up the sweatshirt to actually look at myself squarely. I never liked what I saw when I looked in the mirror. And the reason I didn't like it had nothing to do with my appearance. In the end, it all came down to one thing: a child's vision of himself as to how he would look when he grew up. Back between the ages of seven and ten, I always envisioned myself growing up into your well-built, stubble-cheeked, deeply tanned, just-the-right-amount-of-blond-highlights-in-the-hair underwear-model gentleman. Instead, I looked like his younger brother: pale-faced, sweaty-banged, thin-shouldered, beer-bellied-wino, with glasses and an AC/DC T-shirt. So much for being Don Juan.

High school finished in June and I still had a month before first semester at the University of Winnipeg. I'm still wasn't sure what I wanted to be when I grew up, but in your first year of post-secondary, that didn't matter. Everyone was enrolled in some University One program that came into being a few years back. It's basically Grade Twelve all over again, but maybe a little tougher.

Granddad hollered from the other room, telling me to get in the kitchen. I shouted back, saying I'd be right there.

The kitchen table was neatly set: two frosted beer mugs set on opposite ends, a black ashtray in the table's middle.

Granddad turned from the counter, a beer bottle in each hand. He set a bottle beside each mug. I took my seat at the end of the table nearest the door. Granddad always sat at the end of the table farthest from the door. Always. Don't ask me why.

He tilted his mug as he emptied the bottle. I did the same. He held up his mug, as if in a toast, then took a large, satisfying swig. After, he let out an audible, "Ahh." I took a swig of my own beer, the carbon of the beer stinging my throat on its way down.

"I say we should turn in early tonight," Granddad said. "An' tomorrow, we'll get up early an' hit the lake across the way, there." He gestured to the large window opposite us that looked out onto the back property. The yard extended about a hundred feet then tapered off into a man-made lake, cleaned yearly, as well as stocked with fish. A two-minute walk from the yard and there was a path that led up to an old rickety bridge you could sit on, hang your line from and wait until you caught something.

"Sounds like a plan," I said.

He nodded and took another gulp.

I could tell he wanted a cigarette by the way he slouched in his chair, one hand gripping his mug, the other resting on his belly. He looked off somewhere through the kitchen window. As if he could see anything through the darkness that filled it. His eyes went from the window to me to the window again, then back to me, checking to be sure that I knew what he wanted, but was too shy to ask for.

It was kind of amusing at first, seeing how long he could keep up his subtle yet obvious hints that he wanted to smoke. Soon it became annoying. Though Granddad was your Jack-of-all-trades grandfather, I found it disturbing he was acting so childlike.

Knowing it wasn't a good idea, I reluctantly removed my cigarette package from my jeans pocket and dropped it on the table. (I couldn't leave the smokes at home; fishing and smoking go hand in hand.) Granddad made like he didn't notice, but I could see his eyes salivating at the package of coffin nails. Indulging him, I made show of removing a cigarette, putting it behind my ear and putting another between my lips. I paused, building his anticipation. His eyes took me in then peered back out the window. I thought to toy with him, but decided against it, figuring Granddad had already had enough torture from being in the I.C.U.

I held the pack out to him, proffering him a cigarette.

He made like he didn't want it, but then leaned forward in his chair, his arm extended, his fingers just touching the edge of my pack.

"You sure?" he asked.

"Yeah," I said, "go ahead. Just don't tell Grandmama."

He smiled his famous Granddad smile, the stubble on his cheeks scraping against each other in the folds of his skin. "Thanks, kiddo."

He took the smoke and I slid my lighter across the table. He took a swig of his beer and lit up. I grabbed an ashtray of my own from the cupboard over the sink then sat back down.

Granddad said that he was having a good weekend so far. So was I.

***

It was sometime deep into the night, around 3:30, when I heard the tick-tick-ticking of a clock. Hearing such a patterned noise in the silence of a house—in this case, cabin—was normal. What bothered me about the ticking was that, as far as I was aware, Granddad never kept a ticking clock at the cabin. As old-fashioned as he was, his clocks were digital. He was also a light sleeper and even though the ticking was relatively quiet, it still would be enough to wake him.

I wondered if he was awake now and, perhaps, since I haven't spent the night here in so long, if Grandmama had insisted he install the antique analog clock that had been stationed above the stove at their apartment since who knew when, as a little taste of home.

Maybe it was that old clock that was making the ticking.

Granddad wasn't one to be pushed around by anyone—except by Grandmama. She had Granddad wrapped around her old and wrinkled finger. I once asked Granddad why he cowered under her like a puppy in trouble with its master. He responded with a wink, "'Tis called love, kiddo. I may not like it, but let I be doomed if I don't make her smile by doin' what she wants now and again. You'll know what I mean when ya find yerself a cute little honey one day. I guarantee that. Jus' you wait and see, boy."

Rubbing the sleep from my eyes, I rolled over and tried to ignore the *tick-tick-tick* that seemed to have grown louder over the past ten seconds. I cleared my mind and waited for the drowsiness hanging over me to turn into full-fledged fatigue and whisk me away to La La Land, far away from the noise.

I started to slip away, that *good* feeling of inevitable sleep setting in, when the ticking grew even louder. Granddad would surely be awake now. How could he not be? Forty bucks said he'd shut that clock up and in a minute or two he and I would be back asleep. In the morning, neither of us would remember waking.

Tick.

Tick.

Tick.

The ticking was too loud and I could only imagine how loud the ticking was on the other side of my closed door.

Come on, Granddad, hurry it up, I thought. *Turn that clock off!*

Tick.

Tick.

Tick.

I groaned and threw my blankets back, the cool breeze coming from my open window immediately attacking all the skin that wasn't covered by my boxer shorts. I took a moment and let the goosebumps seize me before getting out of bed.

There was enough light in my room to help me find the door. Shivering, I stepped out, and crept through the dark gray of the cabin, the shapes of the furniture vaguely outlined in the subtle amount of available light.

I was right, too, about the ticking being louder out here. Sounds always seemed louder in the dark, too. Who knew why.

Granddad's door was partially open. He was asleep. I could hear his snoring, which was more like a garbled wheezing. Not wanting to disturb him, I followed the sound of the ticking. It got louder toward the back porch. Why the clock was back there, instead of out from where it was practical, I didn't know.

The door to the back porch was closed. There was no lock. Only the door that led from the back porch to the back lot had a lock. Not that the lock would help anyway. It's one of those rinky-dink locks that all you had to do was push the knob then turn it to lock it from the inside. A burglar worth his loot would have no trouble getting through that "impenetrable" security.

"I remember the day when we didn't have to lock our doors at night," Granddad once told me. He got a lock for the back door simply because all the neighboring cabins had one. And he had a lock on the front door, too, so might as well make them match, right?

Anyway, I opened the door. The ticking doubled in volume. I glanced toward Granddad's room to see if he was awoken by it. He wasn't. He was still wheezing in his sleep.

Flicking on the light, I stepped onto the porch, my eyes adjusting to the brightness. As they did, I scanned for the source of sound that had interrupted my sleep. It seemed to be coming from the back corner, beneath a box of historical romance novels that belonged to Grandmama.

There was hordes of other junk in the porch, too—a couple of broken chairs, an old kitchen table, Granddad's tool box, blankets and other old-people antiquities that made you wonder why they even bought such things to begin with (like a faded porcelain ballerina that's missing a leg).

As I made my way to the corner, I stepped carefully between boxes of more junk, tripping over a couple.

The ticking was far louder here. It couldn't be a clock. Sounded more like a bomb (as if I'd ever heard a bomb tick before—only in the movies).

I bent over and wrapped my hands around the back edges of the box of novels. With a mighty heave, I lifted the box and placed it on the vintage kitchen table beside me. I was right. There was something beneath the box of Grandmama's books. Another box, without a lid. On top of it was a well-worn orangey-red towel draped over a smaller box. With the tips of my forefinger and thumb, I picked off the towel.

Tick.

Tick.

Tick.

And there it was: a well-polished, antique wooden box. The box had a lid. The clock's inside. It better be because I didn't like the idea of the ticking coming from somewhere else in that cramped little porch. It'd be a lot of work to find it.

I picked up the box—and opened its lid.

Tick.

Tick.

Tick.

It wasn't a clock. It wasn't a bomb, either. It was a metronome, secured in a blue velvet-mould. Its wooden cover was absent. I watched as its arm rocked back and forth across the ivory front, counting the beat to a song that wasn't playing.

Since we had one of those things at home, I knew how to turn it off.

Granddad's wheezing suddenly increased. It sounded like he was panicking in his sleep. A bad dream, perhaps. His wheezing got louder. I wondered if I should go and check on him, make sure he's all right. I didn't want him back in the I.C.U. He coughed and began wheezing again.

I should go check on him. I suppressed the arm and replaced it under the bracket at the top of the unit. Then . . .

Silence.

Granddad's wheezing faded.

———

The next morning I woke to the neighbor's dog barking and to the twittering of a small bird outside my window. Groggy, I checked my watch. It was close to 10 A.M. Knowing that if I slept in Granddad would have my head, I got up and went to the bathroom before going to the kitchen. We were supposed to go fishing today. Why didn't he wake me?

My ears were expecting to be greeted by Granddad's congratulating me of joining the world of the living. "Look at what just rose from the grave," he usually said.

The kitchen was empty. I took a quick glance around. The living room was empty, too. The blinds were open. So was Granddad's bedroom door. I walked over, knowing he wouldn't be in there (I just sensed it), but went to check on him anyway, just in case he wasn't feeling too well. He was, however, lying peacefully when I went to his room last night after being in the porch, so he should be up now.

He wasn't there. His bed was neatly made, blankets drawn tight then folded in on an angle at the corners of the mattress, military-styled.

I went back to my room, threw on a Megadeath T-shirt and a pair of ripped jean shorts, and returned to the kitchen.

Something suddenly didn't feel right. I gazed out the window above the sink, expecting to see Granddad's truck. I didn't. Instead there was my car, a half-rusted, silver Toyota Camry, parked askew on the graveled driveway.

"What the . . ." I raked my fingers through my hair. The taste of morning-breath suddenly seemed stronger. I looked at my car again, this time noticing the dashboard littered with burger wrappers and beer labels.

"Granddad?" I called into the cabin.

Without putting on my shoes, I went out to my car, shouting for him all the way.

I ran my hand along the hood of the car and reached the driver-side door. The door was unlocked. I opened the door. My keys dangled from the ignition in the on position. Plopping myself down in the driver's seat, I turned the key back in the ignition and turned the car off. Then I tried to start the car. No go. Dead. Drained the battery.

Confused, my eyes roamed over the messy dashboard, the passenger seat that had a case of beer on it, the cigarette butts that had spilled from the ashtray, the butts of two joints stubbed out in the cup holder.

How did my car get here? Did someone drive it here last night? How did all the booze get in here? Certainly not from anyone in my family. My dad gave up drinking, even socially. My mom never touched a drink in her life. My sister, Stephanie, was too young to drink let alone drive a car.

Granddad? No. Even if he did decide to be reckless and booze it up on the way back here, say, if for whatever reason, he drove his truck back to the city and came back here in my car early this morning, it still didn't explain the joints in the cup holder. I didn't think Granddad even knew what a joint was. And who would he get one from, anyway?

My thoughts were distracted when I heard the telephone ring from inside the cabin. Knowing I should answer it or get in trouble from Granddad if it was an important call, I got out of the car, closed the door, and walked to the cabin. My feet were suddenly sensitive to the prickly grass between the cabin and the car.

As I passed the outhouse, I considered the possibility of Granddad being in there. About to go to the outhouse instead of answering the phone, I stopped, reconsidered, then headed over to the cabin, picking up my pace. The phone had rang over eight times. Whoever was calling hadn't given up yet. It had to be important.

Inside, I picked up the old rotary phone mounted next to the refrigerator. "Hello?"

"What are you doing there?" my mom asked.

"What do you mean what am I doing here?" I leaned up against the counter. "Granddad invited me up here yesterday."

She cleared her throat. When she spoke her voice was weak, concerned. "Robert, Granddad was in the hospital yesterday. He died last night."

My insides suddenly felt empty. What was she talking about? Last night Granddad and I . . .

The ashtrays were gone from the table. I placed my palm on the countertop and pulled it away, feeling something dirty on my skin. My hand had a thin film of dust on it. I looked around the cabin. The couch in the living room, the chair, the TV stand, and the coffee table all had white blankets draped over them. Why I hadn't noticed them when I got up . . .

"Are you okay?" my mother asked. "Why are you out there?"

I didn't respond, but instead looked out the window, past my car and to the For Sale sign staked into the ground beside the mailbox near the edge of the driveway.

"Mom, I . . ." But I couldn't finish. My head felt as if my thoughts and memories were scattered like a filing cabinet ransacked by an intruder, the files dumped on the floor.

My disbelief of my mother's claim of Granddad being dead faded a little and was replaced by the hollow pain of heartache.

"Listen," Mom said, "just stay there and Dad and I will come and get you."

"O-okay," I said. My legs wobbled as if they were made of rubber, so I sat down at the table.

About to say good-bye, I heard a ticking in the background, on the other end of the line.

"What's that?" I asked.

"What's what?"

"That ticking."

"It's Granddad's metronome, back when he played the piano."

Granddad? Piano?

Mom went on. "Stephanie's going to play a song for Granddad's funeral. Grandmama insisted she practiced with Granddad's metronome instead of her own, making it more special."

I couldn't believe what was going on.

"Granddad had that metronome beside his hospital bed during his last days," my mother said. "He said the rhythm from it calmed him down and made him less apprehensive about death. I'm surprised it still works, though. It's real old."

"Why?" I asked not really knowing *why* I asked.

"Because," she said, "it stopped its beat when Granddad died, as if the beat was keeping him alive and someone then decided it was time for him to go."

I flashed back to the night before and how I stopped the metronome from ticking. Granddad's garbled wheezing stopped then, too. How could I have . . . if I did . . . . I wasn't sure what I was thinking. I didn't kill him. But given last night, maybe I was somehow in a place outside of time, out of reality.

Needing to be alone, I said good-bye to Mom. She said she and Dad would be out here this afternoon. I told her that was fine and hung up.

I went back to my room, grabbed a cigarette and lit up.

Here's to you, Granddad. Here's to you.

RAG-MAN

Every time I come here I always wonder the same thing: what does it take to have your work hung in an art gallery?

If you take the time to think about the amount of *actual* physical effort that was put into some of the work that decorates its walls, you come to realize that talent or skill has nothing to do with it.

When I look at some of the paintings I try to imagine what the artist was doing while creating it. Were they painting with precision and care against a very expensive piece of canvas or were they sitting upon it, splashing about in child-like joy, seeing what happens when you combine blue with red?

I've been walking through an area dedicated to more abstract paintings but most of the pieces were just a bunch of sprits and sprays of various colors on a solid-tone background.

Disgusting.

Being an artist myself I think it's rather shameful these untalented, crappy painters can sell their work, and the more prestigious and skillful artist gets completely overlooked. I'll never understand it, but that's not why I come here. I come here to look at the paintings that *deserve* credit. I come to get lost in the pictures and escape reality for an hour or two every week. I allow my creative and somewhat over-imaginative mind to take control of me and throw me into any circumstance it sees fit—adventure, horror, erotica, mystery—it doesn't matter. I just like getting away from the pressures of everyday life, and on my low income this is the only vacation I can afford. Yep, that's me, Peter Fox, starving artist.

I still live with my parents even though I am twenty-three years old. I don't have a career or anything like that. My main area of expertise is wandering aimlessly from job to job and keeping a long yet diverse resume. Right now I've been dabbling in writing and hope to someday sell a short story or two to a science fiction or horror magazine. Maybe a publishing house like *Tongue and Castle,* if they are interested.

Maybe.

Even though my body and mind ached for a classic adventure starring myself and a couple of women with large chests, where I played the hero and they played the damsels-in-distress, I had to hold myself back because today I was keeping a different agenda. I came here to find an image that could inspire something to write about. So far, all of the pictures sucked even though I've seen those same images a thousand times before.

On a nearby bench where elderly tourists came to sit and discuss the latest sore bones in their body or their most recent gut-wrenching bowel movement, I sat down and felt the life drain out of my legs. It felt so good after being on my feet all day. I sat there staring blankly into space at a picture of a mother cradling her newborn child.

My mindless gaze was interrupted by a warm wind blowing in my ear. I turned swiftly to see if anyone I knew was next to me, but I found nothing, only the vacant seat beside me. It was probably my hyperactive imagination so I simply resumed my stare. The mother in the stained-glass painting looked on her child with care, her eyes expressing she knew she was holding somebody precious. All mothers felt that way about their kid, but this one knew her child was different from all the rest and, very bluntly, better than all of them as well.

My eyes were about to shift to the cradled infant when that warm air caressed my ear again. This time it was a lot warmer, almost hot. I took another look around and, like before, found nothing. I got up slightly spooked and continued walking past the painting and stopped at a nearby sculpture encased in glass. Many have seen this image before, but everybody looks at it differently. It was a small statue of Christ on the cross, hanging by His wrists and welcoming death with open arms.

For the past number of months I have been debating my faith. Is God real? Where is He, then? Why haven't I been touched like the tens of millions who have? These were questions that ran through my mind constantly and, as of late, I've been receiving some answers.

Sort of.

Now I'm able to feel a presence, something slightly tangible, something that wasn't there before. It wasn't there all the time but more often than not I felt as if someone was standing next to me. They stood next to me now as I looked at the cross. My heart almost wept as I looked upon the sculpted face of Christ, His eyes crying out "I love you," when that warm air that touched me moments ago gripped me again. Not just my ear this time but on my face and hands as well.

I let out a yelp loud enough to create an echo in the large room. This soft blowing wind burned my skin and grew more and more intense. I looked around, hoping it was just the heat vents in the building blowing on me as if it was personal, but found none.

I took a few steps back and the burning persisted. This could only mean one of two things: either I was getting violently ill or that I was going crazy.

Just when I thought I could bear it no more the heat let up and my face and hands cooled. Taking a deep, soothing breath I walked briskly toward the exit. My inspirational painting could wait. It was time to go home to bed so if I was indeed coming down with something, I could sleep it off.

Involuntarily my fast walking turned into a slow jog. Something was behind me.

I debated whether I should glance back or not but stuck with the latter knowing that if someone *was* following me, looking back at them might make matters worse. Turning to my right I left the exhibit devoted to religious art and entered a vast and almost maze-like room with environmental-inspired paintings hanging on every wall. Even though I've been through here many times before I always find myself getting lost. Probably the same way parents got lost when they visit their child's school for a play.

A knot formed in my left side and the signs I was a heavy smoker became evident. My jog turned into a walk then I stopped briefly for another satisfying gulp of air. Shortly after an announcement came over the intercom saying the gallery would be closing in five minutes and we should all conclude our viewing. The lights began to dim and I could already hear people starting to leave.

I looked around. The paintings that hung over one-story high appeared to be taking on new life. The images that were supposed to express life's beauty suddenly became dead and grim. Even the mood of the paintings began to grower darker, like that one of the farmer bailing hay. Looked more like he was packing dismembered arms and legs instead.

Still walking, I heard a small clicking sound from underneath me and the next thing I knew my feet were tangled and I fell head first into the tiled floor. A hard *thud* echoed inside my skull and a pain formed above my eyes. Pulling myself a few inches from the floor I paused briefly in disbelief, then positioned myself so I was sitting up, my butt cheeks feeling the cold floor beneath me. Somehow my shoelace became untied and it tried to kill me. At least my imagination thought it did.

I ran my hands through my hair expecting to find a lump or a pool of moisture or a soft spot where the top of my head had been opened, but found nothing. Frustrated, I got up and walked slowly in the direction of the exit.

I could see it now, walking through the front door at home and my mom asking me why I looked so stoned. *Gee, Mom, a cold ceramic tile kissed me. It was so passionate it almost knocked me out.*

Yeah, right.

I had forgotten about the notion that someone had been following me until a shadow that was not my own appeared near my feet. I quickly turned around ready to give anyone that was behind me a hard punch, but again found nothing.

The throbbing in my head intensified as my heart fiercely pumped away. In fact, it was beating so hard it hurt with a dull, throbbing ache. I was panicking, and when I tried to speak to self-soothe, my mouth produced nothing, causing me to choke on what felt like a vice around my neck.

Anxiety swept over my body and the world turned into a dream. The only solid recollection I had was I had to get out of the building. I walked down the hall as if I was drunk, trying so hard to keep a grip on reality. Everything I was ceased to exist and now I was just a staggering man trying to keep his eyes open, straining to remember which way was out. Fear had become second nature to me; made my clothes stick to my body. I turned left at a T-junction certain it would take me downstairs and then outside.

Two to three minutes and I would be out. Thank God!

Moisture now saturated my black, matted hair and a salty taste met my lips as sweat found its way into my mouth. I loosened the top button on my plaid shirt, hoping to release some heat and cool down. As if that was a cue to my stalker, that strange intense heat plowed into me and drained me of life. I immediately removed my shirt to reveal the white KISS T-shirt that I wore underneath.

Sensing insanity was inevitable I began to decipher the situation. Was I hallucinating? Was I lying unconscious on the art gallery's floor and this was all a dream? I didn't know and to a large degree I didn't care. I just wanted to leave.

Footsteps formed behind me and a heavy breathing filled the room. It was not my own.

I panicked and screamed, completely frustrated at not being able to see the cause of the breathing and not knowing which way was up. I jumped around to face my enemy ready to rip their heart out if they were the ones who were causing me all this pain. But there, standing in front of me, was a tall, thin man with dusty, tattered rags for clothes. His face was partially concealed by the floppy hat he wore, but the lines of age that graced his face distorted his image entirely. He had no eyes, just black holes that felt as though they were looking right through me.

I waited for him to make a move, but instead this Rag-man just stood their staring into my soul. After what seemed like an eternity he raised his bony fingers and signaled for me to come closer. If I followed his instructions I would be a complete fool and probably not live to see tomorrow. I had to be dreaming. This had to be a nightmare of my overly-imaginative mind trying to freak me out. Yet, regardless of all the thoughts that raced through my head, I knew that this *was* real.

My mouth was dry and my throat felt like cotton, and as much as I wanted to run away I was incredibly drawn to the Rag-man.

Struggling to put life into my legs, I forced myself away from him and ran in the other direction. Footsteps began to follow and the heat intensified. I was burning; my skin began to boil. Making my way down the stairs rather quickly I thought I saw someone in the corner of my eye. When I looked more closely, I saw it was only the security guard sitting at the front desk. I was relieved it wasn't anybody else.

I looked back at him again and my bones jumped out from under my skin. The Rag-man had taken his place. He grinned at me from under his big, floppy hat and his eye-less glare sent a shudder of fear throughout my entire body. My jog became a full sprint as I ran toward the exit.

Finally, the door to the outside world was only a few paces away and with satisfaction I knew I would finally be rid of the Rag-man forever.

I slowed down so I wouldn't crash through the glass-laced door, then gripped its handle and gave a good solid push.

I was free.

Upon my entry into what was supposed to be the front steps leading up to the building, I found myself back outside the religious exhibit inside the art gallery where I originally fell and banged my head. Before, when I was here, I was the only one, but now there were a handful of people milling about with a few of them gathered around together in a circle. I came over to see what was going on. They were gathered around someone lying on the floor.

I stepped in further to take a closer look and through my hazy gaze I saw that it was me, blood pooled around my head.

Shock shook me through and through.

A hand gripped my shoulder and turned me around.

It was the Rag-man. "Welcome home," he said.

MR. JITTERBONES

In London's East End they celebrate Hallowe'en. Jack McClay thought that after what happened last autumn, they wouldn't celebrate it anymore. Not after the deaths of those five prostitutes. Their killer was never caught. No one knew who did it. But rumors abounded. Some still maintained it was a fellow dubbed "Leather Apron," while others suggested it was Prince Edward (though this rumor was scarcely heard). Others thought it was the work of a cult. Either way, the women were dead. Jack now hated the fact that he shared the namesake of their killer, Jack the Ripper. Or, at least, that's what the papers had named him. The East End still hadn't recovered from that terrible autumn and Jack thought no one wanted to see anyone parading around in a costume this year.

He was wrong.

The sky was overcast with gray clouds, a hint of rain on the air. Though it was October 31st, the snow had yet to fall. It had been a warm autumn so far. The pale light of London's street lamps created shadows around the buildings, in the cracks of the cobbles. Anyone with even a hint of imagination could picture a secret killer lurking there, in the shadows, clad in black, ready to strike. But Jack knew better. He knew these streets well. After all, he grew up on them.

Abandoned when he was just seven years old, he remained on the street, struggling to live day-to-day, finding food in trash cans or in the scraps people left on their plates in restaurants. He didn't mind the hard life, though. It was all he knew. There was never a better way. He was twenty years old now. He couldn't recall his parents' faces if he tried. All he could remember about them was their warmth, the security he felt when he was around them. But that was memory. Almost myth.

Clad in a brown overcoat and matching trousers, he made his way to the alley behind the Ten Bells. He had been living there for almost a year.

Last autumn, he was living in an alley near Miller's Court, but after Mary Kelly got her throat cut, he couldn't stay there any longer. He knew her, too. She used to work the corners around there, propositioning men for any amount they would be willing to pay for ten minutes of her company. She was beautiful with long hair, captivating eyes and a well-formed figure that spoke of youth. She was close to his age, as well; only twenty-five. He was sorry she died and often wondered what she could have done that made a madman stop by her abode one night and cut her to pieces.

Near his home now, Jack stuffed his hands in his pockets but not before pulling up the collar of his jacket around his neck. A breeze was picking up.

Off on the next street he heard the lilt of a woman laughing and the shout of a man hollering at someone, the clip-clopping of hooves against the cobbles and the sound of a wagon's wheels as they rolled along the street. It was London. It was the East End. Poverty and despair hung on the air like smoke in a pub. It made his flesh crawl. But, it was all he knew and he had resigned to it long ago.

Jack approached his home: a large wooden crate turned on its side against the rear wall of the Ten Bells. The owner, Mr. Harris, said he could stay there as long as he stayed out of trouble and minded his own business. At Christmas last year things got rowdy at the Ten Bells and a fellow had tried robbing the place. Jack happened to be in the bar that night and apprehended the robber before any harm could be done. Mr. Harris was indebted to Jack. The back alley was now his.

No one came down the back alley anyway except the occasional prostitute and her client. On those nights, Jack would leave and come back a half-hour later. Thirty minutes was more than enough time for the man to get what needed doing done and the woman to collect her pay.

It was just after six now. The children would be along soon. The parents would want them indoors early. Bad men came out at night. Bad women, too. A dog barked in the distance.

Jack crawled inside his crate and sat down. In the corner was his pillow and an old copy of the *London Times,* dated August 12, 1889. He had read it over twenty times. There was nothing better to do some days.

In the other corner he had an old potato sack and within it, a small wooden box that he found in the trash one evening. In the box were the treats for the children: mints, a few chocolates. Nothing spectacular. But the children were thankful, their parents usually unable to afford them any treats. Hallowe'en was a special time for children.

"Wonder what they'll be wearing tonight," Jack said to himself.

The children's costumes were usually just their parents' clothes, the boys with mustaches painted on their faces with charcoal, the girls wearing an old dress of their mother's. They pretended to be grown-ups. A few of the "richer" kids—though no one was rich in the East End— dressed as vampires or undertakers or corpses. Some of the girls dressed as witches. The costumes were rudimentary and only when inspecting their guise closely did you see what they were supposed to be. But the kids' hearts were in it and that's what was important. Hallowe'en was a chance for them to be free of their daily burdens and a chance to just be children.

Jack smiled at the thought of Frederick—Freddy—coming by. Last year, Freddy wore his father's apron and rubber gloves and pretended to be a butcher. Jack wondered what Freddy would be this year.

Probably the same thing, he thought. He didn't know if Freddy could afford a new costume. But he looked forward to seeing the kid's dirty blond hair, blue eyes and dirt-smudged cheeks again.

A constable's whistle shrilled a few streets over followed by the clamoring of footfalls and some shouting. Sounds carried easily in the East End, with its low buildings and open spaces.

Jack glanced up at the moon peeking in from behind a cloud.

The children would be along shortly.

————

The children had come a half-hour later, all rags and smiles, anxious for their treats. There had only been ten of them; few children came by the back alley of the Ten Bells. But Freddy hadn't come. Each time a child came by, a small cloth bag open to receive a chocolate or mint, Jack hoped that Freddy would be the next kid to receive something. After nine of the kids came, Jack had only one piece of chocolate left. By the tenth kid, a little girl wearing her mother's dress and a kerchief over her head, Jack had to turn her away and tell her he had nothing to give her. The girl, so sweet, still said thank you and gave him a curtsey before moving on to her next stop.

Safely tucked away in the corner of his wooden box, was Freddy's chocolate.

I 'ope you come by t'night, ol' chap, Jack thought.

He glanced up at the sky. The moon sat in the middle of a swirl of clouds, a nimbus around the moon. It was quarter after ten. It was late. *Then again, I guess you won't be. Yer mum wouldn' let ya out this late, if she 'ad any sense. There are bad men about. Maybe she'll come by wit' ya? Maybe not as I know she 'as te get up early to work at the bookstore. Your dad? Let's 'ope so.*

It was after eleven when Jack finally gave up waiting. Downhearted, he placed the wooden box in the potato sack and shoved it in the corner of his crate. Scrunched up off to the side was his blanket. He straightened it and lay his head down on the hard floor, draping the blanket over him. It didn't provide much warmth and he could already feel the chill of night settling in his bones.

It wasn't long before it began to drizzle and soon after that, the rain came steadily, drumming a soothing rhythm against the top of the crate. A few drops leaked through the cracks in his roof and he shivered when the cool drops soaked through his blanket and jacket.

Just another night in the East End.

———

After midnight it was still raining. Jack was having a hard time staying asleep. He awoke every fifteen minutes or so, the thunder crashing in the sky jolting him out of slumber. It was nearly black in the alley; the only light came from the lamps on either end of it, lighting the streets that ran adjacent to his home. There weren't any people out. All had gone indoors once the rain really started to come down.

At the next flicker of lightning and crash of thunder, he sat up, blanket drawn about his shoulders.

"Te 'ell wit' sleepin'," he muttered. The only problem with not having a proper home was there was nothing to do when sleep failed to pass the time.

He thought of Freddy again and of his butcher costume from the year before. Now that he thought of it, he was surprised Freddy wore such a costume, what with all the talk of Leather Apron and Bloody Jack. But, it was all Freddy had, he supposed. Couldn't hold it against the kid. Children were supposed to be allowed a good time as much as adults were.

Rain ran off the top left corner of the crate. Jack reached over, cupped his hands beneath the runoff, and filled them with water. He brought his hands to his mouth, slurped some of it, then used the rest to wash his face. The cool water helped clear his head.

The thunder rumbled then crashed with power. It echoed on the air. The sound faded away after a few moments and was replaced by complete silence. Then . . .

Clik-clakity-clak-clak. Clik-clakity-clak-clak.

Silence again. Jack thought the sound to be his imagination. He brought his knees to his chest and wrapped his blanket around them. Chin on his knees, he closed his eyes, hoping to doze off.

He thought of how he would obtain breakfast the following morning. He might find some change on the cobbles. Some usually could be found in front of the Ten Bells, the change having spilled out of the pockets of the drunkards as they stumbled along home. He might need to go into town, where it wasn't as poor, and beg. He hated having to do that. All Londoners stuck up their noses when an unfortunate from the East End bothered them for money.

"We'll see," he said.

Clik-clakity-clak-clak. Clik-clakity-clak-clak. It was like two sticks tapping against each other.

His eyes shot open. This time he knew it wasn't his imagination. He inched his way to the edge of the opening of the crate and peered both ways up the alley.

No one was there.

"Bugger," he said. *Whoever's doin' that oughtta let up an' lemme sleep!*

He leaned against the inside of the crate and closed his eyes. The rain was letting up though it still kept a steady drumbeat against his roof. He was glad he was indoors . . . in a manner of speaking. There was a time when on rainy nights he didn't have anywhere to go and had to brave the weather by cramming himself up against door frames or steps partly covered by an awning, just to keep relatively dry. He was glad he had found this crate and that Mr. Harris was so hospitable in letting him use his alley.

The night wore on.

Clik-clakity-clak-clak. Clik-clakity-clak-clak. Clik-clakity-clak-clak.

Jack snarled. "That does it!" He threw back his blanket, crawled out of his crate and quickly got to his feet.

The alley was bare of any life. Just a few trash cans, some litter, and puddles twinkling in the lamplight.

"Who's there?" he called. No one answered.

The thunder rumbled but didn't crash. The rain had eased even more, just dribbling now.

With a huff, Jack went back into the crate and pulled a cigarette out of a beat up old pack from his breast pocket. He pulled a match out of the other breast pocket and struck it against the crate's sharp wooden corner. He lit his cigarette and tossed the match in a puddle not far from him. It went out with a *fitsz*.

As he drew heavily on the cigarette, the sound returned.

Clik-clakity-clak-clak. Clik-clakity-clak-clak.

A thud on Jack's roof. Empty and hollow; thick-soled boots on wood. It was above him, whatever it was. He wanted to get out of the crate and see what caused the noise but, heart suddenly pounding, something told him he shouldn't. He decided to wait.

Silence. Silence for an eternity. Was it still there? Whatever it was? It could have been something that had fallen off old Mr. Harris's roof and landed on the crate. His crate was right up against the brick and mortar. It surely was possible.

He dragged on his cigarette, the sizzling sound of its cherry burning away at the paper and tobacco somewhat soothing.

A dull thud, but not as loud as before. Movement. Something was up there.

Jack tucked in his legs and inched his bottom along the inside of the crate so he was against the far wall. Another thud and then a splash as whatever it was jumped off his roof and landed in the puddle beside the crate. *Clak-sploosh!*

A cat? Maybe. Cats were common in the alleys. But a cat doesn't wear thick-soled boots. So Jack waited, listened, wanting to see if any more sounds would come. Then . . .

Clik-clakity-clak-clak. A pause. Then another *clik-clakity-clak-clak.*

Jack put the remainder of his cigarette out on the worn sole of his right shoe and crawled to the crate's entrance. His heart thumped rapidly in his chest.

Clik-clakity-clak-clak. Clik-clakity-clak-clak. Clik-clakity-clak-clak. It was moving around.

He swallowed a hard lump in his throat, like a small stone. He could almost hear it splash as it hit the rainwater in his stomach. There was a tickle in his throat and he coughed. His palm immediately shot to his lips, too late to conceal the sound.

A footstep on the cobbles.

Clak.

Jack breathed heavily through his nose. The tickle was still there and he so badly wanted to clear it. And he did. He couldn't help himself. The phlegm rising then settling in his throat suddenly seemed loud in the dead air.

Play it safe, he told himself. *You'll wind up buggered, if ya don'.*

He peered through a crack in the wood beside him. There wasn't enough light to see anything. All he could see was a smudge of black and a little of the brown of the wet street. Even the light from the street lamp at the end of the alleyway was dim.

"Hmph," he whispered.

For a long time there wasn't any more clacking. The only sound was the runoff water finding its way off roofs and to the puddles on the streets.

Gathering his courage, he crawled out of the crate.

A man was beside it.

The man wore a top hat; no hair, just skin so thin you could see the bone underneath. His eyes were enormous, round, bugging out of his head. The irises were as black as charcoal and surrounded by a thin ring of white. He wore a torn tuxedo, the bowtie untied and hanging unevenly around his neck. The cummerbund that looked to be once bright red was now a tarnished maroon, as if it had been covered in dirt for a hundred years and only recently recovered. Curls of smoke drifted faintly from the man's ears, as if his insides were on fire. And there, held in his right hand, hanging casually at his side, was an ax.

The two men stared at each other for a long time; Jack didn't know for how long. The moment was broken when the man's deep red lips curled up in a snarl, revealing crooked, yellow teeth.

Jack's left heel began nervously tapping at the ground. The man just stared at him. Jack's mouth was so dry his tongue stuck to the roof of it. He gathered as much spit as he could to free it. When he spoke, his voice was weak, barely heard.

"Wh-who are . . ." He took a breath. "Who are ya?"

The man didn't respond but instead came a few steps closer.

Clik-clakity-clak-clak. Clik-clak.

So it was him who had made the noise. Jack glanced up to the roof of the Ten Bells and wondered how this man could have jumped from that high up and not hurt himself or broken his legs. The man shuffled a few steps to Jack's left.

Clik-clakity-clak-clak.

'Is bones click when 'e moves, Jack thought. *Mr. Jitterbones.* It was as good a name as any.

Mr. Jitterbones continued to eye Jack, his pale thumb rubbing up and down the hilt of the ax handle. The tarnished gray steel of the ax's blade was stained a deep maroon, matching that of Mr. Jitterbones's cummerbund.

When it was apparent Mr. Jitterbones wasn't going to answer him, Jack asked again, "Who are ya?" He liked how his voice had gained some backbone. The man was in *his* alley. He dropped down on *his* roof. Trespasser.

Mr. Jitterbones raised his ax to waist height and took a step closer to him, bones clacking.

"Fine," Jack said, arms outstretched, "ya don' wanna talk? Then the 'ell wit' ya. I don' need this."

There was a long silence. "Go on. Get!" Jack shouted and pointed down the alley.

Mr. Jitterbones grimaced and brought the ax shoulder-level and grabbed hold of its handle with both hands. He took a step closer. There was a small click of his bones.

Jack's heart sped up again. He didn't want to have to fight but if that's how this was going to pan out, so be it. He looked both ways down the alley. *There's ne'er a flatfoot around when ya need one.*

"All right, ya don' wanna leave? Fine." And he brought up his fists.

The way Mr. Jitterbones looked at him right then was like that of an adult looking at a child who wanted to fight: You have no hope, son, I'm bigger and stronger than you.

Mr. Jitterbones bowed, one hand one way, the one with the ax going the other. He straightened . . . then came at Jack. Jack moved but not quickly enough and the ax grazed his shoulder, cutting through his jacket and into the muscle.

"Arrggh!" he screamed and his left hand went immediately to the wound. Dumb move because, using the vulnerability to his advantage, Mr. Jitterbones sliced at his left side and tore a chunk of meat out of that shoulder as well.

Jack staggered back a step, blood already soaking through his jacket. Mr. Jitterbones advanced. *Clik-clakity-clak.*

For someone who looked as fragile as a skeleton, Mr. Jitterbones moved, albeit clumsily, with great speed. Jack swung at him. Mr. Jitterbones ducked and his ax went for Jack's thigh, tearing the trousers and slicing off a sliver of meat. Warm blood flowed down Jack's leg. He daren't look, but he did anyway and cringed when he saw a bloody mess of brown fabric, the pinky-red of flesh and a bit of the beige of his skin.

With his other leg, Jack kicked Mr. Jitterbones, his foot connecting with bone-man's stomach. It was like hitting a bag filled with gravel. Mr. Jitterbones ambled back a few steps . . . then straightened. He snarled, his lips again curling up to show his yellow, crooked teeth.

Jack tried to call for help but his voice was caught somewhere between the fire in his legs and his shoulders. He was surprised that no police officer had crossed the mouth of the alleyway yet, or that Mr. Harris hadn't come out to see what all the ruckus was about.

There was no use in fighting Mr. Jitterbones, not unless he wanted to be slowly hacked to pieces.

Then a thought occurred to him: *Is Mr. Jitterbones the Ripper? 'E's cuttin' me up. Jus' like those girls that were done in.* It certainly seemed possible but Jack couldn't wholly convince himself of it. Jack the Ripper had this phantom-like air about him; he was mysterious. Mr. Jitterbones was merely a butcher. No finesse, no mystery—just plain carnage. Then again, Bloody Jack was like that as well.

Before he realized what he was doing, Jack began hobbling down the alley, trying to get away.

Mr. Jitterbones stormed after him. *Clik-clakity-clak-clak. Clik-clakity-cla*—there was hot pain in Jack's right calf as Mr. Jitterbones cleaved off another piece. Blood spilled from the wound and ran down his ankle, puddling in his shoe. He fell and Mr. Jitterbones was on top of him.

The bony man turned him over, pinning him. Mr. Jitterbones was light and Jack could have easily thrown him off but nothing was registering right now, nothing but the thought of that blood-stained ax coming down on his face or neck and ending his poor, meaningless existence.

"Freddy . . ." Jack heard himself say. His voice was weak and cracked. *Freddy didn' come by t'night. Didn' see 'im. Couldn' give 'im 'is chocolate. Couldn' do nothin'. Couldn' . . .*

Mr. Jitterbones's dark eyes glared at him, the rings of white around them so bright in contrast they looked almost like halos. Then Jack saw something he never expected. There, like a reflection in a murky puddle, he saw Freddy's face flash across Mr. Jitterbones's and, just as suddenly, was gone.

"Fr-Freddy . . ." he stammered. An image of the boy's tussled blond hair, dirty cheeks and bright blue eyes danced in his mind.

Mr. Jitterbones grimaced then grunted. He raised the ax to Jack's face.

"Please . . . please . . . I beg ya . . . lemme . . . lemme l-live . . ." Jack said, pleaded. He supposed that this dark creature must have heard these same pleas before . . . many times before. Had Freddy said the same thing, or had he been so terrified of the man with the clicking bones and torn tuxedo that smelled of garlic and trash, that he didn't know what to say?

The ax's blade grazed along Jack's neck. He could only lay there, trembling, his heart pounding so hard he was finding it difficult to breathe. The ax's blade was warm at its edge; cool along the blade's side. Jack swallowed, the rise of his Adam's apple putting pressure against the ax's edge. The blade tore the skin as a result and a drop of blood leaked from, then rolled, down his neck.

Mr. Jitterbones looked surprised this had happened, but he also looked pleased.

"I'm s-sorry," Jack said. He didn't know why he said it but it seemed fitting. He must have done something wrong for Mr. Jitterbones to want to murder him.

Jack tried to move, tried to push Mr. Jitterbones off him. He grabbed the bone-man by the neck, squeezing, hoping to cut off any air going into this ghost of a man (if he needed to breathe, that was). Smoke trailed out of Mr. Jitterbones's ears, tainting the air with its smell, like dried corn left on the fire too long. With his bony fingers, Mr. Jitterbones grabbed Jack's wrist and pressed on the tendons just below Jack's palms. Jack felt his fingers curl and the strength go out of his hands. The next thing he knew, both his wrists were pinned to the damp, cool pavement above his head.

That's when the ax came down. All Jack saw was darkness. Something wet splashed his face.

———

There was a mist on the air, gray mixed with salmon-pink. It didn't smell like anything but it sure *felt* like something; like a dusty wind but warmer. Jack took a step forward and heard the stirring of water. He looked down; he was up to his knees in a warm, murky, red and brown liquid. Blood? No, couldn't be blood.

Jack waded further into the misty air, hardly able to see anything. He waved at the fog with his fingers. The pink smoke swirled as he did but just as quickly brought itself together again. Like pawing at water or raindrops.

Where am I? he thought. *Where . . .* Then he remembered. Hallowe'en. Mr. Jitterbones. The ax with the bloodstained blade. The alley. His crate.

The children and the chocolates and mints. And Freddy. Freddy didn't come tonight.

He bent down and touched the red and brown liquid. It was oily and smelled like trash. Like Mr. Jitterbones. The bed of this red river was soft and cushy, like walking on a sponge or damp pillow. Then Jack remembered the cut on his neck from Mr. Jitterbones's ax. He touched where the wound would be. There was a small, damp scratch but nothing worse. He checked his shoulders and legs, all seeming fine albeit a bit sore.

Thank God, he thought. *I'm alive. But . . . am I? I'm jus' dreamin', that's all. Gotta be. 'Afta be.* Yet he wasn't able to convince himself. In dreams, no matter how real they seemed, there was still a "padding" to them, an air of reassurance that what you were witnessing couldn't possibly be real and, when you awoke, though your heart was pounding, you recalled that reassurance and smiled in relief it was just a nightmare. But not here. Not in this place of pink smoke and oily reddish-brown water.

Jack's senses were alive. He could still feel the grease on his fingertips from having touched the water. The murky pink mist had a texture to it as well, like the tiny dots you saw in mist when it rose off the streets in the morning. The smell of trash from the water still lingered in his nostrils. He dare not taste it. He didn't want that filth inside him. But this was real. It had to be.

He put his fingers to his temples. "Jus' calm down. You'll be al' right. Jus' 'ang on a tick. All will be well. 'Asta be."

"Jack?"

Jack dropped his hands and looked around. "Who's there?"

"Jack, it's me. Do you have a candy?" The voice was high, a boy's voice. It was hollow and echoey and seemed to come from all around.

Jack whirled about, the water splashing around his knees, making his thighs wet as he did. The warm water soon cooled and gooseflesh formed on his skin. The hairs on his arms and neck stood on end.

"Who is it? Who's there? Tell me!"

"It's me, Freddy."

"Freddy?" He whirled around once more. "Freddy, where are ya?"

"I'm here, Jack. Honest."

Jack sloshed through the oily swamp, pawing at the mist that hung in the air, as if parting the blinds of a window, hoping it would help him see better; but the pink mist remained as thick as ever.

"Freddy! Freddy, call my name so I can find ya!"

But Freddy didn't call his name. Instead, the boy said, "We're inside him, Jack. We're inside the skeleton-man. He sounds like two sticks hitting each other when he walks, too."

"I know, Freddy. I know 'e does. Where are ya?"

"I'm here. I'm here. Promise."

The boy wasn't making sense. Jack stopped his trudging and put his head between his legs. The sharp garbage-scent of the water made him stand upright almost immediately. Mucus caught in the back of his throat. He thought he was going to throw up. He didn't. Instead he swallowed and waited.

Legs tired, knees sore, he so badly wanted to sit down. There was nowhere to sit.

"I saw the girls, Jack," Freddy said. "I saw 'em and they came up to me and gave me a hug."

Girls? "What girls, Freddy? Which ones? There's no one 'ere." His voice was quiet, tired.

It was a few moments before Freddy answered. "The ones who went missing last year. There's five of them and they're all here. All of them. One says she knows you. Says her name's Mary. Do you know her?"

Yea, Freddy, I know 'er. I knew 'er. I know 'er.

Suddenly, the water stirred and blurred shapes appeared below its surface. Jack swallowed, the sharp taste of mucus still lingering.

Five women rose out of the water, surrounding him. Their pale white faces were pruned, their skin having been in the water too long. Their dresses were in tatters, the dark material clinging to them, outlining their skinny, starved bodies. The brown and red liquid dripped off them slowly, ran down their faces and gaunt necks and collarbones, almost in slow motion. All had eyes set in a ring of gray.

Slowly, they waded toward him. Jack stood at the ready—ready to grab whichever one attacked him first. But there, off a ways in the pink mist, was Freddy, looking on.

"Freddy?" Jack said. "What are they doin'?"

"It's okay," Freddy said.

The women came closer, arms reaching out toward him.

"It's okay. They've come to take you home."

Mary grabbed Jack by the shoulders and pulled him down into the water. The others joined her, and there, echoing throughout the murky liquid, was the low drum of two sticks tapping together.

About the Author

A.P. Fuchs is the author of many novels and short stories, most of which have been published. His most recent book, aside from this one, is *Zombie Fight Night: Battles of the Dead*, in which zombies fight such classic monsters as werewolves, vampires, Bigfoot, and even go up against cool foes like pirates, ninjas, and . . . Bruce Lee.

A.P. Fuchs is also known for his superhero series, *The Axiom-man Saga*, and is the author of *Blood of the Dead*, the first novel in the shoot 'em up zombie trilogy, *Undead World*. He also edited the zombie anthologies *Dead Science* and *Vicious Verses and Reanimated Rhymes: Zany Zombie Poetry for the Undead Head*.

Fuchs lives and writes in Winnipeg, Manitoba.

Visit his corner of the Web at
www.canisterx.com

Check out the *Undead World Trilogy* at **www.undeadworldtrilogy.com**

And follow him on Twitter at:

www.twitter.com/ap_fuchs

COSCOM ENTERTAINMENT

Where Imagination is Truth

www.coscomentertainment.com